MEDICAL ERROR

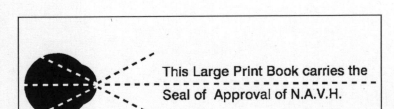

PRESCRIPTION FOR TROUBLE SERIES

MEDICAL ERROR

MEDICAL SUSPENSE WITH HEART

RICHARD L. MABRY, M.D.

THORNDIKE PRESS
A part of Gale, Cengage Learning

GALE
CENGAGE Learning·

Detroit • New York • San Francisco • New Haven, Conn • Waterville, Maine • London

Thorndike Press, a part of Gale, Cengage Learning.

Thorndike Press® Large Print Christian Mystery.
The text of this Large Print edition is unabridged.
Other aspects of the book may vary from the original edition.
Set in 16 pt. Plantin.

LIBRARY OF CONGRESS CATALOGING-IN-PUBLICATION DATA

Mabry, Richard L.
    Medical error : medical suspense with heart / by Richard L. Mabry.
       p. cm. — (Thorndike Press large print Christian mystery)
    (Prescription for trouble series)
    ISBN-13: 978-1-4104-3302-2
    ISBN-10: 1-4104-3302-1
    1. Women physicians—Fiction. 2. Large type books. I. Title.
PS3613.A2M43 2010b
813'.6—dc22   2010036690

Published in 2010 by arrangement with Abingdon Press.

Printed in Mexico
1 2 3 4 5 6 7 14 13 12 11 10

For my wife, Kay, whose love made life
worth living
once more. In my writing endeavors,
she is my biggest
fan, always encouraging mc to do my
best work. I couldn't
do it without her —
nor would I want to.

And for my grandchildren: Cassidy
Ann, Kate, Ryan, and
Connor. I hope that, as you grow up,
you'll think maybe
your Grandad wasn't too bad a writer
(even if there aren't
any pictures in this book).

ACKNOWLEDGMENTS

I want to express my appreciation to my wonderful agent, Rachelle Gardner, as well as to my great editor, Barbara Scott, and everyone at Abingdon Press. Thanks for letting me play on your team.

I'm grateful for the support and encouragement of so many writer friends as I struggled to master the craft of writing and discover the ins and outs of publication. I've learned from each of you. Thank you for the kind words that came just when I needed them. There are too many of you to mention individually, but you know who you are. You have my sincere gratitude.

My long-time friend, attorney, and golf partner, Jerry Gilmore, has been an insightful and supportive reader of my first drafts. Let the record show that any good traits demonstrated by the attorneys in my books are modeled on Jerry, while any legal errors are my own responsibility.

As always, my wife, Kay, has read every word of this novel. She's been lavish with her praise, kind with her criticism, and spot-on with her suggestions. Thank you, dear, for always being there. You make it all worthwhile.

To my readers, you have my undying gratitude for buying my books and giving me feedback, both positive and negative (but mostly positive, I hope). I want you to expect a good reading experience when you pick up one of my novels, and I hope I never betray that trust.

— RICHARD L. MABRY, M.D.

1

Eric Hatley's last day alive began routinely enough.

He paused beside his brown delivery truck, shifted the bulky package, and turned in a tight circle to search for the right apartment.

Shouts filled the air. Firecrackers exploded all around him. A dozen red-hot pokers bored holes through his gut.

The package flew from his arms. He crumpled into a privet hedge at the edge of the sidewalk, clutching his midsection and recoiling when his fingers encountered something wet and slimy.

A wave of nausea swept over him. Cold sweat engulfed him.

Eric managed one strangled cry before everything faded to black.

Dr. Anna McIntyre bumped the swinging door with her hip and backed into Parkland

Hospital's Operating Room Six, her dripping hands held in front of her, palms inward. "Luc, tell me what you've got."

Chief surgical resident, Dr. Luc Nguyn, didn't look up from the rectangle of abdomen outlined by green draping sheets and illuminated by strong surgical lights. "UPS driver, making a delivery in the Projects. Got caught in the crossfire of a gang rumble. Took four bullets in the belly. Pretty shocky by the time he got here."

"Find the bleeding source?"

"Most of it was from the gastric artery. Just finished tying it off."

Anna took a sterile towel from the scrub nurse and began the ritual of gowning and gloving made automatic by countless repetitions. "How about fluids and blood replacement?"

Luc held out his hand, and the nurse slapped a clamp into it. "Lactated Ringer's still running wide open. We've already pushed one unit of unmatched O negative. He's finishing his first unit of cross-matched blood. We've got another one ready and four more holding in the blood bank."

"How's he responding?"

"BP is still low but stable, pulse is slower. I think we're catching up with the blood loss."

Anna plunged her hands into thin surgical gloves. "Lab work?"

"Hematocrit was a little over ten on admission, but I don't think he'd had time to fully hemodilute. My guess is he was nine or less."

Anna turned slightly to allow the circulating nurse to tie her surgical gown. "Bowel perforations?"

"So far I see four holes in the small intestine, two in the colon."

"Okay, he'll need antibiotic coverage. Got that started?"

Luc shrugged. "Not yet. We don't know about drug allergies. His wallet had ID, but we're still working on contacting next of kin. Meanwhile, I have Medical Records checking his name in the hospital computer for previous visits."

"And if he's allergic —"

The nursing supervisor pushed through the swinging doors, already reading from the slip of paper in her hand. "They found one prior visit for an Eric Hatley, same address and date of birth as on this man's driver's license. Seen in the ER two weeks ago for a venereal disease. No history of drug allergy. They gave him IM Omnilex. No problems."

The medical student who'd been assisting

11

moved two steps to his left. Anna took his place across the operating table from Luc.

Luc glanced toward the anesthesiologist. "Two grams of Omnilex IV please."

Anna followed Luc's gaze to the head of the operating table. "I don't believe I know you. I'm Dr. McIntyre."

The doctor kept his eyes on the syringe he was filling. "Yes, ma'am. I'm Jeff Murray, first-year anesthesia resident."

A first-year resident on his own? Where was the staff man? "Keep a close eye on the blood and fluids. Let us know if there's a problem." Anna picked up a surgical sponge and blotted a bit of blood from the edge of the operative area. "Okay, Luc. Let's see what you've got."

In the operating room, Anna was in her element. The green tile walls, the bright lights, the soft beep of the monitors and whoosh of the respirator, the squeak of rubber soles as the circulating nurse moved about the room — all these were as natural to her as water to a fish or air to a bird. Under Anna's direction, the team worked together smoothly. Conversation was at a minimum, something she appreciated. Do the job in the OR, talk in the surgeons' lounge.

"I think that's got it," Luc said.

"Let's check." Anna's fingertips explored the depths of the patient's belly with the delicate touch of a concert violinist. Her eyes roamed the operative field, missing nothing. Luc had done an excellent job. He'd do well in practice when he finished his training in three months.

Anna stepped away from the table. "I think you're through. Routine closure, leave a couple of drains in. Keep him on antibiotic coverage for the next few days."

Luc didn't need to hear that, but she figured the medical student did. She might as well earn her assistant professor's salary with a little low-key teaching.

She stripped off her gloves and tossed them in the waste bucket at the end of the operating table. "If you need me —"

"Luc, we've got a problem. Blood pressure's dropping, pulse is rapid." A hint of panic rose in the anesthesiologist's voice.

The scrub nurse held out fresh gloves, and Anna plunged her hands into them. "He must be bleeding again. Maybe one of the ligatures slipped off."

"No way," Luc said. "Everything was double-tied, with a stick-tie on the major vessels. You saw yourself; the wound was dry when we finished."

"Well, we've got to go back in and look."

Anna turned to the anesthesiologist. "Run the IV wide open. Hang another unit of blood and send for at least two more. Keep him oxygenated. And get your staff man in here. Now!"

Jeff snapped out a couple of requests to the circulating nurse before turning back to Anna. "He's getting hard to ventilate. Do you think we might have overloaded him with fluid and blood? Could he be in pulmonary edema?"

"I want your staff doctor in here now! Let him evaluate all that. We've got our hands full." Anna snatched a scalpel from the instrument tray and sliced through the half-dozen sutures Luc had just placed. "Deavor retractor." She shoved the curved arm of the instrument into the edge of the open wound and tapped the medical student's hand. "Hold this."

Anna grabbed a handful of gauze sponges, expecting a gusher of blood from the abdomen. There was none. No bleeding at all within the wound. So why was the blood pressure dropping?

"Pressure's down to almost nothing." The anesthesia resident's voice was strained. "And I'm really having trouble ventilating him."

Dr. Buddy Jenkins, one of the senior

anesthesiologists, pushed through the swinging doors. "What's going on?"

Anna gave him the short version. "Blood pressure's dropping, pulse is climbing. We've gone back into the belly, but there's no bleeding. And there's a problem ventilating him."

Jenkins moved his resident aside, then slipped a stethoscope under the drapes and listened for a moment. "Wheezes. And no wonder. Look at his face."

Anna peeked over the screen that separated the patient's head and upper body from the operative field. Her heart skipped a beat when she saw the swelling of the lips and the red blotches on the man's face.

"It's not blood loss," Jenkins said. "He's having an anaphylactic reaction. Most likely the blood. Did you give him an antibiotic? Any other meds?"

Anna's mind was already churning, flipping through mental index cards. Anaphylaxis — a massive allergic reaction, when airways closed off and the heart struggled to pump blood. Death could come quickly. Treatment had to be immediate and aggressive.

"He had two grams of Omnilex," Luc said. "But his old chart showed —"

Jenkins was in action before Luc stopped

15

speaking. "I'll give him a cc. of diluted epinephrine by IV push now, then more in a drip." He turned to the anesthesia resident. "Get that ready — one milligram of epinephrine in a hundred milliliters of saline."

"Luc, you two close the abdominal wound," Anna said. "I'm going to break scrub and help Dr. Jenkins."

Jenkins handed her a syringe. "Give him this Decadron, IV push. I need to adjust the ventilator."

Anna injected the contents into the patient's intravenous line. She said a quick prayer that the epinephrine and steroid would turn the tide, that they hadn't been too late in starting treatment.

The team battled for almost half an hour, at first gaining ground, then losing it steadily. Finally, Jenkins caught Anna's eye. They exchanged glances. There was no need for words.

She sighed and stepped away from the table. "I'm calling it." Her voice cracked. "Time of death is 11:07."

Luc let the instrument he'd been holding drop back onto the tray. Jenkins picked up the anesthesia record and began to scribble. Murray, the anesthesia resident, turned back to his supply table and started straightening the mess. The medical student looked at Anna. She nodded toward the door, and he slipped out of the room. She didn't blame him. This was probably the first patient he'd seen die.

Anna tossed her gloves and mask into the waste container. She shrugged, but the tension in her shoulders gripped tighter. "Any idea why this happened? The blood was supposed to be compatible. He'd tolerated Omnilex before. What else could have caused it?"

No one offered an answer. And she certainly had none. But she intended to find out.

The OR charge nurse directed Anna to the family room, where she found Hatley's mother huddled in a corner, twisting a handkerchief and occasionally dabbing at her eyes. The room was small and quiet, the lighting was soft, and the chairs as comfortable as possible. A box of tissues sat on the table, along with a Bible and several inspirational magazines. Soft music playing in the background almost covered the hospital sounds drifting in from the nearby surgical suite.

Anna whispered a silent prayer. She'd done this dozens of times, but it never got any easier. She knelt in front of the woman.

"Mrs. Hatley, I have bad news for you."

Anna stumbled through the next several minutes, trying to explain, doing her best to make sense of a situation that she herself couldn't fully understand. When it came to the matter of permission for an autopsy, Anna wasn't sure of the medicolegal situation here. Hatley had died after being shot, but his injuries weren't the cause of death. Would she have to call the County Medical Examiner and get him to order one? The weeping mother solved the problem by agreeing to allow a postmortem exam.

There was a light tap at the door, and the chaplain slipped into the room. "I'm sorry. I was delayed." He took the chair next to Mrs. Hatley and began speaking to her in a low voice.

Anna was happy to slip out of the room with a last "I'm so sorry." Outside, she paused and took several deep breaths.

It took another half-hour for Anna to write a chart note, dictate an operative report and final case summary, and change into clean scrubs. She was leaving the dressing room when her pager sounded. The display showed her office number followed by the suffix "911." A "stat" page — respond immediately.

As she punched in the number, Anna

wondered what else could possibly go wrong today. "Lisa, what's up?"

"Dr. McIntyre, there are two policemen here. They want to talk with you. And they say it's urgent."

Nick Valentine looked up from the computer and grimaced when he heard the morgue attendant's rubber clogs clomping down the hall. The summons he knew was coming wasn't totally unexpected. After all, he was the pathologist on autopsy call this week, which was why he was sitting in this room adjacent to the morgue of Parkland Hospital instead of in his academic office at the medical school. But he'd hoped for some undisturbed time to get this project done.

The attendant stuck his head through the open door. "Dr. Valentine, you've got an autopsy coming up. Unexpected death in the OR. Dr. McIntyre's case. She asked if you could do it as soon as possible. And please page her before you start. She'd like to come down for the post." The man's head disappeared like that of a frightened turtle. More clomps down the hall signaled his departure.

There was nothing new about an attending wanting a postmortem done ASAP. You'd think they'd realize there was no hurry anymore, but that didn't seem to stop them from asking. At least she was willing to come down and watch instead of just reading his report. Nick turned to the shelf behind his desk and pulled out a dog-eared list headed "Frequently Needed Pager Numbers." He ran his finger down the page. Department of General Surgery. Anna E. McIntyre, Assistant Professor. He picked up the phone and punched in her number. After he heard the answering beeps, he entered his extension and hung up.

While he waited, Nick looked first at the pile of papers that covered half his desk, then at the words on his computer screen. He'd put this off far too long. Now he had to get it done. To his way of thinking, putting together this CV, the *curriculum vitae* that was so important in academics, was wasted effort. Nick had no interest in a promotion, didn't think he'd get one even if his chairman requested it from the dean. But his chairman wanted the CV. And what the chairman wanted, the chairman got.

The phone rang. Probably Dr. McIntyre calling back.

"Dr. Valentine."

"Nick, this is Dr. Wetherington. Do you have that CV finished yet?"

"I'm working on it."

"Well, I need it soon. I want you to get that promotion to associate professor, and I have to be able to show the committee why I've nominated you. Don't let me down."

Nick hung up and rifled through the pile on his desk. Reprints of papers published, programs showing lectures delivered at medical meetings, textbooks with chapters he'd written, certificates from awards received. His professional résumé was pitifully small, but to Nick it represented the least important part of his job. What mattered most to him was what he was about to do — try to find out why the best efforts of a top-notch medical staff had failed to save the life of some poor soul. If he did his job well, then maybe those doctors would be able to snatch some other patient from the jaws of the grim reaper.

His phone rang. "Dr. Valentine, are you about ready?" the morgue attendant said.

Nick looked at his watch. Almost half an hour, and Dr. McIntyre hadn't responded to the page. He hated to start without her, but he might have to. "Give me another ten minutes."

While he waited, Nick figured he might as well try to make Dr. Wetherington happy. Now, when did he deliver that paper before the American Society of Clinical Pathology?

And who cared, anyway?

Anna's administrative assistant met her at the doorway to the outer office. "Dr. McIntyre, I didn't know what to do."

"That's all right, Lisa. I'll talk with them." Anna straightened her white coat and walked into her private office, where two people stood conversing in low tones. Lisa had said, "Two policemen," but Anna was surprised to see that one of them was a woman.

The man stepped forward to meet Anna. "Doctor McIntyre?"

Anna nodded.

He pulled a leather folder from his pocket and held it open for her inspection. Anna could see the gold and blue badge pinned to the lower part of the wallet, but couldn't read the words on it. The card in the top portion told her, though. It carried a picture beside the words, U.S. Drug Enforcement Administration.

Lisa had been wrong. These people were from the DEA, not the police. Still, an unannounced visit from that agency made most doctors sweat. You never knew when some innocent slip might get you into trouble.

The man flipped the credential wallet

closed. "This won't take long."

"Good. I've just finished an emergency case, and I still have a lot to do." Anna moved behind her desk and sat.

"Your chairman said you'd give us as much time as we need."

Anna glanced pointedly at her watch. "Well, have a seat and let's get to it. What do you need from me?"

The man lowered himself into the chair, his expression slightly disapproving. His partner followed suit. "We have some things we need for you to clear up."

"Could I see those credentials again?" Anna said. "Both of you."

They obliged, laying the open wallets on the desk. Anna pulled a slip of notepaper toward her and began copying the information, occasionally glancing up from her writing to match the names and faces on the IDs with the people sitting across from her. The spokesman was Special Agent John Hale, a chunky, middle-aged man wearing an off-the-rack suit that did nothing to disguise his ample middle. Anna thought he looked more like a seedy private eye than an officer of the law.

The woman, the silent half of the pair so far, was Special Agent Carolyn Kramer, a woman who reminded Anna of a California surfer, complete with perfect tan and fault-lessly styled short blonde hair. The resemblance stopped there, though. Kramer's eyes gleamed with a combination of intelligence and determination that told Anna she'd better not underestimate the woman. Kramer wore a stylish pantsuit that had probably cost more than Anna made in a week. How could a DEA agent have money for an outfit like that?

Anna handed the badge wallets back to Hale and Kramer. "All right, how can I help you?"

Hale pulled a small notebook from his inside coat pocket and flipped through the pages. "Doctor, recently you've been writing a large number of Vicodin prescriptions, all of them for an excessive amount of the drug. Can you explain that?"

"I don't know what you mean," Anna said. "I'm pretty sure I haven't written any more Vicodin 'scripts than usual, and I certainly haven't changed my prescribing practices."

Hale nodded, stone-faced. "What are those practices?"

"I prescribe Vicodin for postoperative pain in many of my patients, but always in carefully controlled amounts, usually thirty pills at a time. By the time they've exhausted that first prescription, I can generally put them

24

on a non-narcotic pain reliever. It's rare that I refill a Vicodin 'script."

Apparently, it was Kramer's turn in the tag-team match. She picked up a thick leather folder from the floor beside her chair, unzipped it, and extracted a sheaf of papers held together by a wide rubber band. "Would you care to comment on these?" Her soft alto was a marked contrast to Hale's gruff baritone.

Anna's eyes went to the clock on her desk. "Will this take much longer? I really have things I need to do."

Kramer seemed not to hear. She held out the bundle of papers.

"Okay, let me have a look." Anna recognized the top one in the stack as a prescription written on a form from the faculty clinic. She pulled it free and studied it. The patient's name didn't stir any memory, but that wasn't unusual. She might see twenty or thirty people in a day. The prescription read:

VICODIN TABS

DISP. [#100]

SIG: 1 TAB Q 4 H PRN PAIN

At the bottom of the page, three refills were authorized. The DEA number had been written into the appropriate blank on the lower right-hand corner.

Anna squinted, closed her eyes, then looked again. There was no doubt about it. The DEA number was hers. And the name scrawled across the bottom read: Anna Mc-Intyre, M.D.

"Can you explain this?" Kramer asked.

A familiar vibration against her hip stopped Anna before she could reply. She pulled her pager free and looked at the display. The call was from the medical center, but she didn't recognize the number. Not the operating room. Not the clinic. She relaxed a bit when she saw there was no "911" entry after the number. If this was about the autopsy, she'd have to miss it.

Hale picked up the questioning as though there had been no interruption. "What can you tell us about all these prescriptions for Vicodin?"

"I suppose the most important thing I can tell you is that I didn't write them." She rifled through the stack, paying attention only to the signature at the bottom of each sheet. "None of these are mine."

"That's your number and name, right?" Kramer said.

"Right. But that's not my signature. It's not even close."

"Can you explain how someone else could be writing prescriptions on your pads using your DEA number?" Hale asked.

"I have no idea." Anna made no attempt to keep the bitterness out of her words. "Sorry, I've just lost a patient, and I'm not in the best of moods. Can't we wind this up? I didn't write these 'scripts, and I don't know who did."

Obviously, Hale didn't want to let the matter go. "You're sure there's nothing you want to tell us?"

"What would I have to tell you? I said I don't know anything about this."

Kramer spoke, apparently filling the role of good cop. "Take a guess. Help us out here."

Anna felt her jaw muscles clench. These people were relentless. She had to give them something, or this would never end. "I really don't know. I mean, we've got an established routine, and all the doctors here are pretty careful."

Kramer pulled a silver ballpoint from the leather folder and twirled it between her fingers. "Why don't you walk us through that routine?"

Anna wanted to follow up on Hatley's

autopsy, talk with her department chair about today's events, eventually sit down and try to relax. She was drained. The agents, on the other hand, seemed to have unlimited time and energy.

"Doctor?" Kramer's voice held no hint of irritation. Patient, understanding, all the time in the world. Just two women chatting.

"Sorry." Anna tried to organize her thoughts. "The prescription pads in the clinic are kept in a drawer in each treatment room. That way they're out of sight, although I guess if someone knew where to look, he could latch onto one when no one was in the room." She looked at the agents. Kramer simply nodded. Hale scowled. "Hey, we know it's not perfect, but that's the way we have to do it. Otherwise, we'd waste all of our time hunting for a pad."

"And do you ever forget and leave the pads sitting out when you've finished writing a prescription?" Kramer asked.

"Sure. Especially when we're in a hurry." Anna's cheeks burned.

Hale turned a page in his notebook and frowned. "How about your DEA number?"

"You'll notice those aren't printed on the forms. Each of us has to fill in our number."

"Maybe someone else had access to your number. Do nurses ever write the prescriptions for you?" This came from Kramer. Anna felt as though she was watching a tennis match, going back and forth between the two agents.

"When we have a nurse in the room with us, yes, she'll write the prescription. I don't know what the other doctors do, but I sign the prescriptions after she writes them. And I add the DEA number to the narcotic 'scripts myself."

The questioning went on for another half hour. Anna's throat was dry, her eyes burned, and she felt rivulets of sweat coursing between her shoulder blades. Finally, she'd had enough. "Look, am I being charged with something? Because if I am, I'm not saying another word without a lawyer."

Hale replaced his notebook in his pocket. Kramer picked up her folder and purse. They let the silence hang for a moment more before exchanging glances, then standing.

"Right now, we're simply investigating, Doctor," Hale said. "You may be hearing from the Texas Department of Public Safety and the Dallas Police as well. Also, since your DEA number and identity have been compromised, I'd advise you not to prescribe any controlled substances for now.

You'll receive formal notification in writing tomorrow about applying for a new permit."

The agents walked out, leaving Anna with her hands pressed to her throbbing temples.

Nick stepped back from the autopsy table, pressed the pedal under his right foot, and spoke into the microphone hanging near his head. "No other abnormalities noted. The balance of findings will be dictated after review of the histopathology specimens and the results of the toxicology tests. Usual signature. Thanks." He turned away from the body and gestured to the morgue assistant to close the incisions. "I'll be in the office if you need me. Thanks for your help."

Nick removed his goggles and stripped off his mask, gown, and gloves. He was standing at the sink outside the autopsy room, drying his hands, when he heard footsteps hurrying down the corridor toward him. He turned to see a woman approaching. The attractive redhead wore surgical scrubs, covered by a white coat. As she neared him, he could make out the embroidered name above the breast pocket: Anna McIntyre, MD. She stopped in front of him, and the set of her jaw and the flash of her green eyes told Nick she was in no mood for light banter.

"Dr. McIntyre?"

She nodded.

"Nick Valentine. I paged you, but when you didn't answer I had to go ahead and get started. Sorry."

She waved away his apology. "No, it's my fault. I couldn't break free to answer your page. What can you tell me?"

"Why don't I buy you a cup of coffee and I'll tell you what I've found so far? If we go to the food court, we can get away from the smell down here."

She hesitated for a few seconds. "Okay. Lead the way."

It seemed to Nick there was a Starbucks on every corner of every major city in the U.S. Most important to him, however, was the one here in the basement of the Clinical Sciences Building at Southwestern Medical Center. As he waited to order, he sniffed the rich aromas that filled the air. The smell of coffee never failed to lift his spirits. Maybe it would do the same for the woman who stood stoop-shouldered beside him. For most doctors, caffeine was the engine that helped propel them through long days and longer nights. Maybe all she needed was a booster shot.

When they were seated at a corner table with their venti lattes, Nick filled her in on

31

his findings at the autopsy he'd just completed. "That's about it," he concluded. "I'll sign the death certificate with the preliminary cause of death as anaphylaxis due to an unknown cause."

"But you won't have a final diagnosis until —"

"Right. I'll review the tissue samples and the results of the toxicology screen, but I doubt that we'll find anything there. I'll have some tests run on the blood samples I took, and maybe that will help us. I'll need to research whether there's a good blood test for a drug reaction or latex allergy. The long and short of it is that we may never know the real reason he developed anaphylaxis and died."

"I hadn't even thought of latex allergy," she said. "But that's pretty rare, isn't it?"

"Less than one percent of the population. Seen in people chronically exposed to latex: surgeons and nurses, industrial workers, patients with lifelong indwelling catheters." He felt himself slipping into his lecture mode and made an effort to pull back. "I mean, we could talk about all these uncommon things, but I'll bet you learned the same thing in medical school that I did. When you hear hoof beats —"

"Think horses, not zebras." She managed

a tiny smile. "Yes, I know. So we should concentrate on the blood or the antibiotic. If it was the blood, there's a problem in the blood bank because he got one unit of unmatched O negative, which should have been okay, and one unit that was supposedly compatible by cross-match."

"The residuals in both bags of blood are being re-typed and cross-matched against your patient's blood as we speak. We'll know the answer by the time we finish our coffee." He drank deeply from his cup. "Don't you think an antibiotic reaction is the most likely cause?"

She took a sip of coffee. "Probably, although I hope not. Choosing an antibiotic wasn't a routine matter, because we didn't know if Hatley had any drug allergies. The resident — one of our sharpest ones, by the way — thought he'd see if we could get the information another way. He had medical records check for a previous visit for the patient. They found a recent emergency room visit by the patient where he tolerated Omnilex. Since that antibiotic's the best choice to cover spillage from a perforated bowel, I agreed with Luc when he ordered it."

"But —"

"I know. If you give that drug to a patient

who's allergic to it or to penicillin, their reaction is likely to be severe — like this one. But I thought, since we had that history of tolerance, it was okay." She blinked hard. "I should have known better. Should have made him use a different drug."

Nick sensed he was treading on thin ice here. Maybe he should change the subject. Besides, he wanted to know more about this woman. "You know, I've seen you in the halls, but we've never actually met. Did you train here?"

She hesitated before reeling off what had apparently become a stock answer. "Raised in Oklahoma. Graduated from med school in North Carolina. Duke, actually. Lucky enough to get a surgery residency here at Parkland, and when I finished I was offered a faculty position in the Surgery Department. I've been here a little less than a year now."

Nick held up a hand, palm out. "I know better. You don't get a surgery residency here because you're 'lucky.' You get one because you're good. Let me guess. AOA at Duke?" If Anna was Alpha Omega Alpha, she must have been in the top ten percent of her class.

"Right. But I don't guess it's enough to be bright if you foul up and cost a patient his life." She drank from her cup, and Nick noticed that she swallowed several more times after that.

Nick was barely aware of the activity around him, the ebb and flow of people, the sounds of pagers punctuating dozens of conversations. All he saw was Anna. She was one of the most attractive women he'd encountered in quite a while. But he was certain there was more to this trim, green-eyed redhead than striking good looks. Right now she was focused on medicine — it was obvious she cared a great deal about her patients, and this loss hit her hard — but Nick had a sense that in a different setting she'd be fun to know. And he intended to see if he couldn't arrange that. Anna shifted in her chair. He couldn't let her leave yet.

"Wait a minute," he said. "Aren't you curious about me at all? There may be a prize if you can answer all the questions later."

Did he see the ghost of a grin? "Sure. Why not? What's your story — the *Reader's Digest* version?"

Nick moved his cup aside and leaned forward with his elbows on the table. He wasn't sure how much longer he could draw out their time together, but he was determined to give it his best shot. "My roots are

Italian. Named for my grandfather. He was Nicolo Valentino when he got off the boat, changed his name when he got his citizenship. I'm Nicolo the Third." He ticked off the points on his fingers. "Worked my way through premed at Texas Tech. Got into the med school there by the skin of my teeth. Managed to get a residency in pathology here at Southwestern. When I finished, they had an opening in the department." He held out his hand, palm up, fingers spread, thumb tucked under. "So here I am — four years in the department, still an Assistant Professor. Up for promotion now, and I suspect that if I don't make it they'll cut me like a dead branch from a tree."

Nick's last sentence rang a faint alarm bell in his head. He had to finish that project or the chairman would be royally ticked off, but it only took Nick a second to put that chore out of his mind. He was sitting with the most beautiful woman he'd ever met. He wanted to get to know her better, and he intended to keep her here as long as possible, even if it meant incurring Dr. Wetherington's wrath.

2

Anna strode down the hall toward her office when a familiar voice stopped her. "What's your hurry?"

She turned and glared at Dr. Buddy Jenkins. "Some of us have responsibilities."

"What are you so upset about, Anna?" The anesthesiologist's easy East Texas drawl almost sent Anna into orbit. Didn't he remember that a patient had died today, one who might have been saved if the anesthesia resident had picked up on the diagnosis in time to start proper treatment? Or if Jenkins hadn't been out in the hall having a cup of coffee and chatting with a colleague about the Cowboys or some other sports team?

She had to unclench her teeth before she forced the words out. "Buddy, why was that resident alone in there?"

"Well, I might ask the same thing about Luc Nguyn. He was doing the case without staff supervision until you scrubbed in to check his work. And that's because you trusted him — with good reason." Jenkins sipped from the Styrofoam cup he held. "Murray's inexperienced, but he's okay with the routine stuff. I was there with him to get the case started. I was staffing two rooms today because one of the other faculty anesthesiologists is out sick. I popped in and checked on things periodically, and everything seemed to be going fine. It's unfortunate that Murray missed the signs of anaphylaxis until it was well-established." He opened his mouth, but closed it again without saying more.

Anna sighed. "I know, Buddy. I shouldn't be taking it out on the anesthesiologist. Luc should have thought of anaphylaxis too. Hey, I should have thought of it. After all, it's ultimately my responsibility. And you know as well as I that doctors can't be right most of the time. We have to be right all the time."

"Never happen," Buddy said. "We all make mistakes. We just have to learn from them and move on."

"Well, I'm not moving on until I get the answer to this one. There was no reason that patient should have had that reaction in the first place."

"Fine. Happy hunting. I'll see you at M&M, and we'll kick it around some more." Buddy lifted his cup in a silent salute, then walked away.

He'd see her at M&M. Not the candy. Anna wished it were. No, this was Morbidity and Mortality Conference, the meeting each month when the staff discussed their patients who had suffered adverse consequences from treatment. "Morbidity" sounded so much better than "something went wrong." And "mortality" was more acceptable than "they died." But when it came to assigning blame, there was no sugar coating here.

Anna dreaded the upcoming M&M conference, where the death of Eric Hatley would be discussed. Until then, she intended to keep looking into why he had died. Was it possible that the anesthesia resident had given the wrong medication? Or mismanaged the anesthesia in some way? She kept coming back to the fact that Dr. Murray was inexperienced and on his own.

Or did the blame rest with Luc? A preventable death would leave a black mark, not only on his record but also on his conscience. She'd heard of situations like this that ruined promising careers, sending gifted surgeons into specialties where they could avoid having to make rapid-fire, life-or-death decisions.

Her pager brought her back to the moment. She recognized the number immediately: the chairman's office. She knew what Dr. Fowler wanted to discuss, and it brought more questions to her mind. Would she even be around to look into this case? Or would she be embroiled in something that didn't involve the death of her patient, but rather, the death of her professional career?

Anna squirmed in her chair and tried to ignore the lump stuck in her throat. "Dr. Fowler, why didn't you call and let me know those DEA agents were coming?"

"Because I didn't know. They came by and asked my administrative assistant how to find your office. I never saw them, never knew they were here." Neil Fowler adjusted the knot of his tie, leaned back in his chair, and looked across his desk at Anna. "Tell me what they said."

She took a deep breath and launched into a retelling of her session with Hale and Kramer.

As he listened, Fowler's expression revealed nothing. He'd been chairman of the Surgery Department for ten years — the

youngest chairman at the medical center —
and had a reputation for being stern but
fair. Anna figured he'd seen it all and dealt
with it before. Maybe that's why he could
appear so calm. But this was all new to her.

When Anna finished, Fowler fixed her
with calm, gray eyes. "And they told you
they'd be terminating your ability to write
for narcotics?"

"I'm supposed to receive a special delivery
letter tomorrow from the DEA. And they
said 'suspended,' not 'terminated.' "

Fowler leaned forward and rested his
hands on the desk in front of him. "Anna,
I'm not going to prejudge this matter, and
I'll try to help if I can. But first, I have to
ask you this. Did you write those prescriptions?"

"Absolutely not!" She was surprised at the
fervor of her answer. "Sorry. I didn't mean
to jump at you. No, I did not write them."

"All right. Here's where we need to go.
First of all, before you leave the office I'm
going to get Laura Ernst on the phone, and
you're going to tell her what just went
down."

"Who's she?"

"She heads the legal department at the
school. If you end up being charged with
something, you'll need your own lawyer.

41

But I want Laura to be aware of this from the get-go." For a second, the corners of Fowler's mouth lifted a fraction. "Laura's wound pretty tight, but in a fight you'll be glad to have her on your side."

Anna's brain was moving about a mile a minute. "What about my clinical work? I can't write for any narcotics, but I guess I could get somebody else to sign those prescriptions."

"Uh-uh. I know without asking what the Dean is going to say when he's told about this." Fowler looked at the diver's watch on his wrist. "Which I'm about to do in half an hour." He held up a hand to forestall the words that were on her lips. "He's probably going to suggest I suspend you from clinical duties until this is settled."

"Suspended?"

"Doesn't matter what word you use. Actually, the President would probably suggest that I find a way to terminate you, but that's because he's afraid this might bring some bad publicity to the medical center. The Dean's more realistic and a bit less motivated by perception and politics. Be that as it may, I'm pretty sure Dean Dunston is going to feel it would be good for you to be out of sight until this thing is settled and you're cleared. Anyway, don't worry, because you won't be suspended."

She breathed a sigh of relief.

"Well, not as such," Fowler said. "Instead, you're going to take a vacation for a while."

"But I don't have any vacation time coming," Anna said.

"As of this moment, you've suddenly become eligible for a two-week leave for special study and personal enrichment. Don't sweat the paperwork. I can handle that."

"What am I supposed to do during this time? And what happens after that?"

Fowler tented his fingers. "You're supposed to use that superior intellect that made me hire you to figure out how somebody got hold of your narcotics number and 'script pads and started playing Dr. Feelgood. When you do, take that information to the DEA or the Department of Public Safety or whatever agency has jurisdiction, and clear your name."

"What if I can't?"

The chairman removed his wire-rimmed glasses and began polishing them with a spotless handkerchief. When he'd finished, he looked directly at her and said in a low voice, "Have you heard the expression, 'failure is not an option?' "

"Yes."

Fowler nodded once.

The silence stretched on for a long moment. Then the chairman turned his attention to the stack of papers in front of him.

Anna swallowed hard. "I see."

As Anna changed clothes in the women's dressing room, she felt the glances of surgical nurses and female physicians burning into her back like live coals. She was sure that everyone at the medical center already knew about the death of her patient. She was willing to bet that by tomorrow they'd be whispering about something else: that she'd been accused of writing bogus narcotics prescriptions. Maybe Dr. Fowler was right. She should get out of here.

She pulled out of the faculty garage and started toward home, navigating on automatic pilot. Maybe she'd stop at Blockbuster for a movie to get her mind off her problems. Have a quiet dinner in front of the TV, soak in the tub, try to forget for a few blessed minutes. Then a quick mental review of the contents of her refrigerator changed her route. Better stop by the grocery store as well.

Anna wove up and down the aisles of the store with frequent stops to add items, not sure when she'd have time to shop again.

Sort of like laying in provisions for a siege, she told herself. On her trip down the second aisle she visited, she noticed the clunking sound and the tendency of the cart to pull to one side like a car with a flat tire. By the time she discovered the malfunction, it seemed easier to battle the balky conveyance than unload her groceries into another one. After all, what was one more inconvenience on top of what had already happened? Surely things couldn't get any worse. At least, she hoped that was the case.

When she reached the head of the checkout line, a pimply-faced clerk with a faint smile on his face but none in his voice began scanning her items. He met her eyes long enough to say, "May I have your Reward Card, ma'am?"

Anna found her keys, buried as usual in the deepest, darkest corner of her purse. The clerk thumbed through the plastic tags until he found the right one. He swiped it several times and finally tossed the keys back onto the counter. "The tag's too worn. Won't scan. What's your phone number?"

She repeated the number to the clerk while she swept the keys into her purse and transferred the last of the items from her cart onto the moving belt. Whether the clerk's heart was in his work, his hands moved swiftly, and in a moment the items were scanned and bagged. "That's $62.48."

Anna had pulled out her wallet along with her keys and was ready with her Master-Card. She swiped it and watched the screen, waiting to confirm the amount and sign. She was still waiting when the clerk said, "Ma'am, swipe it again. I'm getting an error message."

She complied.

"Ma'am," the clerk said, "there's a problem with your card. Do you want to use another one?"

"I only brought this one. What's the matter with it?"

"This account is over its limit. Do you want to write a check? Pay with cash?"

The impatience in the clerk's voice made Anna glance around. The man behind her was shifting from one foot to the other, and the line was building.

"I don't have my checkbook," she said. "And I don't have that much cash. I . . . I'll come back."

She didn't even think about the groceries. All she could think about was getting away from the irritable clerk, away from the exasperated looks of the people behind her in line.

She screeched out of the parking lot,

impatient to get home and call the credit card company. There was no way her card was over its limit. Somebody owed her an explanation.

Nick put down the phone and massaged his chin, running his fingers over the scratchy stubble as he thought about the information he'd just been given. Both units of blood received by Eric Hatley werc totally compatible with the patient's own blood. The lab director herself had done the cross-matches in duplicate. No question about it. The blood wasn't the source of the allergic reaction that had killed the man.

"Still here?" The morgue technician stood in the open doorway and raised his eyebrows as though to ask, "Why?"

"Yeah," Nick replied. "I want to work on some stuff, and it's a lot quieter over here than in my academic office."

"Right. Those folks in the drawers back there don't make much noise, do they?"

Nick frowned. He understood that when you worked around death all day, making jokes about it was a normal defense mechanism. But it still didn't make him like the practice. He kept quiet and eventually the attendant took the hint and left with a cheery, "Well, it's quitting time. I'm out of here."

His unfinished project stared back at Nick from the computer screen, the cursor accusing him with every blink. He really should finish it today. But first he wanted to let Anna know what he'd found out about the blood. There was no question in his mind that talking with her took precedence over making his chairman happy. Wetherington was never happy anyway, so why worry about it?

Nick opened the faculty directory and dialed Dr. Anna McIntyre's office number. Her administrative assistant answered on the first ring.

"This is Dr. Valentine. I'm trying to reach Dr. McIntyre. Is she there?"

"I'm sorry, Doctor. She's left for the day."

"Oh." Nick looked at his watch. A bit after four. Sort of early in the day for Anna to be leaving, but — "Well, what time does she usually get there in the morning?"

The woman cleared her throat. "I've been told that Dr. McIntyre will be on leave for at least two weeks. Could someone else help you?"

That didn't make sense. The likelihood that a junior faculty member in her first year would have two weeks of accrued leave, let alone be permitted to take it in one block, was about the same as a meteor hitting Neiman Marcus at noon tomorrow. Had the chairman suspended her? Was she in trouble over this patient death? If so, that made his call even more important.

The assistant's voice interrupted Nick's thoughts. "Doctor?"

"Sorry. I guess I could page her."

He started to hang up when he heard a rattle of words and brought the receiver back to his ear. "What was that?"

"I said her pager is sitting on her desk. I saw it just a few minutes ago. I really think she doesn't want to be disturbed."

Nick could feel his temper bubbling to the surface. He shoved it down and tried to keep his voice calm. "All right, could you give me her home number?"

"I'm afraid we can't do that. Why don't I transfer your call to the chairman's office? Maybe Dr. Fowler can help you."

"No, don't bother. Thanks." Nick hung up before she could respond. He didn't want to go through Neil Fowler to contact Anna. And he didn't want to leave a message. It was dawning on him that what he wanted was to see Anna McIntyre again.

He swiveled back to his computer and looked at the screen. He sighed and closed the document. Then he logged on to the Internet. It shouldn't be hard to find Anna.

Being home didn't defuse Anna's anger and frustration. She took the time for a quick shower and a change into more casual clothes. Back in her living room, she pulled a folder from her desk drawer, kicked off her loafers, and slumped into an easy chair with a Diet Coke and the cordless phone, ready to do battle with the credit card company.

She flipped through the folder until she found her last MasterCard bill. She dialed the wrong number once, then navigated a maze of electronic commands, entered her account number, and confirmed her mother's maiden name to an operator who seemed only mildly interested in the process. Finally, she was able to speak to someone about her problem.

"How may I help you?" said the slightly accented voice on the other end of the line.

"My card was declined today because I'm supposedly over my credit limit. I have my last statement right here. I made a payment only a week ago, and I should be nowhere near my limit. Can you tell me what's going on?"

"I'm so sorry." The operator's tone didn't

match the words, but Anna figured that she'd settle for action instead of sympathy. "Let me pull up your account."

Anna took a long gulp of soft drink while she waited.

"Oh, my."

Anna put down her drink can and sat forward in her chair. "What's wrong?"

"Well, it appears that we actually tried to get in touch with you today about your account, but there was no answer at your home number."

For the first time, Anna noticed the blinking red light on the answering machine. "What were you calling about?"

"According to my records, in the past two days there have been numerous charges to your account, and at the present time it's almost two hundred dollars over your credit limit."

"That can't be right."

"No problem," the operator continued, apparently unfazed by Anna's tone. "Your payment history has been good, so if you like, I'm sure we can extend your limit."

Anna felt her heart descend into her shoes. This was definitely not what she needed on top of all her other problems. "I don't want my credit limit extended. I want you to remove those charges. They're not mine. I can tell you exactly how much I've used my card in the past week." She fumbled in the folder and withdrew a few charge slips. "I charged gasoline a week ago, then a meal at El Chico, a blouse at Dillard's, and two days ago I bought some things at CVS pharmacy. That's it. That couldn't have put me over my limit. You must have my account mixed up with somebody else's." She heard the panic creep into her voice but couldn't stop it.

"I'm sorry, Mrs. McIntyre. Could your husband have made some of these charges and not told you?"

"It's Doctor McIntyre, and I'm not married. I'm the only person with this card."

This time there seemed to be genuine sympathy in the operator's reply. "Oh. I'm afraid what we have here may be a case of unauthorized usage. If you'll hold for a moment, I'll get a supervisor on the line."

Anna found herself automatically saying, "Thank you," before the full import of the operator's words registered. "Unauthorized usage?"

"Unfortunately, it's not that uncommon. The supervisor will get more information from you and confirm a security breach. Then she'll cancel your card and arrange to have a new one sent to you by express courier. You should have it tomorrow afternoon. Will there be someone there to sign for it?"

"Yes."

While the saccharin strains of music on hold played in her ear, Anna considered what this meant. It would be an inconvenience to be without her card for a day, but she had a VISA card she could use until the new MasterCard arrived. Being at home to sign for the delivery would be a pain, but she'd work it out somehow. And she was pretty sure she wouldn't have to pay for the things charged to her account by someone else. Clearing up the mess left behind by whoever hijacked her credit card would be a major nuisance, but somehow she'd get through it. The question that stuck in her mind, going round and round without an answer, was how someone had gotten hold of her credit card information. And did this have anything to do with her DEA number being compromised?

Nick looked at the address written in blue ballpoint ink on his left palm, what he'd once heard called the primitive version of a Palm Pilot. It had taken him twenty minutes of computer surfing to dig up a home phone number for Anna McIntyre and only a few clicks after that to uncover the physical address that went with it. Truly, with the growth of the Internet there was no longer any such thing as privacy.

Now that he was here, he had to wonder why this had seemed so important to him. Because he wanted to help her solve the question of why her patient died? Or because he was excited about seeing Anna?

He eased out from behind the wheel of his Honda Civic and squinted to see the numbers on the doorposts of the duplex. There it was, on the left. He marched to the door and rapped firmly. He made himself wait a measured thirty seconds before repeating his knock, this time a bit harder and longer.

Nick was rewarded with a faint call from inside. "Just a second."

It was closer to two minutes before the peephole darkened for an instant, then the door opened and Anna McIntyre greeted him. She wore a hip-length Dallas Cowboys T-shirt over faded jeans. Her feet were bare, her red hair tousled. Without makeup, the simple beauty of her face shone through. Nick knew that his heart wasn't really doing somersaults, but it sure felt like it.

Anna was talking on a cordless phone as she motioned him inside. She waved him to a seat, pointed to the phone in silent apology, and disappeared into the next room, still talking.

At least she hadn't turned him away at the door. He scanned the living room. Minimal furnishings, but every item obviously chosen with care and taste. He knew how much an assistant professor at the med school made — at least in his department — and he suspected that Anna's personal budget was as tight as his. It appeared that she'd done a nice job with the funds available.

"Sorry." She strode through the door and replaced the phone in its cradle. She scooped up several sheets of paper and shoved them into a manila folder, which she filed in a bottom drawer of the small desk in one corner of the living room. "I've had sort of a personal crisis around here, and I had to finish trying to deal with it."

Nick ran his hand through his dark hair and wished he'd gotten that haircut he'd kept putting off. "I should have called first."

"You wouldn't have gotten through. I've been on the phone for almost an hour, and I refuse to have call waiting. I have trouble enough keeping up with one conversation at a time." She eased down onto the sofa beside him.

Anna had been tense when he saw her earlier today, and apparently, there were still storm warnings flying. He'd love to see her when she actually relaxed. "I'm glad I caught you," he said.

"So, what brings you here?"

Nick hated to jeopardize any chance of turning this into a social occasion by immediately talking about medicine, but that was the reason he was here — or at least, the pretext for the visit. "I got the results of the tests on the blood that Hatley received. Everything checks out. The blood didn't cause the allergic reaction."

Anna frowned. "So it was the antibiotic."

"Probably. But you said he tolerated it only a couple of weeks before."

"Look, I don't have an explanation for it, and right now I have another crisis I'm dealing with." She tucked her feet under her and turned until she faced him. "I know that this afternoon I made a big deal about finding out why Hatley died. Well, it's still a big deal, but unfortunately, it's been overshadowed by some other things — personal things."

"Anything I can do?" Why had he asked that? It was none of his business. But he wanted it to be.

She shook her head. "Nothing, but thanks

for offering. It's a hassle with my credit card company. I can handle it."

"Hey, I've been there. They don't cut you much slack, do they?"

"Not really." Anna rose and took a step toward the door. "I appreciate your willingness to help me dig into the cause of my patient's death. It was nice of you to come here in person to tell me what you've found."

He stood, but made no move to leave. "No problem. Hatley's death is bothering you, and it's puzzling me. And I'd like to cooperate in the investigation." He paused, choosing his words carefully. "And, to be honest, I enjoyed our time together this afternoon. I'd really like to get to know you better. Think that's possible?"

Anna looked away. "I'm sorry. I guess you can see I'm pretty preoccupied, and that's one of the curses of being a surgeon. I'm a linear thinker — one thing at a time. I'll worry at this Hatley case like a dog with a bone, and until I get some answers I doubt that I'll be very social."

"I can wait. Meanwhile, let me help you with the Hatley case."

"Frankly, I can't even see why you want to get involved. It was my patient who died. I'm the one who had to face the family. I'm the one who'll probably get sued."

Nick saw the pain in her eyes, heard it in her voice. "You have every reason to want some answers. Maybe I want answers too. One of the things pathologists are good at is piecing together evidence and coming up with conclusions. This is important to me too. If we can pin down the reason Eric Hatley had that reaction, maybe it will keep another patient from dying."

Anna chewed on her lower lip. "Okay," she said. "We can work together on the Hatley case."

Nick checked the time. Half past seven. "What would you think about doing it over dinner?"

She shook her head. "No, I'm just going to —" She stopped, and her face crumpled.

"What's the matter?" he asked.

"I started to say that I was just going to cook something for myself tonight. But I can't because I don't have anything here to cook. When I went to get groceries this afternoon —" She looked away. "They told me my credit card was maxed out."

Nick knew how that felt. "Hey, I've had that happen to me. This is my treat."

"No, that's not it. The card was maxed out because somebody stole my identity. And I'm in trouble with the DEA. My chairman has put me on what amounts to a two-week suspension so I can hopefully clear my name. And if I can't —" She waved her hand in front of her face as though shooing away a troublesome insect. "I don't know why I'm telling you all this. It's complicated, and it's not your problem."

Nick decided to go for it. "Why don't you tell me about it over dinner? I'm a great listener. And I know where there's a wonderful little restaurant near here. Do you like Italian?"

3

Anna had passed the restaurant several times a week for almost a year without ever really noticing it. From the outside, it looked like the picture in the encyclopedia next to the phrase, "hole in the wall." But once she preceded Nick through the dark oak door with its leaded glass panes, she was glad she'd followed his suggestion to come here.

Along the back wall, six high-backed stools stood empty in front of a zinc-topped bar. A dozen tables were scattered around the room, each one covered by a red-and-white checked tablecloth and topped by a Chianti bottle from which a candle sprouted. The air was redolent of oregano, garlic, and other spices that Anna didn't recognize but definitely wanted to taste. She took a deep breath and felt a few of the knots in her neck muscles begin to unwind.

Anna stole a glance at her companion. She

still wasn't sure why she'd agreed to have dinner with Nick. It wasn't simply his dark good looks, although that was certainly a plus. And he was persistent; she had to give him that. But the main thing was that tonight she'd been as low as she'd ever felt in her life, and Nick's offer of a listening ear had seemed sincere. She found herself relaxing with him. For now, that was enough.

They were greeted by a formidable woman with jet-black hair worn in a bun. "Nicolo," she said, enfolding Nick in a bear hug. "So good- a to see you."

"Thanks, Maria. This is my friend, Dr. Anna McIntyre. I brought her here so I could show off my knowledge of Italian — all six words."

After receiving her own hug, Anna was ushered to a table in the corner and seated with a ceremony that suggested she was a visiting head of state. "Nick," she said, once Maria had scooted away, "this place is marvelous. Do you come here often?"

"No, my usual dinner venue is Burger King. But the owners are family friends, and every once in a while I treat myself to a real meal."

Anna opened her menu and was immediately thrown into a panic. The whole thing was printed in Italian. "I think they gave me the wrong menu."

"You mean because it's not in English? No, that's the way it's done here. But don't worry. You won't be able to order, anyway."

"What do you mean?"

Before Nick could reply, a balding, mustachioed man with a towel tucked into the waistband of his black pants came hurrying up to the table. He engaged in a brief exchange with Nick in Italian. Then the man turned to Anna and said, "Welcome, *signorina*." He lifted her hand to his lips and gently kissed her fingertips before moving away.

"What just happened?" she asked.

"That's the owner, Maria's husband, Benny. Short for Benedetto. He insisted on ordering for us. I'm pretty sure he'll ply us with food until we burst, so I'd suggest you sample each dish but don't try to eat everything set before you."

"You understood all that from such a short conversation?"

"I understood about half the words, but I can promise you that's what he was saying. Trust me. I'm Italian."

"Did they kiss your date's hand the last time you were here?" She felt the heat of a blush on her cheeks as soon as the words were out. Was she flirting with this man she'd only met today?

Nick laughed. "Since my 'date,' as you call him, was a former college fraternity brother who now plays professional football, no."

"Sorry. I didn't really mean to pry."

"No, that's all right," Nick said. "And to answer your implied question, the last real date I had was almost a year ago. She was an obstetrics resident, and I can't even remember her name."

"In the interest of a level playing field, are you going to ask about my last date?"

Nick flashed a shy grin. "No, all I'm interested in is your next date. Can it be with me?"

It seemed to Nick like only a moment passed before he and Anna were sipping cups of coffee and dabbing the last remnants of cannoli from their lips. The courses had been spaced nicely, allowing ample time for talk. The buffer zone of empty tables around them told Nick that Maria had decided to give them privacy. Benny's service had been efficient and unobtrusive. If only the evening didn't have to end.

"Nick, thank you for this," Anna said. "I really needed a lift tonight."

Nick waited while Benny refilled their coffee cups. "Well, I hope this has helped. Do you think you've got things straight with MasterCard now?"

"It gets better, or worse, I guess," she said. "It's not just my MasterCard. The call I was finishing when you arrived was to VISA. I thought I'd better check my limit there, because I'd need to use that one until my new MasterCard arrives. And that's when I found out that my VISA was over its limit."

"Same scenario?"

"Exactly the same. So now both my accounts are closed. The new cards will be here soon, but until they arrive I'm on a cash and carry basis." She shrugged. "It's no big deal. It just complicates things, and I don't need another complication in my life right now."

"And someone has been papering the area with Vicodin 'scripts using your name and DEA number?"

"Right again," Anna said. "My chairman put me on leave until that's sorted out, so I'm in limbo. I can't practice for who knows how long. The only thing that could make it all worse is if somebody ran over my dog — if I had a dog."

Nick could relate to her gallows humor. "You're a victim of the law," he said.

"Which law is that?"

Nick grinned. "My favorite — Murphy's Law. If something can go wrong, it will."

Anna shook her head. "I don't know what to call it, but I certainly don't see how things could get any worse."

Nick tried to pick his words carefully, tiptoeing around the minefield of the tension he saw in Anna. "Is there something I can do?"

"You can help most by doing some research on anaphylaxis. I still can't figure out why the antibiotic killed Hatley. He tolerated it a few weeks earlier when they gave it to him in the Emergency Room."

Nick sneaked a peek at his watch. He'd managed to keep the conversation away from medicine for a half hour or so, but now they were back to the incident that had brought them together in the first place. "And that's all I can do?"

"The other problems are mine, and I have to deal with them," Anna said. "I'm the one who has to make sure this stolen card doesn't ruin my credit. I've heard friends talk about what a pain it is to get those things taken off your record. As for finding out why someone's been writing narcotics prescriptions using my DEA number, I don't have a clue how I'll do that. But one thing at a time, I guess."

"Okay. I'll do what I can. From what I remember, if somebody is allergic to penicillin, they stand a decent chance of being allergic to the class of drugs Hatley received. I'm pretty sure that the generally accepted way to test for penicillin allergy is a skin test, although obviously that's not possible here. What I need is a blood test for allergy to drugs like Omnilex, one I can run on the samples I took at the time of the autopsy. I'll start researching that tomorrow morning."

"Scusi." Benny seemed to materialize at Nick's side. "Would you like anything else?"

Nick looked at Anna and received a brief headshake in response. "No, Benny. That's fine. This was a wonderful meal." He pulled out his wallet and handed over a credit card.

When Benny had shuffled away, Anna said, "Would you at least let me pay my share of this? I can write you a check."

"No, unless somebody's been charging things to my credit card without my knowledge, I think I've got this one covered."

In less than a minute, Benny was back, holding the credit card by his thumb and middle finger much as one would hold a dead rat by the tail. *"Scusi,"* he said. "Nicolo, I'm afraid this is no good."

Nick's heart rate galloped up a notch. He

was pretty sure he was below the limit on his credit card. Barely below it, perhaps, but pretty safe until his next paycheck. Had he joined Anna as the victim of credit card theft? "Benny, are you sure?"

Benny grinned, first at Nick, then at Anna, "Sure, I'm sure. You can't pay with this because we not gonna take you money tonight. Maria and me want this meal to be on us."

"Thank you. That's very kind," Anna said.

"It's our pleasure." Benny turned to Nick. "Maria and me agree. This lady's much nicer than that big guy you had in here last time. He was-a not your type at all."

Nick watched Anna fumble for her keys and wondered why no one had yet invented a woman's purse that would pop out a key ring or wallet with the push of a button. Or maybe they had. He really didn't have any way of knowing, come to think of it.

Anna unlocked the front door, then turned back with it half open. "Nick, thanks for taking my mind off my troubles for a while."

"My pleasure," he said. "Thank you for sharing your troubles with me. And I'll get in touch with you as soon as I research the drug allergy thing a bit more. How shall I contact you? I know your home number, but do you have a cell phone?"

Anna laughed, and Nick could have turned a cartwheel. That smile, that laugh, made the whole evening a success.

"Surprisingly enough, I have all the modern conveniences," Anna said. "Answering machine, e-mail account, even a cell phone. Are you fishing for my number?"

"Busted. I found your phone number and address using the Internet, but your cell and e-mail are another matter entirely. By the way, you can rest assured that tight-lipped assistant of yours didn't spill anything. Matter of fact, I had to hang up before she could sic your chairman on me. I'm brave, but I'm not stupid."

"Okay, you win. Come on in, and I'll write down that information. And you should probably give me yours, since we seem to be linked in this effort." She pushed the door fully open and flipped on the lights in the living room. "Park somewhere. I'll be back in a moment."

Nick chose the sofa, then leaned back, closed his eyes, and let the events of the day unroll on the screen in his mind. He'd started out working on the material for his chairman, bored to tears and frustrated with life in general. Then came a routine autopsy that left him with some unanswered questions. That, in turn, led to the beautiful redhead who, if his nose wasn't fooling him, was brewing coffee and would shortly be sitting down next to him. Life was good.

In a few minutes, Nick sensed movement in the room. He opened his eyes in time to see Anna set two white ceramic mugs on the coffee table. "Hope you don't have an aversion to drinking coffee this late at night. Black with Sweet'n Low, right?"

"Right. Good powers of observation, Doc."

"That's why they pay me the big bucks." Then her smile faded. "Or, at least, why they've paid me so far. Don't know how much longer I'll have a job."

"Don't let it get you down, Anna."

She snuggled down at the opposite end of the sofa from him and blew across the top of her mug. "I'm trying not to. I'll work as hard as I can to straighten things out, but in the end I'll have to trust God."

"I wish I could tell you that'll make everything come out right, but I can't," Nick said. "It's been quite a while since I thought God cared about my problems."

"You want to talk about it?"

"Not really. I shouldn't have brought it up." Way to go, Nick. Nice way to spoil a perfectly good evening. He took a sip of coffee and winced when it burned his mouth. "Let's just leave it at this: I'll work as hard as I can to help you out of this mess. If God intervenes, so much the better. But I'm not going to count on it."

Anna awoke, as she had each morning for years, before the sun came up. She rolled out of bed, stretched, and froze. There was no need to get up early today. No rounds to make. No surgery to perform. No clinics to staff. Not even any paperwork to plow through. She'd been suspended. Well, put on leave, but the effect was the same. Until she could clear herself of the charges against her, she was a doctor without a place to practice.

In the shower, Anna's mind couldn't stay focused. Her thoughts flitted among the problems in her life, rushing back and forth like a rat in a maze. It felt different — sort of empty — not to be heading out the door, coffee in a travel mug, already planning her day. How long would it be before she could get back into that routine? Days? Weeks? The prospect was too depressing to think about.

She still hadn't bought groceries, so Anna ate a piece of dry toast and a cup of coffee for breakfast. What she'd give for a doughnut fix from the medical school's food court, but she couldn't bring herself to go back there. At least, not yet.

After her second cup of coffee, she sat down with a yellow legal pad and began a list. She'd start by addressing the effect of the identity theft on her credit. Based on her experience yesterday, she figured it wouldn't be simple.

More than an hour later, Anna finished the last of several phone calls and heaved a sigh, not so much of relief as of exhaustion. She'd advised all three major credit-reporting entities of the identity theft. They'd promised to make the necessary adjustments to her record, although it might take a little time. That was the good news. The bad news was that, in order to formalize a fraud alert, she had a laundry list of hard-copy material to forward to each company. Then there was something called a security freeze, so no one could open accounts in her name in the future. And it was all going to require copies — lots of copies.

Her first thought was a trip back to the medical school to use the copy machine in the Surgery Department offices. But the prospect of the stares, the questions she was bound to get, made her stop and think.

Maybe she could go to Kinko's instead. She probably had enough in her checking account to cover the cost.

On the other hand, the copier in the department was nice, and it wouldn't cost her a cent to use it. After all, she should probably try to conserve money, since she didn't know how all this would finally shake out. And maybe she'd drop by and see Nick while she was there. Maybe he had more information about the cause of Hatley's death. Besides, she'd enjoyed their time together last night. And she could certainly use a friend right now.

Anna decided it was a wonder Nick had been interested in seeing her again, as distracted as she'd been when they first met. But last night had been better. The meal, the company, Benny's antics — all had brought a smile to her lips when she needed it most. That had to be a good sign.

She gathered up the material she'd need to copy. In the process, Anna paused before the mirror in the hallway. Hair looked okay. Makeup could be a bit better. And maybe she'd change into that new blouse and skirt before she left.

On the drive to the medical school, her little Toyota seemed a bit balky, but Anna put it

72

down to an extension of the bad luck she was having. Maybe she'd gotten some bad gasoline. Maybe it was time to change the spark plugs. She could never recall how often that was supposed to happen. She'd ask around. One more thing to add to the list. She was about a mile from home when the engine coughed three times like a two-pack-a-day smoker, then quit.

She was sitting behind the wheel, trying to restart the car, when there was a tap on the driver's side window. The middle-aged Hispanic man standing there looked pleasant enough. The name over the pocket of his blue work shirt was Ramon. Anna looked beyond him and saw a faded blue pickup parked across the street, a woman in the passenger seat.

"Can I help?" the man said in a voice with only a hint of accent.

Anna measured her options and decided that Ramon was her best one. "Yes, please. It just quit."

After about ten minutes, Ramon peered at Anna from beneath the open hood of her car and said, "I believe it is probably the fuel pump." His brown eyes mirrored the sorrow that was in his voice.

"Can you fix it?"

Ramon shook his head. "No, I am sorry.

My wife and I can give you a ride somewhere if that would help."

Anna recalled the Toyota dealership she passed every day on her way to the medical center. She'd never paid any attention to it until now. "Thanks, but I have a cell phone. I can call for a tow."

Forty minutes later, Anna sat in the waiting room of the dealership, turning the pages of a year-old copy of a magazine without any recognition of the words and pictures. The car had served her faithfully through medical school and residency, as well as two owners before her, owners who had probably not been particularly kind to the vehicle. If this episode wasn't the final chapter for the car, that couldn't be far away. Should she look at another car while she was here?

"May I help you while you're waiting?" It was as though the salesman had read her thoughts.

"I'm waiting for my car to be repaired."

"Why don't I show you some of the bargains we have? You might decide to trade up."

"No, thank you."

"If you change your mind, let me know."

The salesman had no sooner left than Anna heard, "Dr. McIntyre?"

She turned in her chair to find the service advisor standing behind her. "Your car needs a new fuel pump. And we've found a couple of other things." He held out a clipboard. "Here's what it will take to repair it. If you want us to do it, we can get right on it and have you out of here in two or three hours."

Anna looked at the figures. She could afford the repairs — just barely. But maybe she'd be better off putting the money into a new car.

"Let me think about it." She looked around for the salesman, and found him at the coffee machine.

The salesman led Anna on a whirlwind tour of the lot, and after half an hour she sat in his office while his fingers flew over the keys of his computer. "Well, Doctor, I believe we can put you in that car at a price you can afford. Let me get a little information, and I'll run a credit report."

Ten minutes later, the salesman swiveled away from the computer screen, and the look in his eyes told Anna everything she needed to know. "I've done a credit check. I think we might have some trouble financing that car. We can probably do it, but I can't get the interest rate I wanted. And that would make the payments —."

"No, I understand." Anna wanted to argue, but realized how futile it would be. The red flags were already up. Her credit had become suspect. And even though the credit reporting companies had promised to put things right, it wasn't going to happen today.

She found the service advisor and said, "Okay, just do the repair. I'll wait."

"Thanks anyway." Nick Valentine hung up the phone and rummaged through the books and journals scattered in front of him. The desk of his academic office, never the most organized eighteen square feet in the Pathology Department, looked like a war zone. He was computer-literate and often did online searches for information, but at times it was comforting to feel the heft of a textbook in your hands, to mark an important passage with a yellow highlighter. For this problem, he'd pulled out all the stops: a computer search, back issues of journals from the department library, textbooks — old and new — taken from his shelves. And now he'd just hung up from a short, albeit rather unsatisfactory, conversation with the head of the Allergy Division. His head swam with information overload.

He let his gaze rest on Eric Hatley's chart

and the notes he'd made when he reviewed it again. Nothing he'd found changed his mind about the cause of Hatley's death. However, there was one bit of information that puzzled him. Maybe he'd go downstairs and get some coffee to help him think.

"Got a minute?"

The voice brought him instantly alert. Anna McIntyre stood in the doorway. Her shoulders sagged just a bit, even though she had a faint smile plastered on her face. Nick wondered if something more had gone wrong. Then he noticed the two paper cups in Anna's hands.

"I come bearing gifts from Starbucks," she said, advancing and placing one of the containers on his desk like a priest laying a sacrifice on the altar. "I wanted to thank you for the dinner last evening, and for the work you're putting in on the Hatley case."

Nick flipped the lid off the cup and tossed it into his wastebasket, barely hitting his target. He nodded his appreciation and took a deep sip. "No thanks necessary, but you don't know how much I needed this pick-me-up. I've been working all afternoon trying to find a blood test for allergy to Omnilex. Unfortunately, there isn't one, at least not one that's reliable. Mainly because the drug's too new."

Anna eased into the chair across the desk from Nick and took a taste of her coffee. "So there's no way to know for sure whether Eric Hatley had his anaphylactic reaction because of the antibiotic we gave him."

Nick recognized this as a statement, not a question. "His tryptase level came back this morning — sky-high. Hatley definitely had a severe anaphylactic reaction. I just finished the microscopic exam on the tissue samples from the autopsy. Nothing else showed up. Bottom line, there's no question that a massive allergic reaction was the final event. But we can't prove the cause."

"Could this be due to the anesthesiologist giving him a wrong medication of some kind?"

"What makes you ask?"

"The staff man was out of the room. Jeff Murray is a first-year resident, not experienced, not necessarily good under stress. At the time I didn't make too much of it, but as I thought about it later, I wondered if maybe he didn't give Hatley something other than the antibiotic Luc ordered."

Nick shook his head. "No way. I went so far as to go up to surgery this morning and look through one of the anesthesia carts. Other than various antibiotics, I couldn't find anything there that could have done this."

"So I can't blame anesthesia for this."

"Afraid not. But this should interest you." Nick reached past the pile of articles and books on his desk, moved aside Hatley's hospital chart, and picked up a thin file held together by a metal fastener strip threaded through two holes punched at the top.

"What's that?"

"I had them pull the emergency room record for Eric Hatley, the visit that was the basis for your choice of antibiotics. Have a look."

He held out the folder and watched Anna thumb through it the way physicians learn to do, scanning the pages and picking out the important nuggets of information. He could tell when she got to the part that had stopped him cold.

"What do you think?" he asked.

"I think this patient signed in with the same name, address, and date of birth as the man who died on the operating table."

"But?"

"Our Eric Hatley was a middle-aged Caucasian male." Anna looked down at the page where her finger marked the line that Nick knew would get her attention, as it had his. "It says, 'The patient is a young,

African-American male who complains of
___,' "

"Right. Same identifying data. Different people." Nick drained his coffee cup. "Looks like you're not the only person who's had their identity stolen. But in this case, Eric Hatley lost more than his credit cards. He lost his life."

4

Anna stood quietly by as the Emergency Room clerk explained to a young Latino boy that his father would be seen as soon as possible. The boy nodded gravely and rattled off the translation so rapidly that Anna, who prided herself on being able to communicate in that language, couldn't follow the Spanish. The father grimaced, clutched his stomach for a moment, then shrugged in resignation and edged back toward a seat in the crowded waiting room.

When the clerk was free, Anna stepped up to the desk. "Shirley, what doctor's running the ER today?"

The woman turned with a start. "Oh, Dr. McIntyre. I didn't see you standing there. I thought you were on vacation."

Anna leaned over and dropped her voice. "News travels fast around here. Yes, I'm on a leave of sorts, but there's something I need to . . . I have to get some information from

one of the doctors for the project I'm working on. Who's the Pit Boss today?"

Shirley ran her hand through blonde hair
that Anna was willing to bet didn't start out
that color. "That would be Dr. Fell."

"Do you know if he's tied up right now?"

"I think he just slipped back for a cup of
coffee." Shirley pointed the way.

Anna nodded her thanks and headed for
the break room. Just being in the Emergency
Room made her pulse quicken, as she
relived memories of her own time as "Pit
Boss" — the second-year surgery resident
charged with overseeing the ER at Parkland
Hospital, arguably one of the busiest in the
nation. The pressure was tremendous, but
the opportunity to hone one's clinical judgment and skills was almost unlimited.

She recalled the time when one of the
senior staff surgeons had found her sobbing
in the ER break room at the end of her shift.
He'd put a gentle hand on her shoulder.
"What's wrong, Anna?"

She told him about her feverish struggle
to save the victims of a horrible crash on
North Central Expressway. In the end, the
only survivor was a three-year-old child, left
orphaned when his mother, father, and
older sister died. "I did all I could. And it
wasn't enough."

The doctor had eased into the chair beside her. "If you've given it all you had, don't blame yourself when you lose the battle. You can't die with them, you know. If you do, who'd take care of the next one?"

Anna gave a little shudder as she recalled that advice. She'd recently had a patient die — one who should still be alive right now — but for the moment she needed to put any thought of guilt and blame aside. She needed to do something positive. She'd start by questioning the doctor who'd treated the "other" Eric Hatley.

"Dr. McIntyre, what brings you down here? I thought you were on leave." Dr. William Fell was slumped on the couch, sipping from a Styrofoam cup. He started to stand, but Anna waved him back.

"Will, I'm glad you're on duty today. I need to know what you remember about this patient." She held out the emergency room file she'd taken from Nick's office.

He flashed a grin. "Hey, this was two weeks ago. I can't remember the patients from yesterday."

"It's really important. Look at your note. Tell me if it rings a bell."

Will scanned the scrawled note. "Matter of fact, I do recall this guy. In the first place, if you notice the time stamp, he showed up here at two a.m. with a chief complaint of a sexually transmitted disease. I'd just stretched out to take a nap when they woke me. I gave him a pretty good tongue-lashing for picking that time to come in for something like that. Know what he said?"

Anna shook her head.

"Said that he knew we wouldn't be as busy at that time of the morning, and he was up anyway." Will flipped back to the cover sheet. "I remember telling him that, since he had private insurance, he should have gone to his regular doctor during normal hours. He blew me off and asked me if I was going to treat him. I did a quick exam, confirmed my diagnosis with a lab test, and gave him an IM antibiotic. Told him to make a follow-up appointment, but you know they never do. End of story."

"Can you recall what he looked like?"

"Vaguely. Twentyish black male. Taller than me, quite a bit thinner."

"Remember anything else about him?"

Will closed his eyes and Anna could almost hear the wheels turning. "Sorry, nothing stands out. Is it important?"

"Not really, I guess."

"What's this about?"

"The man's name came up in connection with another case, and I'm following up on it," Anna said. "We may have gotten a couple of patients with the same name mixed up. But you didn't do anything wrong, so don't worry about it. Thanks."

"I'll walk out with you," Will said. "It's time for me to get back to work."

They stopped in the hall and Anna put her hand on Will's arm. "Hang in there. It's a tough rotation, but it's worth it — sort of like putting iron into a fire to temper it."

As she started down the hall, Anna couldn't help wondering whether the problems that plagued her right now would temper the iron of her resolve or shatter it.

"Hi, Lisa. I'm picking up some things. Pretend I'm not here." Anna ducked into the sanctuary of her office before her administrative assistant could reply.

She scanned the mail and rummaged through the papers in her "In" box. Nothing that couldn't wait another day. And if things didn't get straightened out pretty soon, none of it would matter anyway. Anna unzipped the backpack she used as a briefcase and pulled out a manila folder bulging with the documents to duplicate. She was still shuffling the papers, deciding how many copies she'd need, when Lisa appeared in the doorway.

"Dr. McIntyre, I know you said to pretend you aren't here, but there are two detectives out there, and they want to speak with you."

Anna decided she was getting entirely too experienced at meeting with members of the law enforcement community. "Have you looked at their credentials?"

Lisa nodded. "Yes. They're with the Dallas Police."

Anna squared her shoulders. "Very well. I'll talk with them."

Lisa paused with her hand on the doorknob. "I want you to know that I think this whole mess with narcotics numbers and forged prescriptions is ridiculous. Nobody in the department thinks you did anything wrong."

"Thank you," Anna said. "I guess you'd better send them in."

The moment the two men — one white, one African American — came through the door, Anna decided she would have pegged them as policemen without any advance warning. Not just because of the wardrobe — off-the-rack sport coats, slightly rumpled dress shirts, shoes obviously chosen for comfort rather than style. No, it was a subtle presence that said, "I'm in charge and I've got my eye on you."

Anna held out her hand. "May I see your

credentials?" She left the men standing while she sat and carefully examined their badges and identification cards. She jotted down their names and badge numbers, adding them to the sheet she'd started for the DEA agents.

Lamar Green was a burly African American with a shaved head and what looked to be a permanent scowl on his face. His whole demeanor said, "Don't mess with me."

Burt Dowling was a rail-thin white man with a pronounced five o'clock shadow and thinning dark brown hair. Whereas Green seemed to jangle with nervous energy, Dowling appeared to observe the world with a touch of disappointment through hooded eyelids.

She handed the credentials back and motioned the men to the two chairs across from her desk. "How may I help you?"

Green pulled a notebook from his pocket but didn't open it. Instead, he fixed her with a glacial stare. "Doctor, we need to ask you some questions about all the prescriptions you've been writing for large amounts of narcotics."

Anna fought to control her temper. "I believe you mean that some prescriptions bearing my DEA number and forged with my signature have turned up. I'm unaware of any evidence that even vaguely suggests I'm anything but a victim in this situation."

Dowling patted the air in a calming gesture. "Doctor, we understand you're upset. Now, it may be that you're as innocent as a lamb." Then, like Texas weather in the spring, his manner turned dark. "On the other hand, maybe you're ticked off that we've found out about this little racket of yours. Now, if you'll come clean about your involvement, I'm sure we can put in a good word for you with the district attorney."

Anna took a deep breath. "There's no need to put in a good word. I'm the victim here. Why don't you get out of here and trace back some of these forged 'scripts to their source? And, while you're at it, maybe you and the DEA can communicate so that I don't have to answer the same questions again and again."

Green stood, apparently trying to use his six-foot-plus height to intimidate Anna. "Doctor, we were hoping you'd be cooperative. We just want you to answer a few questions."

"And then you'll leave me alone?"

"Not quite. We also need to search your home."

Anna felt her blood boiling. "Search my house? Why?"

"Easy, Lamar." Dowling motioned his partner back into his chair before turning to Anna. "It's all part of the process. Do we need to get a warrant?"

Anna's inclination was to dig in her heels, but then again, how difficult would it be for these two men to find a judge who'd sign a search warrant? Why should she spend another day, even two, waiting for them to come back with one? She was innocent, and she knew they wouldn't find anything. "I'll meet you at my home in fifteen minutes."

The detectives were thorough with their search, but — give them credit — they were considerate. Anna had heard horror stories of searches that left homes in shambles, but by the time the men finished, her little apartment would look pretty much as she'd left it that morning.

"What are you looking for, anyway?" she asked Dowling.

"We'll know it when we see it. If you weren't looking over our shoulders, we could finish a lot quicker."

Anna's nerves tingled. When her Irish grandmother told her about second-sight, the gift of knowing in advance that something bad was going to happen, Anna pooh-poohed it. But that's exactly what she felt now. The longer the search continued, the more she regretted her decision not to call an attorney before letting these men into her apartment.

"Better late than never," she muttered. Anna went to her desk and picked up the phone. She found the medical school directory in the bottom drawer under a mass of papers. She rifled the pages, then glanced at her watch: five o'clock. She hoped the person she needed wasn't a clock-watcher.

Anna punched in the number and counted the rings. She was about to hang up, when she heard, "Laura Ernst." Something in the voice told her that the medical center's legal counsel hadn't had a wonderful day.

Well, Anna's hadn't been too good, either, so there wasn't much sympathy in her voice. "Ms. Ernst, this is Dr. Anna McIntyre. Remember, we talked on the phone two days ago."

"Hang on." There was a sound of rustling papers. "Okay, got it. The DEA says your name and number are on a bunch of narcotics prescriptions. As I recall, I told you to sit tight for now. These things usually work out if you're not guilty."

Anna bristled at the last comment, but this was no time to argue. "Well, now two

Dallas Police detectives are searching my home."

"Did they have a warrant?"

"No, I was so mad I just let them —"

"Stop them. Right now. Put down the phone, tell them you've spoken with your attorney. Tell them to get out and not come back until they have a search warrant that spells out exactly what they're looking for and why."

Anna hesitated for a few seconds, then did as Ernst had told her. The detectives tried to change her mind, but there seemed to be no conviction in their arguments. She slammed the door behind them and picked up the phone again.

"They're gone," Anna said.

"Good." Ernst paused. "You know, you may need your own attorney for this. Do you know anyone you could call?"

"No."

Ernst's sigh spoke volumes. "All right. Give me your number. I'll get back to you with a name. I have to make a phone call first."

Nick pulled up in front of Anna's duplex and for the tenth time wondered if it was the least bit over the top for him to see her again this soon. Face it, he decided, the SS

91

Over The Top had sailed when he took her to Maria and Benny's for dinner. He had known the kind of reception they'd give her, and it had been difficult for him to conceal his pleasure at her reaction.

Nick climbed out of the car and reached back for the flowers he'd bought at the supermarket on the spur of the moment. He debated a moment and decided to leave them on the seat. Flowers would definitely be over the top.

With his palms sweating like those of a schoolboy coming to pick up his date for the prom, he started up the walk. When he was halfway to the door, it opened and two men stepped out. It didn't take him long to link the men with the car parked at the curb just ahead of his own Chevrolet. In his experience, only one group drove around in a basic black Ford Crown Victoria with plain hubcaps, a spotlight, and two antennas: cops. What were they doing at Anna's? Had something happened? Had she been hurt?

"Excuse me," he said to the first of the men to reach him — a husky African American who scowled as though someone had just kicked his dog. "What's going on here?"

"Sir, I can't discuss it." The man brushed past Nick, followed in close order by a thin

Caucasian man displaying a similar disposition.

Nick hurried up to the door and rang the doorbell. When there was no answer, he rang it again. He was about to ring for a third time when the door opened.

Anna stood there with her hands on her hips. "I thought I told you —"

"Anna, are you all right?"

She was dressed in the same black skirt and green blouse she'd worn in his office earlier that day. When she recognized Nick, the fire flashing in her green eyes died down and she gestured him in, double locking the door behind him.

"Sorry. I didn't mean to bite your head off," she said. "I thought those two detectives had come back to harass me some more."

"What were detectives doing here?"

"Sit down. Let me put on some coffee. It's a long story."

Twenty minutes and a cup of coffee later, after Anna had explained about the visit from the police, Nick's blood was boiling. "Of course, they didn't find anything, did they?"

Anna's expression told him he'd struck a nerve. Her tone of voice confirmed it. "No, they didn't find anything! Of course, they were still looking when I threw them out, so they could have missed it."

"Sorry. I didn't mean to —"

"I know," Anna said. "I'm just upset. Anyway, I can assure you that there's no money hidden in the coffee can or stashed in the sugar canister. No envelope taped to the underside of the toilet tank cover. Of course, that doesn't mean they didn't look in those places, and everywhere else in the house. At least, until I made them leave."

Nick looked around. "Doesn't look like they messed up your house."

She ran a hand through her hair. "No, I have to admit they weren't malicious. They were clinical about it. Sort of, 'we have to do this, so stand back and don't bother us.' "

"Are they through now?" Nick asked.

"Laura Ernst said they couldn't come back without a search warrant, but I doubt that they're through. They mentioned that one of the things they were looking for was the money from my 'prescription racket' as they called it. Now I guess they'll check to see if I have any secret accounts in the Cayman Islands or Switzerland." She grimaced. "Just wish I did."

Nick drained the last drops of coffee from his cup. "They've got to realize that you're a victim in this whole mess."

"I told them the same thing." Anna picked up the cups and disappeared into the kitchen, returning in a moment with refills for them both. "But I still can't figure out why."

"Why the police are investigating you?"

"No," Anna said. "Why — and how — someone would steal my identity."

Anna stood in the doorway and watched Nick climb into his car and pull away. She closed the door, turned the key in the deadbolt, then went through the house closing blinds. Since the search, she no longer felt secure in her little duplex. Instead she felt dirty, violated.

She wondered about the loneliness she felt now that Nick was gone. They'd only known each other a short time, but she felt a bond forming. Not a good time for that, though.

Dinner for Anna was almost always fast food purchased on the way home or something frozen that she nuked and ate in front of the TV. Tonight the screen was dark. Even the most inane sitcoms were beyond her. Her mind still buzzed like a beehive, filled with incoherent thoughts.

Anna drifted into the kitchen, opened the refrigerator door, and berated herself because she still hadn't made it to the grocery store. She had no milk, no eggs, not much of anything. Finally, she settled for a peanut butter sandwich on stale bread, washed down with a Diet Coke, all consumed while standing over the sink. As she choked down the last bite, she couldn't help wishing she were back at Benny and Maria's restaurant, eating good food, enjoying Nick's company, and totally oblivious to her troubles.

She rinsed her plate, tossed her soft drink can in the recycle container, and leaned against the kitchen cabinet. Anna had never felt so lost, so absolutely bereft of a sense of direction. She remembered what she'd told Nick about her faith during trials. She'd tried to sound confident when she assured him that God would care for her. But right now, her faith was sort of like a south Texas river during a drought: half a mile wide and two inches deep.

In her bedroom, Anna lifted a worn, leather-covered book from the nightstand and flopped onto the bed. She propped herself on two pillows and opened the book to the place she'd long ago marked with a dark blue ribbon. She'd depended on this promise in the past. Maybe the words would help now: "For I know the plans I have for

96

you," declares the Lord, "plans to prosper you and not to harm you, plans to give you hope and a future."

Did God really have a plan to get her out of this mess, to give her a hope and a future? She rested the Bible on her chest and closed her eyes. *Talk to me, God. I'm listening.*

The shrill tone of the telephone startled Anna out of her semi-slumber. She sat up and the Bible tumbled onto the floor. It took her a moment to clear her head and reorient herself. She lifted the receiver, cleared her throat, and said, "Dr. McIntyre."

"Sorry to call so late." Laura Ernst didn't sound sorry. She sounded ticked off at having to deal with this. "It's taken me a little while to get the information I needed."

Anna decided the silence that followed was her cue to apologize, so she did.

"Anyway," Ernst continued, "here's the name and number of the attorney I suggest you call."

Anna scrambled to find a pad and pencil, finally locating both in the bedside table. She scribbled down the information and read it back to Ernst. "Ross Donovan. 214-555-1870. Got it."

"He's a bulldog on cases like this. Of course, he can also be a liar and a cheat,

97

but I've never known him not to do a good job for his clients."

"What do you mean?"

"Call him first thing tomorrow morning. He can tell you what I mean." There was a sharp click.

Anna held the silent phone until a strident stutter tone prompted her to hang up the receiver. What kind of lawyer was this guy? She swung her feet off the bed and hurried to her desk, where she put Donovan's number by the phone. One more call to make tomorrow.

The world didn't look any better or her situation any clearer in the morning. Anna hurried through breakfast and sat at her desk to make some calls. The first was to Ross Donovan. She got a recorded message, asking her to leave a number, which she did.

Anna looked at her watch. Eight in the morning. Too early to expect a quick callback from the lawyer, but not too early for things to be stirring at the medical center. She figured this might be tricky, and it was. It took Anna three phone calls to find a sympathetic clerk in the Medical Records office to track down the name and address of Eric Hatley's mother. With the monthly Morbidity and Mortality Conference coming up in less than a week, Anna wanted to know more about the real Eric Hatley, including the reason someone else would use his health insurance to get treatment.

Her phone rang as she headed out the door. She didn't recognize the number, but the caller ID showed UT Southwestern Med Ctr. The chances that this would be something good ranged from slim to none, but she decided she couldn't dodge the call. Her curiosity wouldn't let her.

"Dr. McIntyre."

"Doctor, this is Laura Ernst. Have you called Ross Donovan?"

"I called and left a message. I'm waiting for a callback."

"Ross isn't an early riser, but he'll get back to you," Ernst said. "Anyway, that's not why I called."

"Oh?"

"My assistant just had a call from the supervisor in Medical Records. You apparently persuaded a clerk to give you contact information for Eric Hatley's next of kin."

No use denying it. "That's right."

"Those records are supposed to be off-limits except as authorized by my office. I hope you don't plan to make contact with the family."

"Why do you say that?" Anna asked.

99

Ernst cleared her throat. "When a patient dies while they're under our care, there's always the possibility that the family might bring suit against us, especially if there's a suspicion of medical error. I've looked into the circumstances of this case, and it appears to me that the proximate cause of the patient's death was the antibiotic you and Dr. Nguyn ordered."

"But —"

"Given the situation, I feel strongly that it's best that all further communication with the family come through our office."

So much for any care and concern from Ernst. Now it was going to be all about protecting the institution. "In other words, you think we're at fault, and we should keep our heads down," Anna said.

"I wouldn't put it that way, but there's something to be said for doing exactly that."

Anna switched the phone to her other hand and flexed the fingers that cramped from their death grip on the receiver. "Well, Ms. Ernst, how do you feel about my expressing my sympathy for this woman's loss? This isn't a statistic she's burying, it's her son. And there are some questions that I'd like to get answered, questions that might shed some light on why Eric died."

"Of course, I can't order you not to

extend your condolences, but I wish you'd do it with a sympathy card, nothing more."

Anna took in a huge breath through her mouth and exhaled through her nose. It came out as more of a snort than she'd intended, but then again, maybe that was the message she felt like sending. "Ms. Ernst, unless I receive a direct order from either my chairman or the dean, I intend to visit Eric Hatley's family. I'll make sure that your office is made aware of any information I might gain. There are some questions that need to be answered, questions that affect the way other patients are treated. I intend to get those answers." Anna took a deep breath and tried to make her voice calm. "I do appreciate your help in my dealing with the police, but on this one I think we're going to have to agree to disagree. Thank you for calling."

Anna pushed the button to end the call and longed momentarily for an old-fashioned phone that she could slam into its cradle. She'd never been fond of attorneys, and this little episode hadn't done anything to change her mind. Nevertheless, as she closed the front door behind her, the tiny seed of doubt Ernst had planted in the back of her mind began to grow. Anna hoped she was doing the right thing.

5

When there was no answer to her knocks, Anna called, "Mrs. Hatley?"

The door opened to the limit of the safety chain, and an eye peered out. "Who are you?" The voice was a husky contralto, the words without inflection, as though the speaker were reciting them from a script.

"I'm Dr. Anna McIntyre. Remember, we met briefly at the hospital? I was with your son when he . . . when he died." Anna shifted uneasily from side to side. "May I come in for a moment?"

The door closed. As she waited, Anna tried without success to recapture an image of Mrs. Hatley from their only other conversation.

A rattle, a couple of clicks, and the door swung open. Mrs. Wanda Hatley stood a head taller than Anna's five feet six. Stick-thin arms and legs protruded from a shapeless flowered housedress. Flyaway brown hair liberally streaked with gray topped a gaunt face. Red-rimmed eyes with amber irises burned a hole through Anna.

"What do you want?" The words were delivered as a challenge, not a question.

"May I come in? I want to talk with you about Eric."

The woman nodded once, then turned and walked away. Anna stepped inside and closed the door behind her. She followed Mrs. Hatley into a living room that contained pieces selected with care. There had probably been a time when this woman took pride in her home. If so, it was long past. Now there was a film of dust on the furniture. The covers on the backs of two upholstered chairs — what were they called? Antimacassars, Anna recalled. These were skewed and wrinkled.

Mrs. Hatley dropped into one of the chairs and picked up a cigarette that smoldered in a half-full ashtray on the end table beside her. "Eric's dead."

Anna eased into the chair opposite. "I know. I was with him when he died. We tried to save his life. We tried everything we could, but it wasn't enough. And I wanted to tell you how sorry I am."

The woman waved away the apology as though waving away the smoke that wafted around her. " 'Sorry' doesn't bring him back."

So much for sympathy. Time to move on. "Mrs. Hatley, was Eric allergic to any medicines?"

For the first time, Anna thought she saw a spark behind that dull façade. "Uh-huh. He almost died a couple of years ago. He went to our family doctor for a Strep throat. Eric had four or five of them a year ever since he was real young. Doc Mercer always gave him a shot of penicillin. Cleared them right up. But this time he had one of those whatchamacallit . . . those allergic things . . . epileptic reactions."

"Anaphylactic," Anna said softly, afraid to break into the narrative now that the woman was talking.

"Yeah, that. Made him swell up like a toad. Doc had to give him two or three shots of that adrenalin stuff. And some cortisone."

In Anna's mind, the pieces dropped into place. A previous severe reaction to penicillin was a warning flag to every doctor who treated the patient after that. Never give penicillin or any of the drugs that might produce a similar reaction. Like Omnilex, the antibiotic the fake Eric Hatley received in the emergency room. The drug that undoubtedly killed this woman's son.

"Mrs. Hatley, do you have any family? Do you have anyone who can be with you right now?" Anna asked.

The woman shook her head, and the curtain of listlessness descended once more. "No family. My husband passed last year. Eric was my only child."

"Do you have brothers or sisters?"

She shook her head.

"Was Eric married?"

Again, the head shake. "No, he lived alone — had a bachelor apartment — but he spent a lot of time here. He took care of me. Bought groceries, ran errands, drove me to doctors' appointments. He was such a good son." She sobbed softly. "Now I don't have anybody."

"Would you like me to get something for you? Can I do anything?"

"Not unless you can bring Eric back." Mrs. Hatley looked up, and Anna felt the eyes bore into her. "A man came by yesterday. Lawyer. Said Eric shouldn't have died. I signed the papers to sue all the doctors and the hospital and everybody. Won't bring Eric back, but it will pay for somebody to take care of me."

"Mrs. Hatley. One of those doctors you're suing is me."

The woman almost spat her response. "I know."

Anna scanned the faces of the group assembled in the department chairman's office and tried to count the allies among them. Unfortunately, other than the chair, Dr. Fowler, she wasn't sure there were any. Laura Ernst, dressed in a tailored navy suit and plain white blouse, frowned and tapped a yellow pencil on the legal pad she balanced on her lap. Dr. William Dunston, the Dean of Clinical Affairs, brushed a fleck of lint off the vest of his gray pinstripe suit.

Fowler leaned back in his chair and polished his rimless glasses with the tail of his white coat. "Anna, why don't you tell us what you've learned about the death of your patient, Eric Hatley?"

Anna cleared her throat. "To recap, Mr. Hatley died from a massive allergic reaction during the final phase of his emergency laparotomy for multiple gunshot wounds. We'd given him antibiotic prophylaxis in the form of Omnilex, after confirming he received that drug without incident during an earlier emergency room visit. The pathologist rendered a cause of death as anaphylaxis due to a reaction to Omnilex. Regretfully, I have to agree."

Dunston clasped his hands over his ample belly. "So there appears to be a conflict between the man's prior tolerance of the drug and the massive anaphylaxis he experienced more recently. What do you make of that?"

"I began looking into it." Anna passed Dunston the emergency room record she'd been holding. "The identifying data on this visit matches what we got from Hatley's wallet. However, if you look at Dr. Fell's note, the patient is described as a 'young, African-American male.' Hatley was a middle-aged Caucasian."

Dunston scanned the record, then passed it on to Ernst, who read it and frowned. "Can you explain the disparity?" the lawyer asked.

"I believe I can." Anna said. "Someone used Hatley's medical insurance information to get treatment. Maybe he didn't want a venereal disease reported to his own insurance company. More likely, he didn't have insurance but was able to steal Hatley's information and use it. I think that identity theft eventually cost Eric Hatley his life."

"And did you later confirm that Eric Hatley had a history of drug allergy?" Fowler's tone was more neutral than Anna might have liked. Was he going to stand behind her?

Anna described her visit with Wanda Hatley. "Had we known of her son's sensitivity to antibiotics of that class, we could have chosen a different drug, and the odds are that he'd be alive today. But we were unable to contact her while Hatley was in surgery. Instead, we relied on the ER record. In hindsight, I think we made the best possible decision under the circumstances. But he died."

"I believe I asked you not to make contact with this patient's family." There was ice in Ernst's voice. "Now I understand that the mother is taking steps to file a malpractice suit against the medical center and all the doctors involved in her son's treatment."

"She talked with that lawyer before I ever contacted her." Anna regretted her sharp tone as soon as the words were out of her mouth. She might not like Laura Ernst, but she needed her as an ally, not an enemy. "I'm sorry. I'm still trying to figure out why Hatley died. I thought maybe I could learn something from his mother that would shed light on the situation. Obviously, I was wrong."

Dunston looked directly at Anna. "Well, the issue here of someone posing as the patient and leaving false information on his medical record certainly muddies the waters. I'll have to leave it to Laura to sort out the legal ramifications of that." He pursed his lips. "From a medical standpoint, it appears that you acted appropriately, but on flawed information. We don't know how this is going to play out, but I'd like to be kept informed of the progress in this case." He shifted his gaze to Fowler. "Please send me a summary of the M&M discussion." Then he swiveled toward Ernst. "I want to be copied on all communication regarding any legal actions." With that, he eased himself upright and left the room.

Ernst was on her feet next. "If I were a plaintiff's attorney I'd be salivating to get my hands on this case."

"But, I —"

The lawyer stopped Anna with an upraised hand. "Dr. McIntyre, I don't want to argue with you. I'm aware that you and Dr. Nguyn took actions that are defensible, actions that fall entirely within the standard of care. But that doesn't mean we're not in for a fight." She retrieved her briefcase from beside her chair and shoved her legal pad into it. "I'm going to want to research this a bit, but it may be that the person really at fault in Hatley's death is the one responsible for that false information getting into his medical records. Whether any action on that front would be civil or criminal remains to be seen, and it still may not affect our liability." She nodded toward Fowler, then Anna. "Please let me know if you learn anything more."

Ernst paused at the door and looked back at Anna. Anna thought perhaps she was going to ask about her dealings with the Dallas Police, inquire whether Donovan had returned her call. Instead, Ernst gave a faint shake of her head, shifted her briefcase to her other hand, and walked out.

Anna started to stand, but Fowler motioned for her to sit. "Hang on just a minute, would you?" He walked to the door and closed it, then returned to his seat behind his desk. "I suggest you let Laura worry about the Hatley case for now. In the meantime, what have you found out about your DEA number turning up on forged narcotics prescriptions?"

"Well, there may be more going on than just that," Anna said. She told him about her credit cards and her compromised credit.

"So you think someone is using your identity, not just to write narcotics 'scripts but to buy things and charge them to you.

Have you figured out how? And why?"

Anna shook her head. "Unfortunately, I don't have a clue, but I intend to keep looking. The latest development is that the police have questioned me and searched my home."

"The police? Not the DEA?"

"Apparently, I'm under suspicion by both."

"Do you have a lawyer?" Fowler asked.

"I called Laura Ernst during the police search. She had me throw them out and tell them not to come back without a warrant. Then she gave me the name of an attorney. I'm waiting for him to call me back."

"Why do you think they wanted to search your place?"

Anna had to unclench her teeth to answer. "They have this idea that I'm part of some grand narcotics scheme. I keep hoping that they and the DEA will finally decide I'm a victim here, not a criminal. Whatever happened to innocent until proven guilty? It all seems so unfair."

Fowler held his hands apart, palms up. "Fair's rarely an option in life. Well, keep me posted. I'll see you back here on Friday for the M&M conference."

Anna waited for some word of encouragement from her chairman. Instead, he said,

"Good luck," and turned back to the stack of papers centered on his desk blotter.

Anna juggled two bulging grocery sacks while she dug for her keys in a purse that strained at the seams. After struggling for what seemed like five minutes, she set her burdens on the front porch. The key ring was, of course, in the furthest depths of her purse. The lock failed to yield to her first couple of tries. She jiggled the key repeatedly and was about to give up when the lock finally opened. Funny, she didn't recall having any trouble like this in the past. Anna peered at the area of the doorjamb around the lock tongue and wondered if those scratches were fresh. Had someone broken in? And could that person still be inside?

She rummaged in her purse and found her cell phone. She had dialed "9-1" before she stopped. This was silly. She was being paranoid. The lock probably needed some graphite, the scratches were old, and she was getting upset about nothing. Besides that, if she called the police every time she saw a shadow, they might not believe her if she really needed them.

Maybe if she went back to the car and got the tire iron out of the trunk —

"What's up?"

Anna was sure she jumped a foot. She swiveled her head around so quickly she heard the bones in her neck crackle. Nick Valentine stood just off the porch, his hands in the pockets of his windbreaker. "Did I scare you?" he asked.

"Yes. Definitely." She took a deep breath. "But I'm glad to see you. What brings you here?"

"I tried to call before I left the med center, but there was no answer."

"My cell didn't ring. I must have been in a dead zone."

Nick shrugged. "We haven't talked in a couple of days, and I wanted to see what you've found out." He reached down and hefted the grocery bags. "Let me give you a hand with those."

"No! Don't go in." Anna put her hand on his arm. "Sorry. I'm jumpy. Probably it's nothing, but when I got home, the lock on the front door was sticking. Then I saw some scratches around it and thought maybe somebody had broken in. I was about to call the police."

Nick laid the bags beside the door. "No need for that. Just give me a sec." He turned and hurried to his car. She saw him pull something from the glove compartment and shove it into his jacket pocket before striding back to the porch. He motioned Anna aside. "You stay out here until I check things out."

"Don't do anything foolish."

"I won't." Nick reached into his pocket and pulled out a small revolver. He held it loosely in his right hand, his index finger outside the trigger guard, the short barrel pointing skyward. "But if someone is hiding in there, they're going to wish they hadn't picked this house."

"That's it. No intruders inside, and no sign that one's been here." Nick jammed the gun into his pocket before retrieving the grocery bags from the front porch. "Where do you want these?"

Nick noticed a strange look on Anna's face as he helped unpack the bags in her kitchen. "Hey, I don't blame you for being suspicious," he said. "But I looked at those scratches around the lock, and I'm pretty sure they're old. And the lock probably needs some graphite."

Anna pulled a chair away from the kitchen table and dropped into it. "No, I'm glad it was nothing. What has me upset is the sight of you with that gun in your hand." She dry washed her face with a hand that trembled slightly. "I guess I didn't expect that."

"Would you like me to put it away?"

"Please."

Nick went outside and placed the gun back in its resting place under a stack of road maps in his car's glove compartment. *Glad I didn't need it. But I'm glad it's there.*

As he walked back into the house, he held out his hands in a "look, they're empty" gesture.

"Thanks," Anna said.

Nick picked up the empty paper bags from the counter and folded them carefully before he sat down across the table from Anna. "I'm sorry. I guess I should explain why I have the gun." He leaned forward with his elbows on the table. "During my first year of med school I moonlighted at an all-night convenience store in Lubbock. If you read the papers or watch the news, you know that's a dangerous job. The owner refused to keep a gun behind the counter. He was one of those who believed that if you handed the robber the money, you wouldn't get hurt." Nick began moving the saltshaker in random circles on the tabletop. "I spent my first paycheck on the training course required for a concealed carry permit. Then I bought this gun. Every night I worked, I had it on a shelf under the cash register." He looked down and closed his eyes as the memories came back, sharp-edged and fresh.

Anna's voice was quiet, almost a whisper. "So it kept you safe."

"In a manner of speaking." He opened his eyes and looked directly into hers. "A guy came in at two one morning, hopped up on speed or something. He pulled a gun out of his belt and pointed it at me. Told me to give him all the money in the register. The way his hands were jerking, I was praying that gun didn't have a hair trigger. I pulled out the bills — probably about seventy dollars — and all the time, my eyes never left that automatic in his hand. The barrel looked about as big as the mouth of a tunnel. Then I thought I saw his trigger finger start to twitch." He shook his head, but couldn't stop the film that was unwinding in his head.

"Go on."

Nick wiped a thin film of sweat from his brow. "I was holding my gun under the counter. I'd grabbed it with my right hand while he was watching my left get the bills out of the cash drawer. I saw that movement and decided it was him or me. I pulled the trigger. One shot in the chest. The coroner said he was dead before he hit the floor."

"You did what you had to do," she said. "He could have killed you."

"Maybe." He dropped his hands on the table and stared into Anna's face. "Unfortunately, the only way to be sure of that had sort of a permanent downside to it. I made a decision, and I stuck with it. Then I put it behind me."

"But you still have the gun."

Nick wasn't sure whether it was a question or a statement, and Anna's tone gave him no clue about what she was feeling right now. "I keep my permit up-to-date, and I carry the gun locked in the glove compartment of my car."

"Why?" In that single word, Nick heard both disbelief and disapproval.

"You can't argue that the parts of town around a hospital are generally pretty unsafe, and the place where we work is no exception. Carjackings, robberies, random drive-by shootings. Back when I was going to church regularly, I recall the preacher saying we live in a broken world. I believe he was right."

"So you depend on your gun to protect you?"

"Sure," Nick said. "What's your protection?"

"The same protection I've depended on

for years — God."

Nick thought there was less than total conviction in Anna's voice, but decided not to challenge her. Instead, he said, "I'm not sure God and I are on speaking terms anymore. I seem to remember some commandment about 'Thou shalt not kill.' So far as I know, that hasn't been repealed, has it?"

Anna brushed her hair aside with a casual and probably unconscious gesture. "I think there's room for discussion there, Nick. You might be surprised at how much God can forgive, if you'll let him."

Nick wanted to believe Anna, but surely the taking of a human life brought too much guilt for even God to forgive. He'd made his decision that day, and there was nothing he could do to change it. "Anna, I appreciate what you're saying. But if I'd depended on God instead of Smith and Wesson, I might have been the one lying dead on that floor. It's a good thing I decided to look out for myself. But now I have to live with the consequences."

Anna put her hand on Nick's arm. "You really don't, you know. But I don't think this is the time to talk about it. I'll just say thank you for being here for me today."

Nick rose slowly, feeling as though he were

a hundred years old. "You know, I was going to see if you'd like to have dinner with me tonight, but now I don't think I'm very good company. Why don't I head home?"

"Please don't. When I was really down, you kept after me until I went out with you. You really cheered me up, and I appreciate it. I'd like to return the favor." Anna reached into the pocket of her skirt and extracted a multi-colored plastic rectangle. "Besides that, I have a new credit card. Why don't you let me test it out?"

Nick forced a smile. Why not? This probably wasn't the greatest time to be alone anyway. "Sure. This time you pick the restaurant."

6

The next morning, Anna took her second cup of coffee to the living room, where the letter lay partially unfolded on her desk, only the DEA seal at the top showing. She brushed her fingertips across the stiff paper — good quality bond, your tax dollars at work — but didn't bother to pick it up and read it. No need. The words were burned into her mind. Just as Hale promised, the letter had come to Anna's office at the med school the day after she met with the two agents. When Anna called the legal office to notify them of the letter and its contents, she got no further than Laura Ernst's administrative assistant. As though reading from a script — and maybe she was — the woman warned Anna to keep Ms. Ernst informed of further developments. No offer of help. Not a drop of sympathy. Just a boilerplate admonition designed to protect the interests of the medical school. The same kind of response Ernst had given Anna about the Hatley case.

Well, in a way, Anna couldn't blame the woman. She probably fielded a dozen calls like this every week, calls from doctors who were worried about malpractice suits or trying to straighten out problems with licensure or attempting to cut through the Gordian knot of regulations that threatened to strangle the independent practice of medicine. Not much fun to work in the legal office of a large medical center.

Anna half-listened to the rest of the woman's instructions, including a reminder not to ignore the embargo on prescribing controlled substances until she was issued a new DEA permit. No danger of that, since she was effectively suspended from clinical duties while this scenario played out.

Since Anna was supposed to use her time off to clear her name, maybe she'd better get started. She went into the kitchen and returned with a fresh cup of coffee. She kicked off her loafers and pulled the phone toward her, berating herself for not thinking to ask Hale and Kramer for their cards. She unfolded the letter far enough to find the phone number at the top. She dialed and was surprised when a real live voice answered, not something that sounded like it came from Star Wars. She asked for either Hale or Kramer, then listened to a series of clicks followed by a string rendition of some semiclassical song she didn't quite recognize.

She'd had her fill of music on hold when she heard a familiar alto voice. "Agent Kramer."

Anna didn't know whether getting the ice queen instead of the rumpled private eye clone was good or bad, but she plunged on. "This is Dr. Anna McIntyre. Do you remember me?"

"Sure, Doctor. You calling to admit you've been selling Vicodin 'scripts on the side?"

Anna wanted to crawl through the phone lines and throttle this woman, even if she had been the nicer of the two agents in her office, although marginally so. "I've told you already, I'm not involved. I'm calling to see if you've found out how someone got hold of my DEA number and decided to play doctor with it. I can't go back to work until this is settled."

"Okay, okay." Had Kramer's tone softened a bit? "It might surprise you, but we're as interested in clearing your name as you are. That would mean we would have discovered who's papering this part of town with those little slips with your name on them." Then the ice crept back into Kramer's voice. "Of course, we haven't given up on the possibility that you're in the middle of the whole enterprise."

Anna searched her memory. What were the names? "Have you talked with Detectives Green or Dowling? They came to see me after I talked with you." She shivered at the thought of that encounter.

Kramer's soft chuckle was out of character for the woman who'd sat across from Anna a few days earlier. "Afraid not. The police and the DEA aren't exactly in the habit of calling to share secrets. Right after we met with you, I talked with one of them — don't recall which one — and they seemed to think you were masterminding a scheme to sell narcotics 'scripts, but I haven't heard anything from them lately."

"So how soon do you think you'll settle this thing? I need a new DEA permit before I can go back to work."

"My crystal ball's a bit cloudy, Doctor," Kramer said. "Check with me in a week and I'll let you know if we have anything."

"Thank you." Anna had to swallow hard to force out the words.

"Of course, if we find something that implicates you, we'll be in touch earlier. You're not planning on leaving town this week, are you?"

After assuring Kramer that she had no such plans, Anna replaced the phone. She shoved the letter aside and tried to think. What else could she do? Call the detectives? No, she'd keep her distance from them. While Hale had seemed skeptical and Kramer cold, Green and Dowling had been downright intimidating, conjuring up visions of rubber hoses and bright lights. She'd avoid any contact with them unless it was absolutely necessary.

Anna felt the frustration of being out of her element. Give her a patient with a difficult diagnostic problem — an acute abdomen, a puzzling set of symptoms — and she was more than competent. But dealing with the law? Not her thing. She needed help.

She dug through the papers on her desk and retrieved the note with Donovan's name and number. Why hadn't he called her back? If she'd had a call from a patient — No, this wasn't medicine, it was the law, and apparently, it moved more slowly than she was used to.

Anna decided to help things along. She punched in the numbers and began to count the rings. On the third, there was a click and a masculine voice said, "Ross Donovan."

"Mr. Donovan, this is Dr. Anna Mc-Intyre."

"Oh, yeah, I just got your message. You were on my list, but I'm glad you called first. How can I help you?"

Anna took a deep breath and launched into a recitation of the events of the past several days, ending with the episode involving the detectives and Laura Ernst's recommendation that she contact Donovan.

The lawyer listened without interruption. When Anna finished, he asked only one question. "Do you want to hire me?"

"That's what I thought this was all about," she said, fighting unsuccessfully to keep exasperation out of her voice.

"So let's meet at my office. Do you have the address?"

"No. All she gave me was your number." The next words came out without conscious thought on her part. "She told me you were very good at things like this. She also told me you were a liar and a cheat. Maybe you can explain that before I hire you."

Donovan laughed, a hearty, full-throated sound. "Dr. McIntyre, I think I can explain it all to your satisfaction. How about coming down here about eleven? 2200 Pacific, suite 1212. We can talk, and if things go well, we can continue it over lunch."

Anna promised to be there. After she hung up, she pulled three blank manila folders from her desk drawer. She labeled them with a fine-point Sharpie: "Hatley," "DEA," and "Police." Anna stuck the contact information for Donovan into the third folder, then pulled a yellow legal pad toward her and began to doodle.

The prescriptions she'd seen appeared to be written on authentic clinic prescription forms. There had been talk at the medical center of changing to tamper-proof prescription pads, but that hadn't been implemented yet. Anna suspected that wouldn't be done until a legal mandate galvanized someone in administration into action, securely locking the barn door after the horse had disappeared over the horizon.

The simplest explanation was the first one that had popped into Anna's mind: a patient took his or her Vicodin prescription home, did a little magic to alter the numbers and patient name, photocopied it, and began selling the results. Or they could have started fresh and simply forged the prescriptions. The pads currently in use could easily be duplicated at any of the hundreds of print shops in Dallas. Even someone who was good with a computer could make up blanks.

Anna kept coming back to the same thing: the DEA number was hers, the name was hers, and they matched. If a patient wasn't the one behind this, it had to be someone who had access to Anna's DEA number. It would most likely be a person at the medical center with whom Anna had regular contact — a doctor, a nurse, a pharmacist. It made her shiver to think that a colleague could be the one responsible for the mess she found herself in right now.

And why would they choose her, use her name and number? Had she done something to make herself vulnerable? Surely she hadn't been any less cautious than all her colleagues. She flinched at the thought that kept intruding itself. Did someone have it in for her?

Names and faces spooled through Anna's head. Start with the patients. She couldn't think of anyone who jumped out as a likely suspect. Maybe if she went over the patient list for her last twenty clinics or so, a name would pop up and trigger a memory. Of course, to do this she'd have to go back to the med school. Could she face the looks she was sure to get from the staff?

Anna set her jaw. Let them stare. She'd stare right back at them, while she searched for the person who was dragging her good

127

name in the dirt and putting her professional reputation in jeopardy.

Ross Donovan looked at the papers heaped on his desk, sighed, and swiveled in his chair to stare out the window at the Dallas skyline. As slow as his practice had been, it was amazing how much stuff accumulated in two weeks away. He swung back and opened the bottom drawer of his desk. He reached down, then pulled his hand back as though a snake were hissing at him from the dark depths of the space. No, not anymore.

Donovan walked through the outer office, trying to ignore the empty desk that was once his assistant's. In the tiny workroom, he moved to the coffeemaker in the corner. He measured out coffee from the almost-empty can, filled the pot at the sink, and pushed the button. As he stood there, listening to the gurgle of the filling pot and enjoying the aroma of the brew, his thoughts ranged far and wide.

He poured coffee into a thick white mug that told the world it belonged to the "World's Best Husband." That brought a chuckle, his second of the day. Must be some kind of a record, Donovan thought. Not many chuckles in his life for the past few months. He sat at his desk, pulled the wastebasket a bit closer, and began to go through the accumulated mail on his desk. Bills went into one stack, letters from past and potential clients into a much smaller one, junk into the trash. He finished his coffee just as he heard the front door open. He swept the mail into his center desk drawer, looked approvingly at the pristine desktop, and straightened his tie from its usual half-mast position. Time to talk with his next client. Time to be a lawyer again. And this time he intended not to blow the chance.

The slow ride up in the elevator gave her plenty of time to change her mind, but Anna was determined to see it through. The building was nice enough on the outside, but the halls were narrow, the walls dingy, the carpet worn. Definitely a low-rent venue.

Suite 1212 was at the end of the hall. The door had a frosted-glass window in the top half, where flaking, faded gold-leaf letters announced to the world that this was the office of Ross Donovan, Attorney At Law. The waiting room held six chairs with worn upholstery, a coffee table with three tattered copies of *D Magazine,* and an empty desk, apparently meant for an administrative assistant. Two doors were on the back wall.

The one on the right was partially open, allowing a view of a coffee machine, metal shelving laden with boxes and papers, and the corner of a sink. The door on the left was closed.

Apparently no one was coming out to welcome her. Anna knocked on the closed door. In less than half a minute, Gregory Peck opened the door. Well, not him, but a handsome man with black, wavy hair, a cleft chin, and sparkling blue eyes that hinted of secrets that could not be shared.

"You must be Dr. McIntyre," he said, offering his hand. "I'm Ross Donovan. Won't you come in and sit down? Would you like some coffee?"

It smelled good, but she decided to pass. "No, thank you."

As she settled into one of the two client chairs across the desk from Donovan, she gave him a quick appraisal. Probably forty years old or thereabouts. Crisp, clean white shirt with cuffs turned back a neat two folds, a conservative blue tie, dark blue suspenders. And although a reappraisal showed her that he wasn't exactly a dead ringer for Gregory Peck, his looks would probably melt the hearts of female jurors from ages sixteen to sixty.

Donovan uncapped a pen — an actual

fountain pen, not a ballpoint, she noted — and pulled a legal pad from a desk drawer. "Suppose you tell me what this is all about."

"Don't you want a retainer or something first?"

He waved away the question. "The TV shows always talk about giving your attorney a dollar to make the relationship formal. If Laura sent you, I suspect we can work out financial arrangements. I assure you that I'll consider anything you tell me to be privileged, even if you decide not to hire me."

Anna digested this and decided it made sense. "One more thing before we get started. Why did Ms. Ernst recommend that I consult you, and in the same breath say that you're a liar and a cheat?"

"The short answer, I guess, is that I am . . . or at least, I was. I lied to her and cheated on her. That was before our divorce."

Anna tried to conceal her surprise. Well, she wasn't hiring a husband. She needed a lawyer. "And I guess when I asked her for the name of a lawyer, she had to call to see if you were free to accept me as a client?"

Donovan grinned, and two dimples flanked the Peck-like cleft in his chin. "Nope, she called to see if I was out of rehab."

■ ■ ■ ■

Anna wheeled into what was probably the last open spot in the faculty parking garage and hurried across the campus. She didn't want to be late for the Morbidity and Mortality Conference, especially today, when she might well have center stage. She wished she'd had time to accept Donovan's lunch invitation, though. He'd left the invitation open, and she might end up having a working dinner with him, depending on how things progressed.

Once she'd gotten past the preliminaries with Donovan, she'd been impressed by his incisive questions and sound counsel. They'd settled on a payment schedule she could meet. He'd advised her to have no more contact with the DEA or the police, assuring her that he would handle all that.

Anna stopped at her office long enough to toss her purse into a desk drawer and snatch up her white coat. The Surgery Department conference room was packed with doctors. The faculty members sat in upholstered swivel chairs scattered at intervals around the long conference table. Third- and fourth-year resident physicians ringed the table, occupying lightly padded wooden side chairs without arms. The more junior residents were scattered around the periphery of the room in plastic shell chairs guaranteed to keep them uncomfortable and awake for the proceedings.

A few medical students, easily identifiable by their short white coats and worried looks, sat together in one corner, trying to avoid being noticed, or even worse, called on. Anna figured that some were here to learn, but most were in attendance because general surgery was a required rotation they had to pass.

The long white coats of the faculty were starched and pristine, in contrast to those of the residents, which ranged between slightly wrinkled and grungy. Although scrub suits seemed to be the uniform of the day, some of the male faculty members wore dress shirts and ties. Anna had chosen a simple white blouse and black skirt, trying for a professional look beneath her white coat. She would have preferred to remain anonymous throughout the entire conference, something she knew was impossible, but she had no intention of calling attention to herself through her choice of clothing.

Neil Fowler moved aside the remains of his box lunch and pulled a stack of papers toward him. Like a ripple around the table, the residents and staff physicians put aside their food. Most conversations died away, some chopped off in mid-sentence. Anna felt the few bites of ham and cheese sandwich she'd been able to choke down trying to push their way back up. She gulped the last of her Diet Coke.

"Let's get this month's M&M Conference underway. We'll start with cases from the junior residents. Shelly?" Fowler took a handkerchief from his pocket and began to polish his glasses, his gaze directed to the far corner of the room. Although two of the medical students exchanged glances, apparently wondering if the chairman's attention was wandering, Anna knew better. She'd attended more than fifty of these conferences, first as a resident and for the past years as a faculty member. Neil Fowler wouldn't miss a word that was said.

After the first presentation, Fowler swept his eyes around the room, focusing one by one on the faculty members, inviting comments. A couple of the more senior faculty had a few words about the management of the case. Each agreed that the morbidity — in this case, a severe postoperative infection that kept the patient in the hospital an extra week — might have been avoided had certain things been done differently. Fowler closed the discussion by mentioning a specific antibiotic that would likely have been more effective. "Moving on. Tim?"

Anna was still processing the chairman's remarks, adding the knowledge to the mental card file she maintained on management of complications, when it hit her. Fowler hadn't looked directly at her since she'd taken her seat. Not at any time during lunch. When he polled the faculty for comments on the previous case, he'd passed over her. It was as though she weren't there. Was this the way it was going to be until she could clear herself of the suspicion that hung over her like a cloud?

Her initial hurt gave way to grim determination. She wasn't about to be kept in limbo until those guys at the DEA found out who was using her information. And as for the Dallas Police, if Green and Dowling were typical examples, she wasn't sure she'd trust them to find a lost dog. They'd probably fine the owner for failing to keep it on a leash. No, she was going to become more actively involved in the process. And she planned to start right after M&M.

Anna's reverie was interrupted when she heard Fowler say, "Luc, how about Mr. Hatley?"

Anna pulled a blank three-by-five card

from the bunch she kept in the pocket of her white coat. As Luc related the events of Hatley's case — his emergency admission, the surgery, the measures taken to replace blood loss and combat the infection that was sure to follow the colon injury — she jotted notes, all the while wishing that she could be the one making the presentation. But it was protocol that the resident on the case detail what happened and what went wrong. After that, the attending was free to speak up, defending where necessary and accepting any criticism alongside the resident.

As Luc wound down the presentation, Anna found her toes tapping in a nervous dance under the table. She picked up her soft drink can, found it empty, and longed for something to counteract the sandpaper-like feeling in her throat.

Anna was trying to organize her thoughts when the door at the back of the room opened, and the anesthesiologist Buddy Jenkins slipped in. He eased into one of the empty chairs along the far side of the room. His eyes met Anna's. Although his expression was carefully neutral, Anna knew what was behind it. Don't try to hang any of this on my resident . . . or on me. Well, she couldn't blame him. She'd probably do the same thing if she were in Jenkins's place. Besides, Nick had pretty well convinced her that the young anesthesia resident's only error had been failing to make the diagnosis early on. But then, neither she nor Luc had picked up on it either. They'd depended too much on that incorrect history, had been too complacent.

"Okay. Dr. McIntyre, your comments?" Fowler's tone conveyed neither approval nor censure.

Anna cleared her throat. "Luc's summarized things pretty well. He put first things first, treated the shock and stopped the bleeding. His repair of the perforated bowel was perfect. Since there was considerable fecal spillage into the abdominal cavity, antibiotic coverage was important." She lifted her eyes from her notes and looked directly at Fowler. "We've already been reminded today how it's possible to have a good surgical result compromised by an infection, and in this case the risk of fatal sepsis was significant. It's unfortunate that, even though we had good information that Mr. Hatley should tolerate the Omnilex, he suffered a severe anaphylactic reaction."

"Who decided on Omnilex? You or Luc?" The speaker was Linda Farley, new to the surgery faculty, fresh out of her training.

Anna was pretty sure that Linda felt the medicine practiced here in Texas could never compare with what she'd learned in Boston at Peter Bent Brigham Hospital, in the shadow of Harvard.

"Luc felt, and rightly so, that Omnilex gave the best coverage in this situation. I agreed."

Linda was like a dog trying to wrest a bone away from a rival. "But if there was any antibiotic allergy, especially to penicillin, Omnilex was almost certain to produce anaphylaxis — which it did."

"I realize that, but —"

"Let's move on." Fowler's voice was calm, but there was no mistaking the way he was taking command of the situation. "There are a lot of 'what ifs,' but in the final analysis, I think there's nothing to be gained by exploring them. We can conjecture all day about how this would have turned out if you'd chosen a safer but less effective antibiotic, or if the anesthesia resident had picked up on the anaphylaxis earlier and started treatment."

Anna saw Jenkins stiffen. If Fowler saw it, he didn't react. He was already closing the chart and opening the next one. "Luc, you and Dr. McIntyre made the right clinical decision based on the information available to you. Unfortunately, there was a bad outcome."

Fowler pulled a sheet of paper toward him and began reading a series of announcements, but Anna had already tuned him out. It was over. She took several deep breaths but still felt claustrophobic. She saw Jenkins slip out, and she wanted desperately to do the same. Unfortunately, the way everyone was packed into the conference room, it would have drawn attention she didn't want. As Fowler continued to speak, Anna uncrossed her legs and put both feet flat on the floor. She rested her hands on the arms of her swivel chair, ready to push up and make a quick exit when the conference finally came to an end. She'd made it through this test. But she knew there were more to come.

Nick looked around the cafeteria. It was two-thirds full of medical school staff — administrative assistants, students, residents and faculty — but he and Anna had managed to score a table with no neighbors nearby. Besides, the buzz of conversation was better than a white noise machine for protecting them from eavesdroppers.

His call had caught Anna as she was walking into her office after the conference. It took some persuasion on his part, but she finally agreed to meet him here so they could talk while he grabbed a late lunch. Thus far, she'd been about as talkative as the Sphinx — although a whole lot prettier.

"You didn't bring up the new information about Hatley?" Nick took a bite of hot dog and wiped the corner of his mouth with a paper napkin.

Anna shook her head. "I was going to mention that I'd found out he was penicillin-allergic. I figured if I didn't say something about it, Fowler would. I mean, I'd already told him about my visit with Hatley's mother. But he moved things along before I could bring it up. I got the impression he was trying to get the discussion over with." She sipped her iced tea. "Maybe he was trying to protect me. Or maybe he was trying to protect the department."

"He knows that Hatley's mother told you he was penicillin-allergic. But does he know about the second Eric Hatley?"

"He learned about it when he and I met with Laura Ernst and the dean," Anna said. "But I'm pretty sure none of them is going to spread that knowledge around. I was afraid that Will Fell, the resident I talked with about the fake Hatley, would be at M&M today and mention it, but he wasn't.

One of the residents told me that Will just got off a twenty-four-hour shift in the ER, and I'm pretty sure he's in dreamland right now."

"So it's not common knowledge that Hatley died because someone stole his identity." Nick took another bite of hot dog and chewed thoughtfully, parsing the implications of what they knew so far. He washed the food down with coffee, wincing as the hot liquid hit his tongue. Anna shoved her iced tea toward him. He scooped out a piece of ice with his spoon and rolled it around in his mouth before continuing. "And you don't want anyone to know yet that you've caught on about the identity theft?"

"I'm not sure how they tie together, but I keep getting the feeling that what happened to me — the credit cards, the DEA number — and what happened to Hatley are linked. I don't know how or why, but if they are, then whoever stole my information had to get it someplace, and I'm betting it was —"

"Here at the medical center," Nick said. "And you don't want to tip your hand while you investigate?"

"Right. I figure it has to be someone around here who has access to my personal stuff." She lifted her glass and drank. "When you change into a scrub suit in the dressing room, what do you do with your wallet?"

Nick's hand went to the hip pocket of his scrub suit. He felt the reassuring bulge. "I put it in my pocket. I keep my change and keys in my white coat, and the wallet goes on my hip. I'm used to feeling it there, where it's safe."

"Exactly. Now think of what a woman does. No woman — at least none that I know — wants to walk around with a bulge in her hip pocket." She held up the small clutch that had been sitting on the table. "Most of the female doctors and nurses around here have either a fanny pack or something like this that they can drop into the pocket of their white coat when they need it. But you don't wear a fanny pack under your surgical gown, and there's no place for a purse there, either. So our valuables end up in a drawer of our desk or in a locker in the dressing room."

"And you think someone got into your purse and stole your credit card information. Maybe got your DEA number off the ID card you carry." Nick pulled out his wallet and flipped through the plastic holders until he came to a small folded blue-and-white card headed Controlled Substance Registration Certificate. "Do you carry

142

yours in your wallet?"

"I do, but probably for a different reason than you do. I'll bet you don't write many prescriptions."

Nick nodded assent. "Not as a pathologist, no. Just occasionally, for friends or family."

"Have you ever written for a controlled substance?"

"One of my buddies wrenched his knee last Friday afternoon playing football. I wrote him for enough Tylenol with codeine to carry him through the weekend until he could see his regular doctor." Nick made the connection quickly. "And I had to look in my wallet to check my DEA number."

"Right. On the other hand, I write prescriptions all day, and I have my number memorized."

"Do you carry your card?" Nick asked.

"I do, but for a different reason. I don't want it lying around where someone could get hold of it. I always thought it was safest to have it in my purse." Anna wadded up her napkin and shoved it into her empty glass. "Guess I was wrong."

7

As though in response to some unheard signal, the cafeteria began to empty. Office workers sighed and marched back to their desks. Doctors gulped their lunches and headed for surgery or clinics. Medical students snatched up their books and drifted out in groups of two and three, trading stories of terrible lecturers and fascinating patients.

Anna looked at her watch. "I should go." She pushed back her chair and grabbed her purse.

"What's on your agenda for this afternoon?" Nick asked.

Anna wasn't sure she had a firm plan. And if she did, should she share it with anybody? Even Nick?

"I smell rubber burning." Nick grinned. "Does it require that much thought to tell me what you're up to?"

"Sorry." She created interlocking rings

with the condensate on the bottom of her empty glass. "I'm not sure I have a plan, other than to snoop around and hope I can recognize a clue if I stumble across it."

"Not much of a plan, but better than nothing I guess," Nick said. "How about dinner later tonight?"

Anna gave him full marks for persistence, but tonight she wanted to be alone. She moved aside a stray strand of hair. "Sorry, Nick. Really, all I want is to pick up some fast food on my way home, sink into a bubble bath, and fall asleep reading the book that's been on my bedside table for a month."

Nick nodded his understanding. "So, tomorrow?" He paused. "No, wait. That's Saturday. I'm covering pathology tomorrow, and I don't want to interrupt our time together if I get called back. Sunday?"

Anna felt the shadow of an idea form. The more she thought about it, the more she liked it. What could it hurt to ask?

"Is the question too hard for you?" Nick asked. "Need to check your Palm Pilot? Trying to decide if we can be alone without a chaperone?"

"No," Anna said. "Just thinking. Sunday would be fine. What did you have in mind?"

"That's usually my only day to sleep in.

How about brunch? Then we can play it by ear. A movie, walk around in the West End, maybe go out to the Arboretum?"

Anna tried to hide her grin, but was afraid it showed in her eyes, if not on her lips. "Are you flexible about those plans?"

"Sure. What do you suggest?"

"Come by my apartment about ten-thirty Sunday morning. Go to church with me. Then we can have lunch and decide how we'll spend the rest of the day."

To his credit, Nick only hesitated for a few seconds. "Sure. What's the dress code?"

"Whatever you're comfortable wearing. Most men wear sport shirts. There are some in jeans. You'll see a smattering of coats and ties, mainly the older members."

"What about you?"

She grinned. "I'll be wearing a dress, but I don't think that's a good look for you. I'd stick with a sport shirt and slacks."

Anna stood in the doorway to the outer office and watched her administrative assistant, Lisa, pound the keys of her computer into submission. Surely by now rumors of all kinds circulated through the department. Although Lisa had already voiced her support, Anna's stomach did a flip-flop as she wondered what kind of reception she'd get from others on the staff.

Lisa's smile seemed genuine. "Dr. Mc-Intyre. It's good to see you. Are you back at work now?"

Anna forced a smile in return. "No, just here to clean out my mail and check my messages. I'm going to close my door. Buzz me on the intercom if it's urgent. Otherwise, pretend I'm not here."

Safely hidden in her office, Anna shoved her purse into a desk drawer and covered it with a file folder. Did that make it safer from prying eyes and searching hands? She grimaced as she realized how ineffective her attempts at security had been in the past. Then again, old habits die hard.

Anna tossed her white coat onto the chair on the other side of her desk and dropped into her swivel chair. Next she heeled off her shoes and shoved them under the kneehole of the desk where she could slip them back on if someone came in. She leaned back, ran her fingers through her hair, and willed her shoulder muscles to relax. M&M was over. One hurdle down, lots more to go.

The always-efficient Lisa had her mail and messages sorted into neat piles centered on her blotter. Anna started by signing operative reports, summaries, and professional

147

letters. Then came the patient information: tissue reports, lab and X-ray, referral summaries. She initialed them all and dictated a few chart notes and instructions for Lisa to pass on to her clinic nurse. The ease with which she'd been able to slip back into her professional persona and forget her other problems didn't surprise her. Her colleagues often kidded that Anna wouldn't notice the start of World War III if she were struggling with a diagnostic problem.

When she was satisfied she'd dealt with the most urgent matters, Anna slipped her feet into her shoes and opened the office door. "Lisa, I'm going down to the break room to get a soft drink. May I bring you something?"

"Oh, no thank you. I was just there for some coffee." Lisa gestured to the Styrofoam cup on her desk.

Anna, like all the other faculty members, generally left her office door open, assuming that her administrative assistant would be at her desk to guard against unwanted visitors. Now Anna saw the fallacy in that assumption. The assistants were away from their desks several times a day: coffee, restroom breaks, trips to the supply room, lunch. Anna closed her office door behind her and waited until she heard it click before she left.

Once she returned to her desk, Diet Coke in hand and shoeless again, Anna decided to tackle her stack of journals before it reached a critical stage and toppled over. She was marking an article with a Post-It note and a scribbled reminder when she heard noise in the outer office. Voices chattered in the hall. A file cabinet closed. Anna looked at her watch and nodded a silent understanding of what was going on. The assistants were leaving. No doubt, Lisa was even now retrieving her purse and preparing to make a quick exit.

Even though they didn't punch a time clock, the administrative assistants came and went with a regularity that was unwavering: In the office by eight a.m. Half an hour for lunch in staggered shifts, with the phones always forwarded for uninterrupted coverage. Out the door by four-thirty. In another ten minutes or so, all the department offices would be empty.

By quarter to five Anna should have the whole department to herself. Then she could nose around the offices without interruption or the need for explanation. She wasn't sure what she'd find, or even what she was looking for, but she was determined to try. She dawdled at her desk for another fifteen minutes, and when she emerged the office staffers were long gone. Of course, the doctors were still in clinic or the operating room and would be for another hour or more. The cleaning people wouldn't come in until later. Now was the time for Sherlock McIntyre to prowl. Anna wished she had Nick, her own private Watson, at her side so she could bounce ideas off of him. That is, if she had any ideas.

It wasn't dark, and Anna knew that there were other people in the building, but still the deserted hallways and offices felt creepy as she wandered systematically through them. Nothing struck her. No one came by and whispered, "I stole your personal information." She had no inspirations. Maybe this detecting was more difficult than it seemed on TV.

Then Anna glanced into the office complex shared by two doctors, Joe Leach and Allen McClay. The outer office was vacant, and their assistant's desk was unoccupied. Dr. McClay's office door was closed, but the door to Dr. Leach's inner office was open. Anna was sure both those doors had been closed when she walked by earlier. She edged into the outer office.

Through the open door of Dr. Leach's office, she heard drawers opening and closing. Someone was in there. Maybe Leach had finished his surgery and was rummaging for something in his always disorganized files. She tiptoed closer just as her chairman, Neil Fowler, emerged from the office with a file folder tucked under his arm. He closed and locked the door before he looked up and saw Anna.

If he was startled, Fowler didn't show it. "Hi, Anna. I thought things went fairly well at M&M, didn't you? I hope you don't think I was cutting you off, but I was afraid that Linda was about to launch into a harangue on how they used to do things in Boston, and I didn't want to give her a chance."

Anna knew she should probably agree and move on. Don't take a chance on antagonizing the chairman. But instead, she said, "Dr. Fowler, what were you doing in Joe's office?"

Fowler held up the file folder. "I needed some of the data he's collecting for a paper we're writing together."

"But how did you get in? I passed by here earlier and his door was locked."

He pulled a ring of keys from his pocket, jingled them, and grinned. "Master key for all the doors in the department. I'm the chairman. Remember?"

151

Anna made some conversational gambit — she wasn't even sure it made sense — and retreated back to her office. She closed the door and leaned against the desk. Of course the chairman would have a master key. She hadn't even thought of that. But how many more were floating around the department? She could hear it now. "Hey, Neil. Let me borrow your key. I need to get into my office, and I forgot mine." Then a quick wax impression — wasn't that the way they did it in the mystery novels? — and pretty soon locked doors presented no challenge.

She chided herself for letting her suspicions run wild. It was hard enough to think that an assistant might yield to the temptation to lift a few prescription pads and copy down a doctor's DEA number in order to turn it into cash or satisfy personal needs. But would another physician do that? No, surely not. On the other hand, she couldn't rule out that possibility.

Well, she'd learned something anyway. Probably more than she wanted to know. And the pool of suspects was larger than ever.

Anna closed the chart and tossed it into the rolling wire cart beside her, on top of all the others that were to be refiled. She shrugged her shoulders, flexed her fingers, and wiggled her toes. She felt as though she'd gone five rounds with a welterweight fighter. She was sore, discouraged, and painfully aware of her shortcomings.

The room was quiet except for an occasional muttered curse as a resident or staff physician struggled to complete long overdue dictation. The Medical Records Department might seem to be a minor cog in the operation of a large medical center like Southwestern, but Anna realized how much power the records staff wielded. How many times had she waited while a misfiled chart was located? How often had she hurried over to this basement room to sign charts and do dictation so her name would come off the dreaded "suspended" list — unable to operate or even admit patients until she'd completed the paperwork that seemed ready to bury her and her colleagues at any minute?

This time she'd come here voluntarily to wade through the charts of almost a hundred patients in search of a clue to the identity of the person who had co-opted her name and DEA number. And it had been a total bust. The names were just that — names. She'd been able to remember a few cases, put faces and scenarios with them, but that hadn't helped. Even though some of her patients weren't the type of people she'd want to go out for coffee with, she couldn't picture any of them being involved in a scheme to produce hundreds of forged narcotics prescriptions.

Anna felt her joints creak as she stood and stretched. The more information she gathered, the less she seemed to know and the wider the circle of suspects grew. She'd thought about going public at the M&M conference with the information about the second "Eric Hatley," the one whose treatment in the ER had led to the administration of Omnilex to her patient. For a moment she questioned her decision to hold back that information — information that would have justified the antibiotic choice she and Luc had made. But this feeling tickling the back of her mind, a feeling that one of her colleagues was tied into the whole identity theft mess, was too strong to ignore. And she didn't want to warn them off until she had more data.

The problem was how to find the facts that would clear her name. And right now, she had no clue.

Nick stared at the cartoons playing on the

TV set in the surgeon's lounge. Bad enough that he had to be here on a Saturday morning to do a frozen section, but wasn't there anything decent to watch while he waited? Apparently not.

The intercom startled him. "We're sending the specimen around right now, Nick."

"Okay, Frank. I'm on my way. Call you when I know something." Nick looked up at the TV in time to see the Roadrunner outwit Wile E. Coyote yet again. To the accompaniment of a triumphant "beep, beep," Nick pushed up from the sofa and strode quickly out of the room.

The routine for a frozen section was straightforward enough. The circulating nurse would hurry to the surgical pathology laboratory with tissue taken by the surgeon. The technician mounted the material and froze it with a special machine called a cryostat, then used a microtome, an instrument that looked like a miniature meat slicer, to shave off thin sections from the specimen onto a microscope slide. The tech stained the sections, the pathologist examined them under a microscope, and in a matter of minutes the surgeon could have his answer and proceed with surgery. Easy enough — when it worked well. Today it didn't.

First the cryostat proved balky, refusing to

freeze the specimen properly. Nick had no clue about how to make the instrument do its job, but apparently this wasn't the first time the pathology tech had encountered such a situation. After a prolonged bit of tinkering with the refrigerant source, the tech finally got the specimen frozen into a hard block, ready to section.

Then the microtome acted up. Theoretically, the paper-thin sections were supposed to fall off the edge of the blade onto the glass microscope slide with only a gentle nudge from a soft brush. Instead, they came off crinkled like the bellows of an accordion, and no amount of teasing would straighten them out. A bit more adjusting, a new microtome blade, and finally the tech was able to apply stain to the specimens and pass them to Nick.

Nick took the first slide and gently blotted the excess stain from around the edges before he slid it onto the stage of the microscope. He scanned the entire section under low power, correlating the images projected onto his retina with the story the surgeon had given him.

"Sixteen-year-old boy," Frank Crawford had said, "presented to the emergency room with abdominal pain, fever, and vomiting. We confirmed an intestinal obstruction and treated him conservatively, but he didn't respond. Now we think he's infarcting part of his small bowel."

"Okay, so the blood supply to that area's been cut off, and he's getting gangrene of the bowel. Not usual, but nothing you haven't seen before," Nick said. "You'll resect that segment, hook everything back up, and he'll most likely recover. What's so special that you think you'll need a frozen section?"

"This doesn't make sense. He doesn't have any of the factors that usually cause intestinal obstruction. And on the CT scan of the abdomen, he's got a bunch of prominent nodes."

"So take some for biopsy. Culture, histology, special stains. I'll make sure all that gets done. Why do you need an answer during surgery?"

"Nick, I've got a bad feeling. Of course, we'll send specimens for all that stuff, but while we're in there I need to be sure this isn't some type of malignancy. It may alter what we have to do."

Frank called it a bad feeling, and Nick didn't argue. After all, he'd experienced and responded to those same gut feelings. A layperson might call them hunches. For a doctor, Nick figured they were the result of disparate facts, stored in some far recess of the frontal lobe, laced together by the subconscious. So here he was, spending his Saturday morning with his eye glued to a microscope.

Nick examined the section of node under low power magnification: definite inflammatory changes, but nothing to suggest a cancer. Then his eye was drawn to one area in particular. He scanned it yet again. The pattern was unique, and the diagnosis fit the clinical picture. Just one more thing to confirm it. Quickly, he swiveled the lens to a higher power. Yes, definitely a non-caseating granuloma. And there was another one. And another.

"What've you got, Nick?" The voice over the intercom was tinny, but still plainly identifiable as Frank's. He was an excellent surgeon, but not known for his patience. Nick knew from experience that Frank had a true "surgeon's mentality." Figure it out, cut it out, move to the next case.

"Let me look at a couple more sections, but I think I've got something for you."

"Is there a malignancy in those nodes?" Frank asked.

"Nothing that I've seen. Let me ask you. What did this kid's chest X-ray look like?"

"Nothing special," Frank said. "One

radiologist thought his hilar nodes were prominent, another one said it wasn't anything."

"Did you do a serum calcium?"

"I don't recall. Probably. We did a full chem panel." There was a pause and the sound of voices in the background. "Read those numbers off to me, would you?" Another pause. "Say that again?"

"What was it?" Nick asked.

"It's 11.2."

"So it's elevated."

"I suppose we attributed it to dehydration," Frank said.

"Nope. He's got sarcoid."

"Are you sure?"

"I'll check out the permanent sections first thing Monday morning, and you'll want to do some more lab work. But, yes, I'm sure. No malignancy. If you get him on steroids pretty quickly, you're going to save him from a bunch of problems."

Frank was quiet for a moment. "And if we'd missed it —"

"But you didn't. Send me some more nodes, including a couple that aren't in formalin so I can get TB cultures. But it's sarcoid, I'm sure."

"Thanks, Nick. Good pick-up. I appreciate you coming in this morning."

Nick stretched to ease the ache in his back. After he thanked the pathology tech and promised to put in a good word with Dr. Wetherington on Monday for a new microtome and cryostat, Nick ambled off toward the surgeons' locker room to change. He stopped in the lounge and drew a cup of coffee. After one look at the mud-like consistency, he decided to wait and visit the Starbuck's downstairs on his way out.

He was standing at his open locker when he heard a noise behind him. Nick turned and saw a man in the uniform of a security guard, standing before a locker on the other side of the room, struggling to insert a key. "Help you?" Nick asked.

"Oh, I need to get into this locker. Dr. Morgan thinks he forgot his wallet when he left last night. He called and asked that someone get it and put it in his office. He'll pick it up later this morning."

The guard finally managed to get the locker open. He swept his hand across the top shelf and frowned. Then he stood on tiptoe and reached to the very back of the shelf. The expression on his face changed to one of triumph, and he pulled out a wallet. "Got it. No wonder he forgot it. Stuck way in the back there."

"How did you get the locker key?" Nick asked.

The guard unsnapped a huge ring of keys from his belt and held it up. "Oh, we have master keys to all the lockers up here. Every once in a while someone has to get into their locker after hours, and they don't have their key."

Nick didn't bother asking the man how he was going to leave the wallet in Dr. Morgan's locked office. He'd already figured that out. What he wondered was how many people were on the security staff of the medical center, and how often that ring of keys got passed around. He hated the prospect of telling Anna that her list of suspects had just expanded.

8

Anna awoke Saturday morning, filled with a
sense of futility. How long had it been since
her world started to fall apart? A month? A
year? No, less than a week. She felt like that
guy in Greek mythology — the name es-
caped her — who was doomed to roll the
boulder up the hill. Every time he made a
little progress, it rolled back. That was her,
no doubt about it. It seemed as though
every time she tried to solve one of her
problems, another one cropped up.

She considered those problems, one by
one. She had new credit cards, but she
didn't know who had been using her old
ones. She'd eventually clear her credit history, but she was sure it would be a time-
consuming and frustrating process. She'd
learned why Eric Hatley suffered a fatal reaction to a medication he should have tolerated, but in the process she'd been hit with
the news that Hatley's mother was filing a

malpractice suit. And when it came to finding out who was responsible for the narcotics prescriptions that bore her name and DEA registration, not only had she made no headway, the harder she looked, the more people she found who could be responsible.

She was a doctor, not a detective. Why was she the one doing all this looking anyway? She heaved a sigh. She was doing it because until she was no longer under suspicion by the DEA and the police she was a woman without a profession. She wanted to practice medicine, to teach, to get her life back. If she wanted that sooner rather than later, she'd better stop sitting here at the breakfast table drinking coffee and feeling sorry for herself. Even though it was Saturday, she should be doing something. Unfortunately, she had no idea what that was.

"Might as well run some errands. I can't foul that up," she muttered under her breath.

Anna rinsed out her coffee cup and set it beside the sink to drain. It took her only a few minutes to make out a grocery list. After that, she'd go by the cleaners, fill up her car, and try to catch up on all those little things she'd let slide recently. She knew that none of this would get her any closer to clearing her name with the law, but at least she could feel as though she'd accomplished something by the end of the day.

The last time she picked up groceries, she drove out of her way to shop in another part of town. Her first inclination was to do the same thing and avoid the grocery store where the pimply-faced clerk had sent her running out the door by announcing to her and the world that her credit card was over the limit. Then she made a decision. No minimum-wage store clerk was intimidating her. She'd walk into that store with her head held high, buy a cart full of groceries, and pay for them with one of her brand-new credit cards.

Anna relaxed when she entered the store and scanned the faces of the checkers. No, he wasn't here. Maybe that was a good sign. She went up and down the aisles, loading her cart, ducking her head to avoid the glances of the shoppers around her. Then she realized that no one but her had any notion of what had happened here a few days ago. And even then, it hadn't been her fault.

The shortest line was in front of a checker Anna knew by sight but not by name, a middle-aged woman with a slightly distracted look behind her corporate smile. She scanned each item, bagged it all with practiced ease, and announced, "Forty-two fifty-three."

Anna cringed a bit when she swiped her new card. Her heart thumped as she watched the display announce, "Awaiting approval." Ten seconds. Fifteen. No, this couldn't be happening again. "What's the problem?" she finally asked.

The checker said, "Let me see that card, Hon." The woman swiped it on the scanner above her register's keypad. She frowned. She swiped it in the other direction. Another frown. She turned the card over, looked at the front, and her frown turned into a look of triumph.

"What?" Anna said.

The checker pointed to a small sticker Anna had managed to ignore. "See this, Hon? This is a new card. When you get it, you have to call this number and have the card activated. That keeps somebody from stealing it out of your mailbox and using it." She handed the card back to Anna. "Got another one?"

Anna remembered that she'd done exactly what the woman described when her new MasterCard arrived, and she'd used that card ever since. When this VISA card arrived, she'd filed it away in her wallet, intending to activate it later. Then she'd forgotten. Today, she'd pulled out the card for the first time, not realizing her error until it was too late. *Way to embarrass yourself again, Anna.*

She tucked the not-yet-active card back into a slot in her wallet and swiped her MasterCard. When the "Approved" message popped up, along with a space for her signature, Anna realized she'd been holding her breath. She took in what seemed like half the air in the room, wondering how long it would take for her pulse rate to slow down again. Who was it that said of life's reverses that whatever didn't kill you just made you stronger? If that was the case, she'd already gotten a lot stronger. She hoped her strengthening process was about over, but a little voice inside her warned that there was probably more to come. Anna's grandmother would have called it "second sight." Nick probably would tell her it was an acceptance of Murphy's Law. Whatever it was called, Anna felt distinctly uneasy as she wheeled her cart out of the store, afraid of what might be next.

Once she'd stowed her grocery purchases, hung up her dry cleaning, and tossed her credit card receipts on the desk for filing later, Anna sat down with the phone and called the number indicated to activate her VISA card. The whole process took five minutes, four of which were spent listening to an operator telling her how important it was for her to purchase a plan that would notify all her credit card companies if her cards were lost or stolen. Anna told the operator thank you very much, and declined the coverage.

She still felt as though she should be doing something. Maybe her attorney had talked with the DEA or the police by now. She didn't know how fast lawyers worked. And would he be in his office on Saturday? If she'd been presented with a difficult medical problem, she knew she'd worry with it until she was on top of it, weekend or not. Maybe he operated under the same philosophy.

Well, she was paying Ross Donovan, so why should she be afraid to call him? Anna found his number, making a mental note to program it into her cell phone's memory, punched the keys, and waited. One ring. Two. Three.

"Ross Donovan." The response was a bit brusque, but not antagonistic. Sort of like, "Hey, I'm trying to get some work done here and hate to stop to answer the phone." Anna knew the feeling.

"Mr. Donovan, this is Dr. Anna McIntyre."

The tone of the response brightened appreciably. "Hi, Dr. McIntyre. You know, we're going to be working together for a while. I'm Ross. May I call you Anna?"

"Sure."

"So was there something you need? I'm afraid I haven't —" Anna heard a muffled thud. "Hang on, I just managed to shove a stack of papers off my desk." A minute passed before the attorney was back on the line. "Sorry. Is there something I can do for you?"

"I wondered if you'd called those policemen." Anna searched her memory, and finally the names popped up. "Green and Dowling. Are they still intent on proving that I'm part of some sinister narcotics ring?"

"I left a call for them yesterday. One was in court, the other was off. They may try to call me this weekend. Once I've talked with them, I'll get back to you. But, as I told you yesterday, if you're innocent, you have nothing to worry about."

Anna wished she could believe that. "What about the DEA?"

"Again, I left messages for both Hale and Kramer. No return call yet. If they're reasonable, I should be able to get you a new DEA permit fairly quickly. There's no doubt that the prescriptions are forgeries. The only question is how someone got your number, matched it with your other information, and started using it to write false prescriptions."

That brought up a question Anna had wondered about. "Could they have picked a number at random, and by chance it matched mine?"

He chuckled. "Sorry, didn't mean to laugh at you. Yeah, they could have picked a number, and the chances of it matching yours are the same as a roomful of monkeys producing the works of Shakespeare. No, whoever's behind this had to know what name went with the number."

"Don't pharmacists check that against some kind of directory or list?"

"Not usually."

"So it still comes down to someone who knew both my name and number."

"Yep," Donovan said. "If I were you, I'd think about someone you work with as the most likely suspect. Maybe we can point the police toward the real criminals and get them off your back."

Anna sighed. "Well, I've thought about it already, and that list is getting longer and longer. Anyway, I won't keep you. If you're in the office on Saturday, I know you must be busy."

"Not as much as you might think. Being in rehab for two weeks to dry out and get my head straight didn't leave me with a bunch of clients."

What could she say to that? "Well, I trust things are going okay for you now."

"So far, so good. You know, one of the things they tell us in AA is not to get too tired or too hungry. I've been working all morning, and it's getting near lunchtime. How about a working lunch?" Donovan correctly interpreted the silence on the other end of the line. "You realize, I wasn't asking you for a date. That would be unethical, so long as I'm working on your case."

"I . . . I really think I'd better take a rain check. Maybe some other time."

"Sure," Donovan said. "And I'll call you when I know more."

The phone call left Anna with feelings she couldn't identify. There was something about Ross Donovan that attracted her, while at the same time setting off all kinds of alarms. He was flawed, but his openness about his problem and the way he handled it were somehow appealing. If there was another invitation for a lunch or dinner — a working one, of course — she might just take him up on it.

Anna shoved the phone out of the way and turned her attention to the pile of unopened mail on the desk. Might as well take care of that. After all, this was supposed to be a catch-up day. The first two envelopes she opened informed her, in what would have been hushed and respectful tones if the letters could have delivered their message aloud, that she'd been preapproved for credit cards with a limit far above her reasonable purchasing power. She tossed them in the trash, but while she opened her bill from the phone company a disturbing thought hit her. She retrieved the two discarded sheets and systematically ripped them into tiny pieces. She opened her fist and loosed a small snowstorm into the wastebasket, thinking that she really needed to buy a paper shredder — today.

The next three pieces of mail were bills, and Anna dutifully put them aside in a stack next to her checkbook. She'd pay them this afternoon. Her credit was more important to her than ever, and she wasn't about to let these go unattended.

She picked up the next envelope and was

171

about to apply the letter opener to it when the phone rang. The caller ID showed an unfamiliar number. Who could be calling her? Someone from the medical center? She was effectively suspended from clinical duties. There was no way that Fowler would be in his office today. She thought of Nick and felt an unexpected flutter.

"Hello?"

"Hey, Anna. How's your Saturday going?"

Anna wasn't sure whether she appreciated or resented the chipper tone of Nick's voice. "I think the expression is 'rowing against the tide.' I've already spent half the day and don't feel as though I've accomplished anything worthwhile. How about you? Aren't you on call?"

"Yep. Had to go in for a frozen section this morning, but things are quiet now. Have you had lunch?"

Anna looked at her wrist and discovered she'd left her watch on her bedside table, not an unusual action for her on a day off. "Is it that time already?"

"My stomach tells me I'm at least half an hour late for lunch." Nick paused, apparently for effect. "I knew it. Mickey's little hand is on the twelve and his big hand is on the six. How about having lunch with me?"

"What about your being on call?"

"No problem," Nick said. "Things are quiet now, and there shouldn't be anything I can't put off for an hour or so. Why don't I show up with some deli treats? We can picnic in your living room. Guaranteed good weather. No flying or crawling critters to interfere."

Anna hesitated. Their relationship seemed to be moving a little fast. Didn't she have enough to worry about? Then again, she liked having Nick around, so what was the problem? "Okay. How long before you're here?"

"Does this answer your question?"

The sound of her doorbell ringing was simultaneous with a fainter version in the phone receiver. She laughed. "Pretty sure of yourself aren't you, Dr. Valentine?"

"Pretty confident, Dr. McIntyre. Besides that, I knew when I bought it that if you weren't home or — perish the thought — turned me down, the food wouldn't go to waste."

Anna rose and started toward the door, dropping the unopened mail on the coffee table along the way.

Nick shifted the wicker basket from his left hand to his right. The woman at the deli had sold him the picnic hamper for what

173

she'd termed a bargain price, probably because he'd spent so much on the food in it. He wasn't sure what made him think he could make this crazy idea work. After all, he'd told Anna only yesterday that he'd be tied up today. She probably had her day all planned out — a day without him. But after doing the frozen section, after hammering out the stack of stuff on his desk that he'd put off for a week, he found that he missed her. He wanted to talk to her, be with her, even smell the floral scent of her shampoo. The way he felt about her . . . it was different than anything he'd ever felt about a woman. And he liked it.

The front door swung open and Anna stood there smiling at him. She was dressed casually: simple skirt and blouse, sandals. Her red hair was pulled back with a band that matched her green eyes. "You're just full of surprises, aren't you?"

"I like to keep you guessing," Nick said. He hefted the basket. "Can I put this down somewhere? I think the lady at the deli threw in some lead weights when my back was turned."

Anna beckoned him in. "Sure. Bring it into the living room. We'll set up a picnic on the coffee table."

Nick pulled a red checked cloth off the

top of the basket and handed it to Anna. "When Nick Valentine brings a picnic, he brings everything except the ants."

"Where did you get all this?" Anna asked. "Red checked tablecloth, picnic hamper, goodies. This is like something out of a movie."

Nick shrugged an "it was nothing" gesture. "I'd heard about this little deli in Highland Park. Family owned, been there for years. I decided to pick up a couple of sandwiches and call you to see if you wanted to share them with me." He shrugged. "I ended up buying all this."

"It's wonderful. But there's so much food."

"As I told you, any leftover food won't be wasted. As for the basket and tablecloth, maybe you can keep them for our next picnic."

Nick wondered why he'd said that. It sounded brash, assuming that there'd be more picnics, more time together. *Don't rush her. Take it easy. Be cool.*

Anna scooped a pile of mail off the coffee table. "Let me clear this off so I can spread the cloth." Two letters on the bottom of the pile slipped from her grasp and fell to the floor.

Nick set the basket on the floor and

stooped to retrieve the mail. "Let me get those." One letter had landed address side up, and his eyes brushed across the return address: Metro Clinical Laboratories. "This looks like a lab report."

Anna smoothed the wrinkles from the cloth and began to pull items from the hamper. "Oh, that's probably mine. I had my annual physical a couple of weeks ago. I suppose my doctor ordered some kind of new test that the lab at the med center wasn't set up to do yet, so he sent it to an outside lab."

Nick frowned, but hurried to erase it before Anna looked up. "You know, I'm in the pathology department. If there's a test out there that we can't run, I haven't heard about it."

"Well, Dr. Pathologist, in that case, why don't you open it and see what it is? And if I have trouble interpreting the results, I've got an expert on hand."

Nick fumbled with the envelope. "Are you sure, Anna?" There was no levity in his voice now. "This is confidential stuff. Look." He held out the envelope and pointed to the large red letters in the lower-right-hand corner: CONFIDENTIAL.

"I don't mind if you know my cholesterol or my triglyceride or whatever. Go ahead. I almost have our picnic set up, and I don't want to stop."

Nick ran his finger under the flap and pulled out a single sheet of paper. He scanned the results with a practiced eye. Then he looked at the top of the page and double-checked the name and address of the patient. Finally, he asked, "What's your date of birth?"

"Why do you ask?"

"Just making sure this is really your report."

For the first time, Anna looked up. "July seventh."

"That matches," Nick said. "Did your doctor talk with you about ordering any unusual tests?"

"Nick, you're scaring me," Anna said. "What is it?"

He handed the report to her. "You'd better see this yourself."

Anna put down the loaf of sliced sourdough bread she was holding and looked down at the report in her hand. "Why did Dr. Reed order these? And why were they sent to a lab outside the medical center? The names of the tests are vaguely familiar, but I can't quite place them."

Nick eased onto the sofa and patted the cushion beside him. "Anna, sit down."

She sank into the seat, the picnic forgotten. "I don't understand," she said.

"Let me take your questions in order." Nick's voice was quiet, his tone sober. This wasn't the Nick who'd walked in her front door a few moments ago, the one who made her perk up. He'd changed. And it wasn't good. "First, Dr. Reed must have ordered these tests because he had reason to suspect a serious illness."

"What kind of —"

"I'll get to that. Second, he probably sent them to an outside lab because he was being considerate. By and large, our lab personnel at the medical center are professionals. They respect patient confidentiality. But sometimes they let things slip. He didn't want this information to get out."

Anna took a deep breath. She couldn't recall feeling this way since she waited for the dean's office to post the list of those who'd passed their courses and would receive their MD degree. When the list went up, she almost turned away without reading it. She ached to know the verdict but was afraid of what she'd see.

"Anna, are you okay?" There was concern in Nick's voice. "Can I get you something to drink?"

"No, I'll be fine. Go on." Anna tried to

swallow, to move her heart out of her throat as she waited for the other shoe to drop.

"You're right about the tests. You don't deal with them every day, but I do." Nick held up the paper. "If this first one is positive, it's followed up by another. If that one is positive, they do a third. If they're all three positive, then we do a confirmatory test. Even then, some clinicians insist on a fourth assay as sort of a fail-safe. If that's positive, there's no doubt."

"What are you saying?"

It seemed to Anna that Nick shrank back a bit. "You're HIV positive."

She felt as though someone had slammed a fist into her gut. "That can't be true."

"They ran all the tests," Nick said. "To be sure. After all, this is an area where false positives and false negatives can be disastrous."

Anna shook her head, as though trying to dislodge what she'd just heard. "No, no. I mean, there's no way I could be HIV-positive." She stopped, trying to figure out how to couch her reply. "I haven't had any exposure."

"Sure you have." Nick's tone was neutral, nonjudgmental. "You've been in patient contact for what? At least the last three years of med school, three or four more in residency, then in practice. Didn't you ever notice a hole in your glove during surgery? Maybe you had a little cut on your hand at the time but paid no attention to it. Did you accidentally stick yourself with a needle? Sure you've had exposure. It doesn't take sexual contact to contract AIDS. Blood exposure to non-intact skin will do it."

Anna felt the initial adrenaline rush of fear fading. Think logically, she told herself. Think about it. Once more she looked at the report, this time a lot more carefully. Studied it as though her life depended on it, which in a way, it did. She moved past the lab values themselves, and concentrated on the heading of the report.

That was her name, her date of birth. She didn't know her insurance number offhand, but she was willing to bet the designation at the top of the page was correct. Her home address was right, down to the added four digits after the ZIP code, numbers that Anna never could remember. And she could see why her doctor might have had the report sent to her at home, to protect her privacy. But why would Gary . . . wait a minute! The name of the requesting doctor wasn't Gary Reed. And the address wasn't the faculty clinic on Harry Hines Boulevard. No, the order came from Dr. Khalid Mahmood. The facility was the Metro Medical Center on Grand Avenue. This test was sent to the lab by what Anna often heard called a Doc-In-The-Box, a walk-in clinic, one located in one of the more depressed parts of Dallas.

"Nick, I found it. I know what happened," Anna said.

"You mean you know how you were exposed?"

"No. I mean I think I know how this test was done using my name and insurance information."

She saw the doubt in his eyes, knew he was probably thinking she'd gone somewhere she wasn't known to have the test done. How was she going to convince him that she was an innocent victim? And why did she care so much about what he thought?

Anna handed the report to Nick and watched his face as he took the paper. He didn't look down at it. He looked at her, like he was giving her a lie detector test with his eyes. Finally, he lowered his gaze and tapped the top portion of the report. "Anna, this is your name. Your address. The fact that the test was done at an out-of-the-way clinic doesn't change that."

She shook her head. "Can't you see? The

same thing's happened to me that happened to Eric Hatley. Someone's using my identity to get medical care. They got hold of my insurance information and used it the same way they used my credit cards and DEA registration. This is just another part of the identity theft."

"It makes sense, I guess. I want to believe you. But these test results —"

"Besides the fact that I know these aren't my tests. Think about it logically. It came from another clinic. That implies that I was trying to keep the results a secret. If that were my intent, would I have asked you to open the envelope? No, I'd have made sure the envelope stayed hidden while you were here. Hey, I'd have opened it myself the moment it arrived."

She watched Nick's frown deepen, then gradually fade. "Okay, I see what you mean. But let's say this isn't your test. What can you do about it?"

"I've got an idea. It's crazy, but so is everything that's happened to me so far."

Nick handed the report back to Anna. "What's that?"

Anna began to pace. "I've been thinking about the credit theft and the narcotics thing separately. They're not. I've had a vague feeling they were related, but now I

182

think they're part of something a lot bigger. Someone — we don't know who — got hold of all my personal information. They either used it themselves or passed it on to other people. If I trace one of these incidents back to the source, I've got my answer."

"You keep saying that you're going to do this," Nick said. "What happened to the 'we' that we talked about? Did I get thrown off the team?"

Nick was right. Her problems seemed to be piling up faster than she could deal with them by herself. "You're right. Two heads are better than one. We'll brainstorm this and figure out our next move." She surprised herself by reaching out for Nick's hand. "But you do believe me, don't you?"

Nick took the offered hand and squeezed, and his expression changed. "Yes, I believe you. I don't understand it all, but we'll figure it out." He dropped her hand and pointed to the forgotten picnic, now all laid out. "But can we do it while we're eating? After all, low blood sugar hinders the thinking process. Isn't that right, Doc?"

Anna relaxed as she saw that Nick had apparently accepted her innocence. "Sure," she said. "Let's eat."

The picnic, once it started, involved more eating than talking. Anna found that the afternoon's events hadn't blunted her appetite. "My compliments to your deli," she said, wiping mustard from her lips with a paper napkin.

"Thank you. I think —"

A pager went off and they both jumped. Anna's hand went to her waist in an automatic gesture that ended in frustration when she recalled that her pager was still on her desk at the medical center. She wasn't on call. No one wanted her.

Nick thumbed the button, looked at the display, and frowned. "Gotta call in. Okay if I use your phone?" When he hung up, the frown had turned to a look of disgust. "I have to go back to the medical center. There's a medicolegal autopsy they want done ASAP."

"Go on. I'll clean up here."

"Should I come back when I've finished?" The look on his face made it clear that he wanted to do just that.

"Can I take a rain check? I'm beat. And there's nothing either of us can do about any of this before Monday." Anna wrapped the remaining two sandwiches and a handful of cookies in one of the napkins and shoved them at Nick. "Take these with you. You're more likely to want them than I am. And thanks for the picnic. I enjoyed it."

When Nick stopped at the doorway, Anna thought he might be about to turn back and kiss her. Would she let him? The question became moot when he said, "I've enjoyed it too. Don't forget. I'll be by at ten-thirty in the morning."

She closed the door, leaned against it, and replayed the scene in her mind. If the question of the lab report hadn't come up, would the afternoon have ended differently? She wondered.

9

Anna awoke before the alarm sounded. She looked at the clock, tried to recall what day it was, struggled to define the feeling at the back of her consciousness that something was supposed to happen today. It had nothing to do with work — she was still on unofficial suspension. It was . . . Sunday. And Nick had agreed to attend church with her.

She kept reminding herself that she should be cool. Nick was a friend, nothing more. She didn't have time or space in her life for anything else, certainly not with everything swirling around her. But she did her makeup with extra care. Then she spent an unusually long time in front of her open closet door. Anna didn't have a lot of clothes — her budget was far from limitless — but she'd bought wisely, choosing good quality things that set off her red hair, green eyes, and pale complexion. She finally chose a simple green dress.

At ten-fifteen she started fidgeting. By ten-thirty she was checking her watch every fifteen seconds. At ten-forty, her phone rang.

"Anna, this is Nick. I'm so very sorry."

She felt as though she were on a roller coaster that had just started to drop. He was going to cancel. She'd scared him off by asking him to go to church with her. "That's okay, Nick."

"No, you don't even know what I'm apologizing for. I got a call this morning from George Race. He's the pathologist on call today, and his daughter is being christened this morning. The doctor who was supposed to cover for him got sick, and he needs me to work — at least until noon."

Anna felt her heart start beating again. She was a doctor. She could understand a situation like this coming up. It had nothing to do with her invitation to church. "Of course you have to cover for him, Nick. I'd be disappointed if you didn't."

"I'll be through at noon. Can we still have lunch together?"

Anna rummaged through the notes scattered on the coffee table in her front room. There it was. "I can do better than that. Some friends are having a party this afternoon. There'll be food there."

"Will I know any of these people? Are they

doctors? Neighbors? What?"

Anna gripped the phone a bit tighter. Better tell him the truth. "It's a group from our church. They're a lot of fun. And there'll be tons of good food."

"How can I turn that down? When can I pick you up and what can I bring?"

It wasn't that Nick didn't believe Anna when she said this party wouldn't be like church. It was just that perhaps her idea of "church" was different from his. Oh, well, at least he'd have a chance to be with her.

"Looks like a pretty big party." Nick squeezed his car into a parking space a block away from the house that Anna said was his target.

"Not too big. And I think you'll like these people."

He climbed out and hurried around to open the car door for her. She looked ravishing in a green blouse and tan slacks. Then again, Nick recalled that she looked great in scrubs and a wrinkled white coat too. Maybe it wasn't the clothes.

"Thanks for coming," she said as they approached the house.

"Wouldn't miss it," he said. *Well, I would have but it gives me another chance to be with you.* He stabbed at the doorbell.

"Everyone's around back." A middle-aged man hurried up the walk behind them, two grocery sacks in one arm and a large plastic bag of ice in the other.

"Thanks, Chet," Anna said. "Nick Valentine, this is your host, Chet Conway. Chet, Nick is a colleague of mine."

"Nice meeting you. Come on this way." Chet nudged a gate open with his foot, and led them through into a large fenced backyard filled with chattering people. People talked in small groups while others bustled back and forth between the kitchen and a long table loaded with food. "Nick, help Chet with those sacks. I'll put this pie down and see if his wife, Martha, needs a hand."

Chet shoved a sack into Nick's arms and said, "Napkins, paper plates, plasticware, cups. Find the nearest person in the kitchen and then run like the wind. Otherwise you'll be drafted." He laughed. "When you escape, find me and I'll introduce you around."

Nick did as he was told. Soon, he stood with Chet and two men whose names he had already forgotten, trying to follow their conversation without being drawn into it.

"I don't know what we're going to do with those people in Congress," the first man said. "No wonder our country's going to the dogs."

"We've always had bad people around. Doesn't mean they can't be good leaders," Chet said.

"Yeah, but it's more likely to happen if they're decent in the first place. Isn't that right?" The second man looked at Nick with a "back me up on this" expression.

Nick managed a shrug.

Chet grinned. Nick had seen that grin before. It was the expression of a staff physician when a medical student made a statement that wasn't going to stand up under close scrutiny. This could be good.

"Why don't we consider some of the leaders in the Bible? Would you agree they were good people?" Chet said.

The first man nodded. "Sure."

Chet grinned. "Start with Moses. Great leader. Led the Israelites out of captivity. God gave him the Ten Commandments. Moses was bound to be a pretty good guy? Would you sign off on that?"

The first and second man looked at each other, apparently wondering where the trap was. "Sure," they said in unison.

"Remember where Moses was before all that? He was hiding in the desert, because he'd killed a man," Chet said.

The men didn't seem to have an answer for that, but Chet wasn't through. "Ready for another try?"

"Sure," the first man said, not quite so eager now.

"King David," Chet said. "Saved his people by slaying Goliath when he was just a kid. Became king of Israel. Wrote the Psalms."

"Yeah, and the Messiah came from his line," the second man said. Surely this one was a winner.

"Remember what David did after he was king? Lusted after another man's wife and had her husband killed by sending him to the front lines. There's your good man."

Nick let the rest of the conversation wash over him, as he thought about what he'd heard. Nick always figured he'd blown his chance with God when he pulled that trigger. Maybe he'd been wrong.

Meanwhile, the game — for that was what it had become — was in full swing. One man would give an example of a leader. Another would point out his flaws.

"Peter. Lead apostle. Called 'the rock.' "

"Hot-tempered firebrand who cut off a man's ear in a fight. Denied his Lord three times when the chips were down."

Nick eased away. He'd heard enough to start him thinking. No, this hadn't been "church, the second installment," but there'd been some good stuff thrown around.

"Enjoying yourself?" Anna eased up beside him. "I'm sorry I left you alone for a bit, but I had to help get the food on the table. Ready to eat?"

"Sure," Nick answered. He pointed to the group of men he'd just left. "I don't remember those guys' names, but are they on the church staff or something? They were slinging Bible stuff around right and left."

"Chet, the host, is an insurance agent. Charlie, on the left, is a mechanic. Rick, on the right, is a dentist." She looked around and pointed. "The only minister I see here is the man in Bermuda shorts and flip-flops. That's Robert, our pastor."

Nick reached for Anna's hand, and she allowed him to take it. Together, they strolled toward the long table, where people were already lining up with paper plates in their hands. During the meal, Nick managed to take a polite interest in the conversations that flowed around him, but his thoughts kept coming back to one point: God probably hadn't written him off when he'd killed that holdup man. Maybe he had a second chance coming.

On Monday morning, Anna's phone rang

while she toasted an English muffin.

"Anna, this is Ross Donovan. Hope I'm not calling too early."

She caught the muffin as it popped from the toaster and immediately dropped it on a plate. "No, not at all. What do you have for me?"

"Agent Hale at the DEA finally returned my call. He agreed to meet with me this morning. Kramer will probably be there too. Do you want to come?"

Anna sucked at her fingers until they stopped burning. "What do you think?"

"I think this is the part where I tell them that if they have anything solid, show me a warrant for your arrest. If they don't, then back off, give you a new DEA permit, and let you get on with your life."

"Should you push them like that?"

"Did you tell me the truth when you said you had no knowledge of or involvement with those false narcotics prescriptions?"

"Yes."

"Then it's time to bring it to a head." Donovan's voice took on an edge. "At your first meeting, if they really had something, they'd have brought you in for questioning at their offices. Instead, they came to you and gave you the obligatory nudge, the one they always hope results in a confession. It

193

didn't. Now they're letting you twist in the wind while they check out other leads. It's time that came to a halt."

"Tell me where to meet you."

"Come by my office at nine-thirty this morning. We'll talk some more and drive over there together."

Anna was about to hang up when she thought of another question. "What about the Dallas Police?"

"They haven't returned my calls. Let's deal with the DEA first. That'll get you back to your practice."

An hour later, Anna was seated in Ross Donovan's office. She remembered how good the coffee had smelled on her last visit, so she accepted his offer of a cup. Her first sip convinced her that taste and smell weren't always linked. This coffee was so strong she checked the spoon to make sure it hadn't melted after she stirred in the sweetener.

"Coffee a bit strong for you?" Donovan asked.

Anna wiped a tear from the corner of her eye. "I thought I'd had some strong coffee at the hospital, but this tops it. But tastes vary, I guess."

"It's alcoholics' coffee."

She took a cautious sip, but couldn't taste

anything but bitter, strong brew.

Donovan smiled. "No," he said. "Not alcoholic coffee. It's like the coffee you find at AA meetings everywhere. Hot, strong, and lots of it. When you're trying to avoid one addiction, you tend to find a replacement. A lot of alcoholics smoke. Some get hooked on sweets. Most guzzle coffee. I decided there was no reason to kick alcohol only to get lung cancer or diabetes, but I was willing to risk an ulcer."

"If you don't mind my asking, how can an alcoholic practice law?"

"Well, as it turns out, not very well. I managed never to drink before I met with clients or had to be in court. But I made up for it by drinking at other times. And, as my ex can attest, I combined that with running around on her. She tried to straighten me out, but finally she'd had enough. She filed for divorce."

"I'm sorry," Anna said.

"Me too. She'd been practicing law under her maiden name, so a lot of people didn't even notice a change. But the divorce was the slap in the face I needed. A few months after it was final, I went into rehab."

"Do you miss drinking?"

Donovan's laugh was far from mirthful. "Would you miss breathing? Sure I miss it.

It was what kept me alive. I made sure there was always a bottle of Jim Beam right here." He pointed to the bottom drawer of his desk. "Every day, as soon as my assistant left — that was back when I had an assistant — I unscrewed the top of that bad boy and had a few belts. That held me until I could get to the bar."

"Are you . . . do you think you're okay now?"

"Do you mean is your lawyer going to show up drunk sometime? I hope not. But I take it one day at a time. You learn that in AA, because if you don't learn it, you're back drinking."

Anna looked at her watch and Donovan took the hint. "Well, enough about my sordid past," he said. "Let's get ready for our meeting with the *Federales*."

Anna wasn't sure how to take this man. He seemed almost jovial at times. Was this a coping mechanism? Or had he reached the bottom of life's barrel so completely that nothing caused him any fear or worry? Despite it all, she found herself trusting him. Even if his ex-wife had qualified her referral with the words "liar" and "cheat."

Ross was seated alongside Anna in straight chairs across the table from Kramer and

Hale. He recognized the room; he'd been in dozens like it, usually in a jail or police station, with his client sitting across the scarred metal table in shackles and a guard standing right outside the door. The agents had probably chosen to meet in an interview room simply to scare Anna. Judging from what he'd seen so far of his client and her Irish temper, they weren't going to get far with that maneuver.

This was Ross's first time to meet the two DEA agents, and they weren't what he'd imagined. Hale was a week past needing a haircut. His suit looked like he'd slept in it. Kramer, on the other hand, looked like a million dollars. For an instant Ross wondered why she was working in law enforcement, instead of acting or modeling. Then he saw her eyes and revised his estimate.

Agent Hale leaned back and laced his hands behind his head. His coat dropped open, showing an automatic holstered on his hip, something else Ross figured was meant to intimidate his client.

"Counselor, let's cut to the chase," Hale said. "We don't have to share the results of our investigation with you until we file charges against your client."

Ross sat a bit straighter and planted both hands on the table. He fixed Hale with a gaze he hoped was laser-like. "Agent, speaking of cutting to the chase, why don't you admit that you confronted my client and accused her of a crime you knew full well she didn't commit, hoping she might give you some bit of information that would help you in an investigation where you were totally lost?"

Hale came halfway out of his chair. "Now wait —"

"Hang on, there," Kramer put a restraining arm on her partner's shoulder. Her voice had steel behind the softness. "Maybe it's time to put our cards on the table." She looked at Anna. "We recognize that the signatures on the prescriptions bearing your DEA number were forged. So far, we've found no evidence of involvement on your part. You're not totally in the clear yet, but we're willing to cut you some slack if you'll help us. If we issue you a new DEA permit so you can go back to work at the medical center, we'd expect you to keep your eyes and ears open. If you discover something that might help us find the person behind this, can we depend on you to pass it on to us immediately?"

Ross held up a warning hand to Anna. "Don't answer." He turned back to Hale. "You'll call her chairman and tell him you haven't turned up anything to incriminate my client? And you'll communicate that to the Dallas Police Department?"

The expression on Hale's face suggested he'd just dined on a lemon. After a moment, Hale nodded.

Ross suspected that the interview was being taped, and nods don't go into a transcript. "Say it, Agent. Say it for the tape."

Hale swore under his breath. "Yes, we'll do that. I'll make the calls today. It'll probably take us a week to get you a new DEA permit. But I can't promise the DPD will back off. I've talked with Dowling and Green a couple of times. They really believe that the doctor here is mixed up in this some way."

"Thank you for the information," Ross said. "Just make the call."

Hale wasn't through, though. "And Doctor, you'll keep us informed of anything you learn that would help our investigation?"

Ross figured it was time to say "yes" and end the interview. He nodded at Anna, who gave her head a quick up-and-down.

This time it was Hale's turn. "Dr. McIntyre? Get it on the record, please."

"Fine, I'll pass on anything I find out," she said.

There were no handshakes to end the

meeting, just the scrape of chairs and the rustle of papers gathered into briefcases and folders. Ross worked to maintain a poker face. This wasn't a total victory, but it was at least a small one. It was nice to be back in practice again, and especially nice to be doing it sober — and for such a lovely client.

Outside, on the sidewalk, Anna turned and offered her hand. "Thank you for your help."

"Just doing my job," Donovan said. "Now, how about some lunch?"

"I'm . . . uh —"

Donovan patted the air. "Easy there. I'm just offering to buy you a sandwich. Besides that, we can talk. The fact that the DEA's let up a bit doesn't mean you're out of the woods. And I get the impression there's more to this than what you've told me so far." He ticked off the points on his fingers. "Never lie to your lawyer. Never withhold information from your lawyer. Always trust your lawyer. And —" He pointed his finger at her. "Always accept an invitation to eat with your lawyer, so long as he agrees to pay and not charge it back to you."

The Irish have a saying: "He could charm the birds out of the trees." That fit Ross —

at least a sober Ross. Anna relented. "All right. Just a quick sandwich. I have some things I need to do today."

10

Nick looked at the sandwich on his desk and wrinkled his nose. Mondays were always busy, so he generally brought lunch from home and ate at his desk. Today, though, he hadn't done so well as a chef. He lifted the top slice of bread and sniffed at the lunch meat, wondering if he should slice off the green rind or toss the whole thing. The chips he'd sealed in a sandwich bag had been reduced to a greasy mass of shards. The apple, the last one in his crisper, was dry, wrinkled, and totally unappetizing.

He shoved everything back into the brown bag and heaved it into his wastebasket, where it settled with a satisfying *clunk*. Nick looked at his watch. One o'clock. *Wonder if Anna's already eaten.* He picked up the phone, punched in her home number, counted the rings, and felt his heart sink when the answering machine picked up. "Anna, this is Nick. Just calling to invite you to have a late lunch with me. I'll try your cell." He did, only to have his call roll over to voicemail on the second ring. He repeated the message with appropriate variations and hung up.

In the cafeteria, the chicken potpie on his plate tasted like sawdust, although all around him people were shoveling it in with great gusto. He managed to eat about half of it before he pushed it aside. Maybe some coffee and a piece of pie? No, he wasn't really that hungry, something so foreign to him that he toyed with the idea of asking one of his internal medicine colleagues to give him a checkup. Then again, maybe what he felt wasn't due to a bug. Maybe the cause was a certain redheaded surgeon.

How long had he known Anna McIntyre now? A week? Two? Surely not long enough to feel this serious about her. Maybe this wasn't love at first sight, but at the very least it was "strong liking in less than two weeks."

The beep of his pager roused him from his self-analysis. He thumbed the button and checked the display: Dr. Wetherington — probably fuming because Nick hadn't finished his professional résumé for the promotions committee. Somehow, Nick didn't think his chairman would accept the excuse that he'd been too busy spending time with his new girlfriend. Maybe he'd have time to think up a good story on his way to the chairman's office.

"I've only spoken with these guys on the phone. You've seen them in person. What are your impressions of Green and Dowling?" Ross put down his chicken sandwich to listen.

Anna dabbed at her mouth with a napkin and tried to think of the right way to describe these men. "Green frightens me a bit. Remember the football player, Mean Joe Greene, who was supposed to be such a terror? Well, Mean Joe would be a pussycat compared with Lamar Green."

"What about Dowling?"

"So pale you'd think he never saw the sun. Lean and sinewy, losing his hair. Quiet, but I have this mental image of a snake ready to strike at any time."

"Which one would you rather deal with?" Ross asked.

Anna couldn't suppress a shiver. "Neither one. Green would come right after me. Dowling might stab me in the back. They scare me."

"Okay, we'll let that rest," Ross said. "Time to talk about something else."

Anna was surprised to learn that Ross

liked the same kind of music she did, enjoyed the same movies she did, and in general was a real person. As he paid the check, she decided her first lunch with a lawyer hadn't been as bad as she'd feared, especially considering the precipitating circumstances.

They parted in front of the restaurant, with Ross promising to keep Anna posted on any new developments and extracting the same promise from her. She ransomed her car from the parking garage and pulled out onto Pacific Street. The laboratory where the pseudo-Anna McIntyre had received her HIV workup was on Grand Avenue, only a couple of miles in distance but light-years in economic status from downtown Dallas. Anna pulled up a mental map of the streets involved and set a course for the Metro Clinical Lab. She didn't recall the exact street address, but it shouldn't be too hard to find.

When Anna turned onto Grand, the neighborhood changed, and she locked her doors. Ahead, on the corner, she saw a one-story, red brick building bearing a sign in faded black letters: Metro Clinical Laboratory. The parking area at the side of the building resembled a road in Afghanistan after a mortar attack. Holes in the concrete threatened her wheels and suspension as she dodged right and left. She brought the car to a halt in the one empty parking space, the farthest from the building.

Anna checked that the car doors were still locked before retrieving her purse from under her seat. Maybe she should check her messages at home before she went into the building. She flipped open her cell phone and noticed the icon that indicated one new voicemail message. Then she remembered. She'd turned off the ringer before going into conference with the DEA agents. She changed the setting and pushed the button to retrieve the message.

"This is Nick. Just calling to invite you to have a late lunch with me. Guess you're tied up. Call me when you get this message. I . . . uh, I . . . hey, I really enjoyed our picnic."

Anna leaned back in the seat and wondered how this had happened. A month ago she'd been totally focused on her career. Not much of a social life beyond an occasional date that almost never led to a second one. Now her professional and personal life were on the verge of ruin, but she had two men in her life, either of whom could turn out to be the Mr. Right she'd always hoped would come along.

She started to punch the number to call Nick, who had made it onto her speed-dial list soon after their first meeting. Then she stopped. She really ought to go inside and get this out of the way. She could call him from home or at least from the car after she was safely out of this neighborhood.

Anna unzipped her purse, dropped in the phone, and rummaged around until her fingers identified the tiny canister of pepper spray she'd carried since moving to Dallas. She'd never used it, but today she felt better knowing it was there. She moved the canister toward the top of the purse and left the zipper partly open. Then she unlocked her doors, looped the strap of her purse securely over her head and across her body, and stepped out. She beeped the doors locked once more and looked around her.

A half dozen homeless men crouched against the chain-link fence that formed the far end of the parking lot, next to where she'd left her car. They represented a veritable United Nations of colors and ethnicity, but they shared one characteristic: red-rimmed eyes that seemed to stare right through her. The man on the end had a firm grip on the neck of a bottle protruding from a brown paper sack. She watched out of the corner of her eye as he drank, wiped his lips with the back of his hand, and passed the bottle to one of his companions.

Anna dreaded turning her back on these men to walk the seventy feet to the front door. Don't run, she told herself. Just move along. They won't hurt you. She dropped her hand inside her purse and grabbed the pepper spray. Keys in one hand with her thumb on the panic button of the remote, pepper spray canister in the other. Take a deep breath. Start walking.

The walk to the door seemed to take an hour, but she reached it with no consequences worse than a cramp between her shoulder blades from muscles taut as a violin string. Once inside the building, she dropped keys and canister into her purse and looked around for a receptionist.

"Help you?" The Hispanic girl sat behind a scarred desk against the back wall of the foyer. Straight chairs with ripped vinyl seat cushions lined the walls on either side of the room. A coffee table held several tattered magazines and out-of-date copies of two newspapers, the *Dallas News* and *El Sol.*

"I'm Dr. Anna McIntyre. I need to speak with your laboratory director."

"May I ask why?" The girl was civil enough, but apparently used to deflecting questions. She probably had her orders. A routine was in place, and any departure from it would present a problem.

"I'd rather discuss it with the director. Is he or she available?"

The girl shook her head. Anna could almost see the gears turning as the receptionist pulled up the appropriate response from her memory bank. "Our medical director is Dr. Gaston. His office is in Fort Worth, but he makes a visit here once a week. He was here yesterday. Would you like to come back next week?"

"Who's in charge here? I mean, right now, on the premises."

"I guess that would be our chief technician."

Anna took a calming breath. "And that would be?"

"Rhonda Brown."

"May I speak with her?"

"May I ask why?"

The dialogue continued like a bad imitation of an Abbott and Costello routine, but eventually the receptionist waved Anna through the door and into the laboratory. She was met there by a stout African American woman dressed in a flowered scrub top and navy scrub pants, the ensemble covered by a crisp white coat.

"Ms. Brown, I'm Dr. Anna McIntyre."

Anna extended her hand.

"Pleased to meet you, Doctor. And it's not Ms. It's Miss. Anyway, you can call me Rhonda." She took Anna's hand and gave it a brief, firm shake, while never taking her brown eyes off her visitor. "How can I help you?"

"Is there somewhere we can sit down? This won't take long, but there's a bit of explaining that goes with it."

"Sorry, but I've got tests going and two other techs to supervise. If I can't do it right here, right now, you'll have to come back."

Anna sighed. She'd have to keep it simple, leave out the details, and hope Rhonda went along with her request. She told her about the lab report she'd received and asked if there was any way to identify the woman on whom the test had been run.

"Doctor, more than fifty patients come in here every day." Rhonda pointed to the open door to the waiting room. "Most mornings every one of those chairs is filled. As soon as somebody comes in here for us to draw blood, somebody standing along the wall takes the vacant seat. We check their paperwork, ask them to verify their name and birthday, take the sample and move on. So far as we're concerned, you are who your lab slip says you are."

"Well, can I ask the other technicians? Maybe they remember something."

Rhonda was already shaking her head before Anna finished. "Dr. McIntyre, you ever heard of HIPAA?"

Of course, Anna had heard of the Health Insurance Portability and Accountability Act of 1996. Its most important provision, designed to protect patient privacy, had added another layer of paperwork for medical professionals already buried under reams of it. Before any medical information could be revealed, even to a patient's spouse or parent, the proper forms had to be signed. "You're telling me you can't help me because of HIPAA regulations," Anna said.

"I'm telling you that I could get in trouble just by talking to you about this. That patient — the one who told us she was Anna McIntyre — didn't list your name on the HIPAA form she signed."

"But I'm Anna McIntyre. So I can give you permission."

Rhonda shook her head and started to turn away. "Doctor, I've given you more time than I should already. Even if we went through all the legal hassling to get permission to talk about this, I'd still tell you the same thing. All the information we have about these patients is what they give us and what Lola out there at the desk copies off their insurance papers. We don't remember their faces or whether they have green hair or a big eye in the middle of their forehead. All I'm looking for is a good antecubital vein. Then, if the patient doesn't faint in the chair, we slap on a bandage, they're out and somebody else fills the spot before it gets cold." The last words were said over her shoulder and by the time Anna framed a reply, Rhonda was looking over a printer strip as it spewed from an automated analyzer.

It was obvious to Anna she'd gone as far as she could go here, with absolutely nothing to show for her efforts except the start of a massive headache. She thanked Rhonda, who acknowledged it with a wave. Anna turned and made her way back into the waiting room where the receptionist — presumably Lola — hardly gave her a glance before returning to her attack on the keyboard of her computer.

Anna spied a water fountain in the corner. She dug two Extra Strength Tylenols out of her purse, and washed them down with tepid water from the fountain. As soon as she got to a better neighborhood, she'd stop at a convenience store and get a Coke. Maybe the caffeine would help get rid of the headache.

In the parking lot, the collection of homeless men had dwindled to three, all leaning against the chain-link fence. The bag-in-a-bottle she'd seen earlier was no longer in evidence. Anna headed toward her car, fighting the urge to run. Easy now. Just like being in the jungle — don't show any fear. Halfway to her car, she pulled her keys from her purse and thumbed the remote.

"Hey, lady. You got any spare change?"

The largest of the trio, a stocky white man, eased off the fence and began walking toward her. He hadn't shaved in days, and as he got closer, Anna decided he probably hadn't bathed recently either. The other two men didn't move, apparently content to watch the scene unfold.

"I asked if you got any spare change." He was directly between Anna and her car, standing easily with his hands on his hips. His breath smelled of cheap wine and dental decay.

"No. No, I haven't." She tried to move past him, but he moved with her, blocking her way.

"Well, maybe we should just see." He reached out for her purse and tried to wrestle it away from her, foiled for the moment by the strap across her chest.

"Help!" Her screams didn't produce any action from the two observers, who continued to watch with detachment. She tugged at her purse with her left hand, groping wildly for her pepper spray with her right.

The man dropped his hold on the purse and drew back his fist. Anna's hand closed around the spray canister and pulled it free. Her finger was on the button when she felt a jarring pain in the point of her jaw. She caught a glimpse of sky. A loud thud, like a football being punted, filled her head. Then nothing.

Her first thought was that she had to get up. It must be morning. She wasn't sure what she had to do, but she was certain she was late. She started to roll out of bed, only to find that she couldn't move. She was strapped down. And the room was moving — rocking from side to side, bumping up and down. What was going on?

"Just take it easy, miss. Lie back."

The unfamiliar voice didn't reassure her. Just the opposite. She was in some sort of narrow room, and the sound of a siren seemed to be all around her. Where was she? And why couldn't she move? She opened her eyes but the light was dim. Everything was fuzzy, with halos and colored spots making it almost impossible to see anything clearly.

She heard a man's voice, the words faint and echoing as though issuing from a tunnel. "Easy there."

She tried to turn her head but met resistance. A wave of pain drove her back against the bed. What was going on?

"Don't struggle. We have you secured to a stretcher. Your neck's in a collar, in case you hurt it when you fell back on the concrete. Just relax and we'll have you in the Emergency Room in just a few minutes."

She strained to move, but when she flexed her right wrist she felt a sharp prick.

"You have an IV in your arm. Just lie back. We'll be at the hospital soon."

Why was he saying that? What was going on? Another effort to turn her head intensified pain that she thought couldn't get any worse. Her stomach began to churn. She lay back, closed her eyes, and took a deep breath.

"Can you tell us what happened to you?"

The voice was nearer. She opened her eyes, squinted, saw a man bending over her. He was wearing blue coveralls with some type of emblem on the chest. The nameplate over his breast pocket read "Tom."

"Tom." Her voice was raspy. She swallowed and tried again. "What happened? Where am I?"

"Hold on. Let me check your vital signs again."

She felt something squeeze her arm to the point of pain, heard a mechanical whir. She bit her lip from the discomfort before the pressure was released with a low hiss. Tom nodded and made a notation on a clipboard he pulled from somewhere behind him. "Okay. Here's what I know. You apparently fell in the parking lot of Metro Labs. Looks like you hit the back of your head. Lost consciousness. One of the technicians stepped outside for a smoke, saw you, and called it in. We just picked you up, and we're headed to the Emergency Room."

"Hey, Tom." A metallic voice came through a speaker above her head. "Baylor's ER says they're swamped. If she's stable, I'm detouring to Parkland."

"Affirmative," Tom replied. "Let's do it."

She squeezed her eyes shut and tried to concentrate. Her head felt as though an air hose was inflating it to three times its normal size. The pain increased with every beat of her heart. When the wail of the siren dipped, she was conscious of a constant roaring in her head. The ambulance — at least, she figured she was in an ambulance

— rocked and swayed, bringing with it more nausea. She swallowed hard and willed her stomach to be calm.

Think. Why had she been at that lab — the name had already flown from her thoughts — and why did she fall? As her thoughts went around like a carnival ride, going in a circle with no progress, a more important question intruded. Who was she?

11

"Ambulance coming in, Dr. Fell. Female, found unconscious in a parking lot. Vital signs are stable. The EMT says she's starting to wake up."

Dr. Will Fell looked up long enough from the wound he was suturing to nod at the nurse. Then he bowed over his work, careful to give the same attention to this last stitch as he had to the first one. He could still hear Dr. McIntyre's voice. "Resist the temptation to hurry when you're about through. Don't think about the next patient. Think about this one. Every patient should get your full attention until you're finished. That's the only way to practice medicine."

He snipped the ends of the suture and motioned for the aide to apply a bandage. "See that he gets a tetanus shot, wound care instructions, and a follow-up appointment for suture removal in a week to ten days."

Will looked down at the man on the table,

a middle-aged Mexican laborer who'd come in with a nasty laceration of his arm from an industrial accident. The man spoke little English, and Will's Spanish was rough, but they'd communicated well enough.

"*¿Alguna pregunta?*"

The man shook his head. No, no questions. Will figured as much. If the man had any, he probably wouldn't ask them. Keep your head down. Don't call attention to yourself. This was the lesson learned early on. Even if you had your green card, stay away from anyone in authority. Will looked at the technician. "Be sure he understands, would you?"

"No problem." The aide reached into a cabinet behind her and pulled out a sheet that contained wound care instructions in both English and Spanish.

Now he could shift his attention to the next patient. As Will stepped into the hall, he began running through a mental checklist of the causes for unconsciousness. Start with the broad categories: traumatic, toxic, metabolic, neurologic, infectious, vascular. Then again, once you broke them down into individual conditions, the number was staggering. In medical school, Will had once competed with several other students to list as many specific causes as possible for unconsciousness. Will had won with two hundred seventy-two.

Well, if she's already regaining consciousness, his job was a bit easier. He'd definitely look for a head injury, probably check some blood chemistries, a toxicology screen, maybe schedule an EEG to see if this was a seizure. Then, like any good diagnostician, he'd see where his findings took him. That's something else Dr. McIntyre instilled in all her residents. For a surgeon, she had a lot of internist in her — always looking deeper into the problem, taking pride in her diagnostic ability. Look closely; don't rush to judgment. He liked what he'd heard her say once. "You're not a technician. You're a doctor. So be a good one. Anyone can learn to cut. A good clinician knows why and when."

Well, Dr. McIntyre, let's see how much I learned from you. Will tapped lightly on the door of Trauma Room Two and pushed through the door. The EMTs were just unloading the patient onto a gurney and giving their report to the nurse. Will took the clipboard from the lead EMT and studied the scribbled notes.

Jane Doe. No ID on her, no purse or wallet at the scene. Vital signs stable. Neuro exam not remarkable — take that with a grain of salt, since a neurological evaluation done in a moving ambulance might not be accurate. The note said there was no odor of alcohol, none of the sweet smell of diabetic ketoacidosis on her breath. Swelling in the occipital region, bruising at the point of the chin, so there was probably some trauma involved. If she'd fallen, that explained the injury to the back of the skull, but why the bruising on the chin? Had she been in a fight? He'd definitely want a CT of the skull.

"Okay, Doc. She's all yours." The EMT turned back to the patient. "Good luck, lady. You're in good hands."

"Thank you," she said.

Will's head snapped up at the sound of that quiet voice. He covered the distance to the gurney in five quick steps, stopping short to look down at the disheveled form of his mentor, Dr. Anna McIntyre. She smiled weakly and said, "Are you a doctor? Can you help me?"

The man looking down at her seemed so young. Was he a doctor? Or was he a nurse or a technician, even an orderly? Had she made a terrible gaffe by calling him "doctor?" No matter. He had a kind face and she sensed somehow that he cared. Maybe he could help.

"Dr. McIntyre?"

Was the young man speaking to another doctor in the room? That name sounded so familiar. Even the room looked familiar. Why? What was going on?

"Please, can you help me?" she said again.

The man leaned over her. He was wearing what looked like gray pajamas, covered by a white coat with words embroidered over the breast pocket. She squinted. Will Fell, M.D.

"Dr. McIntyre? Don't you know who I am?"

"I'm sorry. Should I? I mean, I can't even recall my own name, so I guess it's okay that I don't know yours."

He turned and gave orders to the woman beside him. Some of the words made a vague sort of sense, but the memories they triggered seemed as disconnected as the pieces of a jigsaw puzzle just dumped from the box. And when she tried to put them together, all it did was make her headache worse.

The doctor turned back to her. "I'm going to examine you. Just try to relax. First of all, follow my finger with your eyes." As the examination went on, there were times when she seemed to know instinctively what was coming next. Most of the time she was right. What could that mean?

The doctor shoved his stethoscope — she wondered how she knew that was what it was called — into the pocket of his white coat. "We're going to take a bit of blood for some lab work. Then the nurse here is going to take you to X-ray for some studies of your head. After that, I'll be back to talk with you some more."

"But you haven't answered my question. Can you help me?"

"Of course," he said. But she could see the doubt in his eyes.

The voice on the phone was neutral, the greeting brisk. "Dr. Simpson."

"Sir, this is Will Fell. I'm a surgery resident in the Parkland ER."

"Yes, I know. You're the Pit Boss. What do you need?"

Will guessed that when you were the chief of a busy neurosurgical service you didn't spend much time in social niceties or idle chitchat. He swallowed hard, more nervous than he'd ever been while presenting at Grand Rounds. "Sir, I need you down here. We —"

"Whatever this is, why can't one of the neurosurgery residents handle it?"

"Dr. Simpson, I think I need a faculty presence. Dr. Anna McIntyre was just brought in to the ER. She apparently sustained some head trauma and lost consciousness. She's awake now, but she's amnesic — not just for the event, it's global amnesia. She's getting a CT of the head right now. I did a neuro exam, and I think it's normal, but —"

"I'm on my way. Meet me in radiology."

Twenty minutes later, Will sat beside Mike Simpson, chairman of the Department of Neurosurgery, watching the man study the images on the computer screen in front of them.

"What do you see?" Simpson asked.

Will squinted, wondering what he'd missed. To him, this was a normal CT of the head. No midline shift, no masses, nothing. What had Simpson seen that he hadn't? "Sorry, sir. It all looks normal to me."

Simpson nodded. "Right. Now why did you get this scan?"

Oh, boy. Will steeled himself for the chewing out that was coming. Every test, especially one with a hefty price tag, required justification. "Well, she had physical evidence of trauma to the head. I wanted to rule out a subdural hematoma. That's a surgical emergency."

"But did she have neurologic signs?"

Will felt drops of sweat coursing between

his shoulder blades. "Uh, well, I wasn't sure."

"You're a second-year resident. You've probably done hundreds of neuro exams. What did you think about this one?"

Will squared his shoulders. "I thought it was normal. But this is a faculty member and I thought —"

"You wanted to be sure. And that was a good decision. But did you think her neurologic exam was normal?"

"Uh . . . yes, sir."

"Deep tendon reflexes brisk and equal. Pupils reactive to light. No papilledema. Sensation intact. So she was neurologically intact?" Simpson turned from the computer screen and fixed him with cold gray eyes. "But she had amnesia. That's abnormal. It's not a physical sign, but recall that one of the elements — the first element — of a good neurologic is whether the patient is oriented to time, place, and person. She isn't, so her neurologic is abnormal. Never mind her pupillary reactions and deep tendon reflexes. So you were right. You had to get the CT." The faintest hint of a smile flickered on Simpson's lips. "Fell, you're a good doctor. Dr. McIntyre told me once she had high expectations for you. When you know you're right, don't back down.

But remember one thing. In our profession, good isn't enough. We have to be perfect."

Will nodded. "So you agree she has no evidence of a subdural?"

"Just a concussion."

"And the amnesia? Should I get a psychiatry consult?"

Simpson shook his head. "Transient global amnesia. A rare consequence of head trauma, especially if there's significant associated psychological stress. I'm betting that within the next few hours she'll start remembering things. By tomorrow, maybe the next day, she should be fine."

"Will all her memory come back?"

Simpson shrugged. "Most of it. Generally these patients don't remember anything about the precipitating event. Other than that, yes, it all comes back to them."

"Do you want her hospitalized for observation?"

"Admit her to my private service with the diagnosis of head injury, rule out subdural hematoma. Neuro signs every hour. You know the drill. Get an MRI of the head tomorrow to make sure she isn't developing anything else. I'll see her before I leave this evening. If anything comes up before then, page me."

■ ■ ■ ■

"Good morning, Will." Anna pulled the covers up to her chin. It wasn't so much a matter of modesty. Goodness knows that had gone out the window along with her clothes when the nurses replaced them with a hospital gown. And she dreaded looking in a mirror. One of the ICU night nurses had taken pity on her and scared up a hairbrush and lipstick, but Anna still felt — and probably looked, she guessed — like a Halloween leftover.

"Morning, Dr. McIntyre." Will was freshly shaved, his scrub suit and white coat were clean and unwrinkled, but the dark circles under his eyes told a different story.

"Will, you were in here off and on all night. Weren't you supposed to go off duty last evening?"

Will suddenly found her chart very interesting. He didn't look up as he said, "Well, I decided to hang around here last night."

"There was no need for that. Dr. Simpson came by last evening. He brought the on-call neurosurgery resident with him and briefed him on my case. You should have gone home for some rest."

"Oh, I snatched a few naps in the call

room. No big deal."

Anna decided not to pursue a subject that was obviously an embarrassment to Will. Instead, she asked, "So, what's the plan?" She grinned. "I mean, I think I know what the plan should be, but I still have some holes in my memory right now."

Will seemed on firmer footing now, talking about something clinical. "Your neuro signs are stable, so we — I mean, Dr. Simpson — will let up on the frequency of checking those. You're scheduled for an MRI this afternoon. If things go well, we can get rid of that IV this evening and start letting you eat and move around."

"And how long before Mike lets me go home?"

"Maybe another day or two. And I'm pretty sure he'll want you on limited activity for a week or so."

Something that had been gnawing at the back of Anna's mind began to burrow forward into her conscious thoughts. She had gone to that laboratory for a reason. All the pieces of the puzzle hadn't put themselves together in her addled brain, but she had the sense that she needed to get back to whatever she was doing. Soon.

Will hesitated for a moment before reaching down and touching her hand, carefully avoiding the IV snaking into the vein just above her wrist. "I've got to go back on duty in the ER, but if you need anything, just have the nurses page me."

"Thanks, Will."

Anna appreciated Will's obvious concern for her. She was independent enough to think she didn't need his help, but it was nice to know it was there. Then she realized that there were a couple of men in her life who'd already shown her that they cared. And she should probably contact both of them.

That led to another thought. Her cell phone. Where was it? The answer came back quickly, and with it another set of problems reared its head. Her cell phone was in her purse. And her purse? The last she'd seen of it, a derelict was tugging it away from her. Purse. Cell phone. Wallet. Identification. Cash. Credit cards. All gone. And her car? What were the chances it was still parked where she had left it? There was so much to deal with. But not now. Not yet. Instead, she closed her eyes and began to do the only thing she felt well enough to do. She prayed.

Nick Valentine frowned at the ringing phone. What now? He wasn't on call, so this couldn't be a frozen section or an autopsy.

He was current on all his dictation, not just the pathology reports — he was scrupulous in keeping current with those — but even the academic and administrative material. The long-delayed curriculum vitae was on Dr. Wetherington's desk, putting an end to almost daily phone calls asking for that piece of material. No, Nick's desk was clean, and his conscience was clear. So why couldn't he have a moment's peace to finish this journal article he'd been trying to read for the past month?

"Dr. Valentine." Nick noticed that he hadn't been completely successful in keeping the annoyance out of his tone, and a glimmer of guilt flitted across his mind.

"Nick?" The voice was a little weak but he recognized it immediately.

"Anna! Where are you? Are you all right? I've been trying to reach you since noon yesterday."

"It's sort of a long story. Right now I'm at University Hospital. They've just moved me out of the ICU and into a room. If you want to come by, I'll —"

"I'm on my way. What room?"

Nick rushed down the warren of corridors from his office at the medical school to the University Hospital, his mind churning. ICU? What had happened? Was Anna going to be okay? He arrived at the elevators but decided they were too slow. He took the stairs two at a time. He paused at the door to her room long enough to slow his breathing, wondering if his pounding heart was a consequence of the stairs or a signal of the emotion he felt. He tapped on the door.

"Come in."

The response was faint, the voice almost unrecognizable. Nick opened the door. What he saw brought the same feeling as his first — and last — roller-coaster ride. His stomach dropped, his pulse raced, and he wanted to turn back the clock and start over. Anna lay with eyes half-closed, lifting her hand a few inches in greeting before letting it fall back on the covers. The bruise on her jaw was a palette of green and blue, a stark contrast with the pallor of her skin. Her red hair was tousled, and her green eyes had none of their usual snap and sparkle.

Nick scanned the monitors recording Anna's vital signs, and he relaxed a bit when he saw the values. He covered the distance to the bed in three long strides. "I've been so worried about you."

"I'm sorry. I guess —" She swallowed with visible effort. "Could I have a sip of water?"

Nick wondered if it was okay to let her drink. She still had an IV in, but there was a Styrofoam pitcher of water on the bedside table, and a flexible straw sat in a half-full glass beside it. He held the water for her, supporting her head with his other hand. She managed three small sips.

"Thanks," she said. "You must be wondering why I didn't call sooner."

"That's not important. I'm just glad you're okay. At least, if they've moved you out of ICU, I guess you are. What happened? What can I do?" Nick had to stop the questions from pouring out. It appeared that Anna was all right now. That was all that mattered.

"I couldn't call you," she said. "I didn't even know my own name for a while."

He sank into the chair at her bedside and covered her hand with his. He felt her flinch and pulled back. "Sorry."

"No, that's okay. Actually, it's nice. Just watch the IV."

He took her hand once more, this time more gently. "I think you'd better tell me about it."

It took a while for Anna to relate the story. Several times she paused, apparently searching to recapture events. "My memory's coming back now," she concluded. "I don't remember exactly how I got hit on the head, but we've sort of pieced together that I was mugged. And there are still a few areas that are sort of fuzzy around the edges."

"So you're going to be okay?"

"Mike Simpson says I'll be fine, although he wants me to take it easy for at least the next week." She grimaced. "I think I'm probably going to push that, though. As soon as he turns me loose, I want to pick up where I left off . . . if I can figure out exactly where that was."

A shadow passed across Anna's face and she turned her head away. She freed her hand from Nick's and wiped a tear from the corner of her eye.

"What's the matter?" he asked.

"I just thought of all the things I have to do. The mugger got my purse, with my phone, my wallet, driver's license and credit cards, everything. I can't do anything until I take care of that."

"Let me help," Nick said. "I can —"

There was a light tap on the door and it swung open. Nick turned to see a heavy-set black woman, a sweater thrown over her dark blue scrub suit, tiptoe into the room. "Dr. McIntyre?"

Anna looked puzzled for a moment. Then Nick saw her expression change, and she said, "Miss . . . Miss Brown? Have I got it right?"

"That's right, Rhonda Brown. You've got a good memory for names and faces."

"Not recently, but that seems to be getting better." Anna indicated Nick. "This is Dr. Nick Valentine."

Nick exchanged handshakes with the woman and offered her his chair.

"Can't stay. I sneaked away from the lab and whenever I'm gone, everything turns to — Well, it gets bad. Got to get back and keep things running." She hesitated, and Nick could tell she was nervous about something. "Look, you need to know something. I'm the one who called the medics. I sneaked out for a smoke just in time to see a wino struggling to get your purse away from you. He decked you, I screamed, and he dropped your purse and ran. I stuck my head in the door and yelled for the receptionist to put down her magazine and call for an ambulance. Then I went back outside to wait with you until the paramedics rolled up. That's when I decided to disappear. Didn't want to be involved, you know?"

"Thank you for calling for help," Anna said.

"Well, that was the least I could do. I kept thinking about that story I learned in Sunday school. You know, the Good Samaritan? All I could think of was 'They passed by on the other side.' I couldn't do that."

"I'm glad you gave me the chance to thank you in person," Anna said. "I know it was hard for you to come."

"You don't know the half of it." Rhonda reached into the shopping bag that dangled from her hand and pulled out a purse. "I didn't trust that gang that's always hanging around in the parking lot. So I grabbed this before they could snatch it and run. Everything's still there: your cell phone, credit cards, driver's license, cash. I even scooped up your car keys and put them in here." She held out the purse.

Anna took it with trembling fingers. "You don't know how much this means to me. Thank you."

Rhonda shrugged. "At first, I figured the money in this would buy me a new pair of Reeboks, with enough left over for lunches next week. But that's the other half of that Good Samaritan story. That guy not only helped out the man who'd been robbed. He paid the innkeeper to take care of him. Besides, I don't need new sneakers, and I'm on a diet."

12

"That's such a relief," Anna told Nick after Rhonda left. "At least I don't have to worry about canceling my credit cards and getting a new driver's license. And my house key is on that ring along with my car keys. I don't like to think about what someone could have done with that."

Nick frowned. "Anna, I wish you'd let this drop. Sure, somebody stole your identity. We can see that. But trying to find out who's behind it can only get you hurt. You —"

"Hold on." Anna held up one hand, careful to choose the one without an IV. "According to Miss Brown, the reason I'm here in this bed is because I was mugged by a derelict who wanted my purse so he could buy another bottle of Thunderbird. It could just as easily have happened on my way to work or the grocery store."

"All right. I guess I can accept that. But I

still worry about you. So would you be careful? And would you let me help?"

Maybe Nick's expression of concern and offer of help came from a sense of duty. But there seemed to be genuine affection there as well. And that brought up the question of how she felt about Nick. Were her feelings for him platonic? Or was something more developing? No, there was too much to think about and her brain wasn't up to it. Not yet, at least.

She realized Nick was still waiting for an answer. It seemed easier to acquiesce than argue. "I'll be careful. And once I'm out of here, I promise we'll talk about what I . . . what we need to do next."

Once Nick was gone, Anna dumped the contents of her purse onto the bedside table and began to go through them. She opened her wallet and held her breath, letting it out when she saw both her new credit cards still in place, along with her driver's license and two very special cards: a wallet-sized ID card confirming her Texas medical license and another with her DEA permit number on it. She would need to be extra careful with those in the future, although short of putting them in a vault she wasn't sure how to protect them.

Anna thumbed through the bills in the wallet, wishing that Rhonda Brown had taken the reward she'd offered. "Nope," the technician said. "I did it because it was the right thing to do, not for money. You just do something good for somebody someday. That'll be enough."

Her cell phone was clipped to an inside pocket of the purse, and Anna was surprised to see that it still held a charge. The display also showed twelve missed calls and eight voicemail messages. She scrolled through the log and saw that, along with six messages from Nick, she had two from Ross Donovan.

She listened to Nick's messages first. There was a definite progression in their tone. The first was a casual invitation to lunch, the next call expressed regret that they hadn't been able to get together, and a third asked if he could see her that evening. The fourth, fifth, and sixth demonstrated his worry when he was unable to contact her at her office, at home, or via her cell phone. Yes, no doubt about it. Nick cared for her. But she wasn't ready to answer the question of how deep her feelings for him ran. Not now. Not with all this hanging over her.

She moved to the messages from Ross

Donovan, wondering if her reluctance to think about a commitment to Nick had something to do with this other man who'd come into her life. The first was fairly businesslike: "Anna, this is Ross Donovan. I enjoyed lunch with you. I think our meeting with the DEA went fairly well. I suggest you call your chairman tomorrow to make sure Hale notifies him that you're in the clear with the agency. I'll see what I can do to get the Dallas Police off your back now. Keep in touch."

So much had happened in the past twenty-four hours; Anna had almost forgotten her meeting with the DEA agents. A new permit and a call from Hale to her chairman should pave the way for her return to work. She wasn't sure how ready she was physically, but she certainly was itching to be back doing what she loved best — practicing medicine and teaching residents.

The next message from Donovan put an end to Anna's improved mood. "Anna, call me as soon as you get this message. Detective Green phoned. He and Dowling want to talk with you. They've agreed to do the interview at my office, but they say if you don't follow up with them tomorrow, they'll issue a warrant to pick you up as a material witness. I don't know what they have, but apparently something new has come up. Call me ASAP."

Anna hadn't yet entered Donovan's number on her cell phone directory, so she had to scroll back and find it in her call log. Her stomach churned as she waited for him to answer the call.

"Ross Donovan." His voice carried a smile, and she could picture his dimples deepening as he spoke.

"Mr. Donovan . . . Ross, this is Anna McIntyre. I won't be able to meet with the detectives today. It's —"

There was no smile in Donovan's voice this time. "Anna, I think they were serious about picking you up as a material witness. You'd better make time for this."

"Ross, a lot has happened since I left you yesterday. You'd better come by my hospital room and let me explain."

Ross Donovan looked up from the yellow legal pad balanced on his knee. It was almost filled with scribbling in the personal shorthand he'd developed over the years. Only he could read it, sometimes only after a second and third effort, but he figured that represented another level of security and privacy for his clients.

"So, Anna, you don't think this attack on

you had anything to do with the identity theft?"

Anna didn't answer, just shook her head. She leaned back against her pillows and closed her eyes, obviously spent after filling him in on the events of the past twenty-four hours.

Ross tapped his fountain pen against his front teeth and looked at the ceiling. "You know, when you came to my office the first time, you started by telling me you had problems with the police and the DEA. I managed to pry the information out of you that someone had stolen your credit card numbers as well. But I get the sense that this problem is even broader than that. What aren't you telling me?"

Anna reached toward the pitcher and glass on her bedside table. Ross rose and poured water for her. He waited until she'd emptied the glass before resuming his seat.

"I guess I need to give you the whole story," she said.

"That usually helps your attorney. Just remember two things. First of all, what you tell me is in confidence. I can't be required to divulge it." He uncapped his pen and sat back.

"What's the second thing?" she asked.

"The other thing to remember is that I've

been a liar, a cheat, and a drunk. So whatever you've done, I've probably done worse."

He grinned when that elicited a chuckle. He sensed that she was teetering on the brink of exhaustion, and he hated to put her through this, but if he was to help her he needed the full story.

A half hour later, he dropped the legal pad to the floor and leaned toward Anna's bed, his forearms on his thighs. "Okay, here's a summary of the problem, as I understand it. Correct me if I'm wrong anywhere." He began to tick off points on his fingers. "First, someone stole your credit card information and maxed out the accounts, temporarily damaging your credit in the process. Second, someone used your DEA number and name to float a bunch of narcotics prescriptions in the area, and although Agents Kramer and Hale are ready to ease up on you, the Dallas Police — for whatever reason — are still intent on proving you're a criminal. And third, both you and one of your patients had your insurance information used by someone else to obtain care. That maneuver cost your patient his life and made you a target for a malpractice suit. It also resulted in your name being associated with a positive test for HIV." He leaned back and spread his hands like a magician showing the rabbit. "Right?"

Anna seemed to sink deeper into the bed, as though she were deflating. "Right."

"So here's what we do. And notice, I said, 'we.' The credit repair isn't rocket science, but it takes a bit of work. As soon as you're discharged, get me the paperwork you've already started. I'll look at it and try to help. But that may have to go on the back burner, because it's not our immediate problem. Our first priority is to keep you out of jail and clear you with the Dallas Police. I'll call Green or Dowling as soon as I leave here and explain to them that you've been hospitalized for a serious head injury. If they insist on interviewing you anyway, I'll start claiming police brutality, infringement of your constitutional rights, and anything else I can think of. After all, you're not competent to answer questions because of your hazy mental condition."

"But —"

"Hey, your mental status may be fine. But we've been given a perfect excuse to delay this interview, and the longer we can put it off, the more information we'll have when it comes time to talk with them. Let me take care of this."

243

Anna nodded her understanding. "And the malpractice suit?"

"I suppose you have malpractice insurance?"

"Yes, the medical school covers me. Actually, all of the state med schools self-insure through a trust. But I think I'd better talk about engaging you to represent me as well. The way Ms. Ernst has reacted so far, I don't get a warm and fuzzy feeling about her."

Ross was silent.

"Oh," Anna said, understanding lighting her eyes. "I forgot."

"Never mind. When we divorced, there weren't many warm and fuzzy feelings on either side."

"But if you represented me, you'd be working with your ex-wife," Anna said. "Is that going to present a problem?"

Ross rubbed his chin. "We'll have to see, won't we?"

"How's the patient today?" Anna opened her eyes and saw Neil Fowler standing at her bedside. He wore a gray scrub suit, and the impression of a surgical cap ringed his forehead.

"I'm a bit wobbly on my feet sometimes, but my memory's pretty much come back."

Anna struggled to grin. "Sometimes that isn't good, though."

Fowler leaned his back against the doorframe and stretched. "Oh, that feels good. I just finished a bowel resection, and my back is killing me." He straightened. "Anna, I know I told you to use your time off to clear yourself of these narcotic prescription charges, but I think it's time for you to stop. I don't know all the details, but if whatever you've been doing is what got you that concussion, it's not worth it. Let me talk with the DEA and see if they're about ready to turn you loose to practice again."

"No need. I've spoken with one of the agents." She made an effort to brush the cobwebs away from her head. "Agent . . . his name escapes me. He's supposed to call you to tell you they haven't found any involvement on my part. They're going to issue me a new number. What I have to do —" Something, some instinct, stopped Anna before she told Fowler her deal with the DEA: have her privileges restored in exchange for keeping her eyes and ears open. She didn't really suspect her chairman of involvement in the counterfeit prescriptions, but then again, she had no reason to exclude him from her list of suspects.

Fowler apparently took her letting the words trail off as just another sign of her recent concussion. He nodded, stretched, and said, "Well, I'm converting your special leave to sick leave. If you're like me, you've got more of those days stored up than you'll ever use. So take the time you need to heal from this head injury. We miss you and we'll be glad to have you back at work, but don't push it."

After Fowler left, Anna wondered why she hadn't fully confided in her chairman. Was it because he had access to all the offices in the department, including hers? How easy would it be for someone in his position to get access not only to her purse but to her personal information, her Social Security number? Was she being paranoid . . . or just careful?

13

Anna stretched and yawned. It was good to wake up in her bed. She luxuriated in the feel of fresh sheets, crisp and clean against her skin. She inhaled the aroma of the coffee that the automatic timer on her coffeepot had already started brewing. Mike Simpson wanted to keep her in the hospital for another day, but she pleaded with him until he gave in, extracting a promise that she take it easy for a few more days. Her definition of taking it easy would probably be different from Mike's, but she had things to do and not even a concussion would stop her. Some coffee and a couple of Tylenols should get her going. Then she'd see where the day took her.

Anna sat in her robe at the kitchen table and nibbled on a toasted English muffin spread with cherry jam. Her mind was already busy trying to decide where in the tangled skein of her problems she might find a loose thread to pull. Repair her credit? She needed to take Ross the paperwork she'd started, but that wasn't urgent. Clear herself with the police and the DEA? Right now, the DEA seemed content to let her alone. As for the police, Green and Dowling had grudgingly agreed to put off the interview until tomorrow, and there was no use worrying about that until she knew what they wanted.

Then there was the Hatley case. She was sure now that his death wasn't due to malpractice, but rather a terrible accident directly attributable to someone using Hatley's identity to put false data into his medical records. Ross had warned her away from digging further into the Hatley case, at least until they saw whether a malpractice case was truly forthcoming. But Anna couldn't get over the feeling that she and Eric Hatley weren't the only two people who'd suffered misappropriation of their medical insurance information. If she could somehow find a pattern, she might be able to trace the enterprise back to its perpetrators. And if she could do that, she'd solve a lot of her problems.

After breakfast, Anna sat down at her desk and went through the mail that had accumulated during her brief hospitalization.

She set a few bills aside to be paid and tossed the junk mail into the wastebasket. Then she recalled her intention to get a shredder, something else that had fallen through the cracks, something more for her "to do" list. Anna retrieved the mail from the wastebasket and shuffled through it to find everything that had her name and address on it. By the time she finished tearing the documents to shreds, her wastebasket looked like the aftermath of a snowstorm.

Maybe she'd better check her bank balance before she paid the bills. She logged onto the bank's website, entered her user name and password, and frowned when she saw the amount shown in her account. That couldn't be right. What had happened?

She clicked on "transactions" and ran her finger down the list on the screen. She didn't recall writing the last three checks that were listed. Matter of fact, she was certain she'd never bought anything from those stores. Was someone . . . did this mean . . . ? No, there was no question. Identity theft and its effect on her finances had just jumped to the head of her to-do list for the day.

Nick Valentine sensed movement in the doorway of his office. He looked up to see

Anna standing there, holding two cups of what appeared to be Starbucks' best.

"Hey there. How are you feeling?"

Anna handed him one of the cups and settled into the chair across the desk from him. "Still a dull headache. Sometimes I feel like I need to brush some cobwebs out of my brain. But all in all, not too bad."

He motioned her to a chair. "What are you doing here? I thought Dr. Fowler told you to take a few more days off."

Anna shook her head, sending her red hair left and right, revealing a few gold highlights Nick hadn't seen before. "I came by to get some papers I left in my office. I need to take them to my attorney." She smiled. "While I was in the building, I thought I'd come by and share some coffee with you."

"That's great." He took a sip. Perfect. Just like the beautiful woman sitting across from him. "Anna, I think we're getting to be more than friends. At least, I hope so. And I hope you feel that way too."

Anna gazed at her coffee cup as though it were a crystal ball. "Nick, I like you a lot. But right now my life is so messed up, I don't think there's any way I can get into the kind of relationship I think you want. Maybe, after things straighten out, that's a possibility. In the meantime, can we continue to be good friends?"

Nick forced a smile. "Sure. And friends help each other. Is there anything I can do?"

Anna rose and dropped her half-full cup into the wastebasket. "Thanks, but I'm not sure myself what my next move needs to be. I'm on my way to meet with Ross Donovan, and we'll map out our strategy then."

The name brought bile to Nick's throat, and he tried to push it down with a sip of coffee. "Don't forget that I'm here to help. Ready, willing, able . . . and sober."

"Nick, don't be that way. Ross has had some problems with alcohol, but he's doing okay now. And don't be jealous that I'm seeing him. I'm in legal trouble, and he's my attorney. If I were in medical trouble, I'd turn to you."

"I just don't want you hurt." Nick wondered if that wasn't a half-truth. The truth was that if Anna began to develop feelings for her attorney, there was a chance it would end in heartbreak for her. But Nick's heart might be broken as well.

Ross Donovan reached for the manila folder Anna held out.

"This is what I put together," she said. "I was on my way to the medical school to make some copies when my car died. By the time I got to the school, something else came up, and I just threw this into a desk drawer and forgot about it." She grimaced. "Sorry."

Ross dropped the folder onto the corner of his desk. "No problem. I'll look through this to make sure you have all the paperwork done right. You can sign the forms, and we'll send them to your credit card companies and the credit-reporting bureaus. I'll help you make sure there's no permanent damage to your credit."

"Unfortunately, something else happened today. I guess you need to know about that too."

He listened, occasionally jotting a note, as Anna told him about her discovery of the checks someone had written on her account. "Have you spoken with the bank?" he asked.

"I stopped by and talked with one of the officers at my local branch. There's no question the checks were forged. What confuses me is that they were written on my own blank checks. The name, the address, even the style of the check — all the same as the ones I've always used."

"Easy enough for someone to get hold of one of your checks and have new ones printed, you know."

"I know," Anna said. "But the sequence of numbers corresponded to my own checks. These followed the last check I wrote. Matter of fact, I haven't written any checks in the past four days, not only because I've been in the hospital, but because I ran out of checks. In church last Sunday, I saw that my checkbook was empty, so that evening I went online and ordered a new batch. They haven't come yet, though. Guess I need to check on that."

Ross was shaking his head before Anna finished. "Here's what probably happened. The online order was picked up first thing Monday and, unfortunately for you, they got right on it and printed them. The checks were mailed out Tuesday morning and arrived at your place Wednesday, while you were in the hospital. Someone stole the order from your mailbox and had a whole day to write checks before you came home on Thursday."

"I never thought about that. I've always had the checks sent to me by mail."

"You've been lucky so far. Doing it that way is fine if someone has to sign for them, but it's risky if they're simply left in your curbside mailbox. Ideally, you should have them delivered to your branch bank for you to pick up. It's even better to get a post office box and have all your secure mail sent there." Ross leaned across the desk. "Is the bank crediting your account?"

"The bank officer said she would check and see what she could do."

"She probably wants you to file a police report before she takes action. We can take care of that."

Ross picked up the phone and dialed, wondering if he'd go to this much trouble if the client across the desk were a sixty-year-old farmer wearing jeans and a flannel shirt instead of an attractive redhead whose green eyes seemed to hypnotize him every time he looked into them.

The day was nice, so they walked the dozen blocks from Ross's office to the police station. It seemed to Anna that the closing of the heavy outer door extinguished not just the sunlight, but all traces of hope. Both the walls and the mood of the building were gray. All around her were men and women engaged in a struggle, some of them trying to preserve their liberty while others tried to deprive them of it, perhaps even of their lives.

Anna fidgeted in her chair. She wondered if the police deliberately chose chairs for their interview rooms that would provide maximum discomfort to the suspects sitting there. Beside her, Ross Donovan crossed his legs after carefully hiking up his pants leg to preserve the crease in his gray pin-stripe pants. His jacket was unbuttoned, showing a blue Oxford-cloth shirt and striped tie. He showed no signs of nervousness, but then again, this was his natural environment. Put him in an operating room, and he'd be sweating like she was now.

Anna started to rise when the two detectives walked into the room, but she stopped when Donovan touched her lightly on the shoulder. Don't show any respect for them. He'd warned her to volunteer nothing and to look at him before answering if there was any doubt in her mind about the information involved.

As usual, Dowling's expression was one of boredom mixed with cynicism, while Green nodded coldly at them and took a seat across the table. Dowling, a marked contrast with his partner in skin color and physique, reached across the table and shook hands with Anna and Ross before seating himself beside his partner. Well, if they were going to play good-cop, bad-cop, the two men were continuing in the roles they'd already established.

Dowling began. "Doctor, we appreciate

your coming in. I'm sorry to hear about your accident. How's the head?"

"I'm fine, thank you," Anna said.

"My client has suffered a concussion," Donovan said. "I'm sure you know that for several days afterward the thought processes can be muddled. Let's be sure to get that on the record."

"We're not on the record, yet, Counselor," Green said with a scowl. "But since you bring it up, let's do that, if you don't mind." He reached to the middle of the table and punched the button on a tape recorder. "This is a record of the interview with Dr. Anna McIntyre by Detectives Lamar Green and Burt Dowling. Also present is Ross Donovan, attorney for Dr. McIntyre. Doctor, do we have your permission to record this interview?"

Anna looked to Donovan, who nodded. "Yes," she said.

"Doctor," Dowling said, "we have previously asked you about numerous illicit prescriptions for large amounts of the narcotic, Vicodin, that have circulated in the community, all of them bearing your signature and Drug Enforcement Agency number."

"Wait a minute," Donovan said. "The prescriptions bore the *forged* signature of my client."

"Sorry," Dowling said, although his expression didn't show it. "They were signed with the name of Dr. McIntyre." He paused, apparently waiting for a comment, then continued. "Doctor, you have denied writing those prescriptions. Would you like to change your statement at this time?"

"No. I didn't write them," Anna said.

"And if we put you under oath?"

"I'd still deny writing them."

"Okay, we won't swear you in at this time, but we may come back to that," Dowling said.

Green fixed Anna with a stare. "Doctor, how well did you know Eric Hatley?"

The sudden shift in subject caught Anna by surprise. "I didn't know the man. I'd never seen him until he was on the operating table."

"And you maintain that his death was an accident?"

"It was the result of a massive allergic reaction to a medication administered during his emergency surgery," Anna said.

"Doctor, why would you administer such a dangerous drug to the patient?"

Anna leaned across the table, trying to drive home her point. "The drug wasn't dangerous. It was Omnilex, a potent antibiotic prescribed and administered quite safely every day. It was necessary to give it because Mr. Hatley had been shot. Bowel contents spilled into his abdominal cavity. Without antibiotic treatment, he could have developed peritonitis and died."

Green shuffled some papers until he came to what he wanted. "This is the death certificate for Eric Hatley. The cause of death is listed as —" He squinted at the paper. "Is shown as anaphylaxis due to allergic reaction to Omnilex. Do you agree with the pathologist, Dr. . . . ?" Green squinted again. "Dr. Valentine?"

"Yes. I discussed the case with Dr. Valentine before he rendered a final cause of death. I agree with his diagnosis."

"So why would you give Omnilex to a man who was so allergic to it?" Green asked.

Anna wondered where this was going. She glanced at her attorney, who gave a slight shrug. Apparently, he was as surprised as she was that they were going over this yet again. "We checked the hospital records and found a prior visit for a patient with the same name, date of birth, and other identifying data as Eric Hatley. At that time, only a few weeks earlier, he had been given Omnilex and suffered no adverse effects."

"Let's talk about that drug," Dowling

said. "You knew that if Omnilex was administered to a patient who was highly allergic to it, the result could be a fatal reaction. Is that correct?"

"Of course. The same can be said of almost any drug."

Dowling's voice was calm, but his words made Anna's stomach clench. "And you didn't know Eric Hatley, had never heard him mention his allergy to that drug, had no reason to try to kill him?"

"Of course not!"

Green dug into his pocket and came out with something he held clenched in his huge fist. "Doctor, I submit to you that Eric Hatley was one of the many people who looked to you for illicit drugs. But he got nervous about it and was about to go to the police and expose the whole setup. You arranged for Hatley to be shot, but the assailant missed. Instead of killing him, he hit Hatley in the abdomen. When he showed up in your operating room, you decided to finish the job by giving Hatley a dose of an antibiotic to which you'd already learned he was highly allergic. I submit to you that you are guilty of the murder of Eric Hatley."

Anna felt her temper rising to the top. Where was this coming from, anyway? "That's ridiculous. You have nothing to suggest there's even a shred of truth in that accusation."

Green flashed perfect white teeth and opened his fist, allowing a pill vial to drop onto the table. Donovan picked it up, looked at it, and handed it to Anna, a stunned expression on his face.

Anna's hand, normally steady under the greatest stress of the operating room, trembled slightly as she took the vial and read the label. "Eric Hatley. Vicodin ES tablets. #100. Take one tablet every four hours for pain. Dr. A. McIntyre. Two refills."

She hardly heard Dowling's voice droning, "You have the right to remain silent . . ."

14

It took a few seconds before instinct and experience made Ross Donovan move. He was pleased that years of alcohol hadn't erased those reflexes. Dulled them a bit, maybe, but they were still there. And this seemed the way to go.

Ross leaned toward Anna and whispered in her ear, "Don't say another word. Don't even acknowledge the Miranda warning."

She turned toward him, her eyes wide, and opened her mouth. He touched his lips with his forefinger and shook his head.

"Doctor, do you understand these rights?" Dowling asked.

Ross spoke distinctly, leaning a bit toward the microphone, making sure his words reached both Dowling and the tape. "Detective, my client, as I clearly pointed out before you began this taping, has recently been hospitalized with a severe head injury. The chairman of the Department of Neurosurgery at the University of Texas South-western Medical School was her attending physician, and I feel sure you'll agree he's qualified as a medical expert. If necessary we can produce an affidavit from him that she's still not completely recovered. Since she is not yet in full possession of her faculties, I find your ambush tactics to be both unethical and bordering on harassment."

"Counselor, don't —"

Ross went on as though Dowling hadn't spoken. "I've advised my client not to say anything further. I will agree to produce her for an interview at some future time when she is able to do so without jeopardizing her rights, but until then I have only one question for you." He paused and looked from Dowling to Green and back. "Are you prepared, at this time, to arrest my client? If so, please produce a warrant."

The room was silent as a tomb as Dowling and Green exchanged glances. Finally, Ross spoke once more. "For the tape, please, gentlemen. Your answer?"

Green spat his response from between clenched teeth. "Not yet!"

Ross rose and took Anna's arm, guiding her to her feet. "Then this interview is over. Please make any future contact with my client through me."

In the hall, Anna said, "Why —"

"No," Ross said. "Not a word until we're on the street."

Outside, Ross said, "Okay, I know you've got a lot of questions. Well, I have some of my own. Let's go back to my office, where we can have some privacy. We'll sit down with some coffee and try to make sense of this mess."

The office was comfortably warm, but Anna shivered. She clasped her hands around the mug of coffee and watched ripples move across its surface.

"All right, take your time. Pull yourself together." Ross Donovan's voice was calm and reassuring. "We'll get through this. Remember, I'm on your side. You've engaged me to be your lawyer. This is what I do. Don't let those two guys get to you. That's what they want."

"Why did he read me my rights? Were they about to arrest me?"

"Normally, police only give the Miranda warning in association with an arrest, but you heard their answer. They don't have enough for an arrest warrant, so apparently they thought they could scare you into an admission of guilt."

"But I swear, I'd never laid eyes on Eric

Hatley, never even heard of him, until I encountered him on that operating table," Anna said. "I didn't arrange for him to be shot. As I understand it, he got caught in the cross fire of a gang shooting in the projects. Obviously, I didn't know he was allergic to Omnilex. If I'd known that, I wouldn't have signed off on giving it."

"Do you know anything about the prescription Green showed us?" Ross asked.

"Nothing. I had no idea Hatley had been using illicit Vicodin." Anna took a sip of the coffee and recalled Ross's description — alcoholics' coffee. If she were a drinker, now would be the time to have some, but she'd just stick with this strong, bitter brew.

Ross flipped to a fresh page on his legal pad. "So this is all news to you?"

"Of course it is. I didn't write any of those Vicodin 'scripts they were talking about, I have no idea who was using them or how they got them. If I did, maybe we could unravel some of the mystery about this whole thing." She took another sip of coffee and put down the cup, pleased to see that her hands were slowly becoming surgeon-steady again.

"Talk me through it once more. The whole thing. The Hatley case. Your credit card and bank problems. The use of your insurance information. I keep thinking there's a common thread that ties all this together. We just have to find it."

Anna thought of the image she'd had that morning. Had it only been a few hours ago? A tangled ball of thread, with her looking for a loose end to pull and unravel. Maybe the two of them, acting together, could find that thread. But when they tugged on it, would it help unlock some of the mysteries, or tighten the knot further?

A tap on the door made Nick look up from the stack of death certificates he was signing.

"Dr. Valentine?" The doorway was filled by the broad shoulders of an African American man whose wrinkled brown suit and out-of-fashion tie suggested a not very successful insurance salesman or a low-level manager. "May we come in?"

"Sure." Nick gestured the man in.

The big man glided into the room with a grace that belied his size. Football, Nick thought, because he sure didn't learn how to move like that as a dancer. The larger man was followed by a lanky white man, dressed in a similar style. They took the chairs Nick offered and introduced themselves.

"I'm Lamar Green," the first man said, flipping open a credentials wallet and holding it out to Nick. The gold shield and photo ID identified him as a detective with the Dallas Police Department. If any further proof of his *bona fides* was necessary, it was provided when the man pulled aside his coat to stow the wallet, giving Nick a glimpse of a handgun, riding butt-forward on Green's left hip.

"This is Burt Dowling," Green said, pointing to his partner, a cadaverous man with a pronounced five o'clock shadow. Dowling also offered his badge and ID.

Nick wasn't too worried by the visit. The police often came to talk with him about some of the autopsies he did on homicide victims. "All right, gentlemen. How can I help?"

Dowling took the lead. "Doctor, did you perform the autopsy on Eric Hatley's body?"

Nick didn't have to look it up — the name was fresh in his mind — but he held up one finger in a "just a moment" gesture and turned to his computer. What were these guys after?

Nick called up the Hatley file, and, still facing the computer, said, "Got it. What about it?"

Dowling unwound the string that held a hard cardboard file folder shut. He pawed through the papers inside and pulled one out. "You listed the cause of death as anaphylaxis due to allergic reaction to Omnilex. Is that still your professional opinion?"

"Sure. No reason to change." Nick swiveled to face the detectives. "Why do you ask?"

Green took up the conversation. "We're just getting our ducks in a row. So you'd be willing to testify in court as to the cause of death?"

"I suppose so," Nick said. "What's this about? Do you have the shooters? Are you trying to make a case against them? Because if he hadn't had the allergic reaction, Hatley probably would have recovered from the gunshot wounds. Dr. Nguyn did a nice job with the surgical repair."

"No, we're mainly interested in the Omnilex reaction. If a doctor knew a patient was allergic to that drug but still gave them Omnilex, they'd expect a severe reaction, just like Hatley had. Right?"

Nick didn't like where this was going. "Right."

Green leaned forward slightly. "And if they dragged their feet a little in treating that reaction, maybe delayed giving the right medicine or didn't give it at all, they could see to it that the patient died. Right again?"

Nick looked Green in the eye. "Now you're into conjecture. And in this case, I've reviewed the records of everything that happened in the operating room. If anyone was slow in making the diagnosis, it was the first-year resident who gave the anesthesia. But Dr. McIntyre got the senior anesthesia staff in as soon as the patient got into trouble. All the doctors worked hard, gave the right medication, did everything that could be done to save Hatley. But, despite their best efforts, he died. That happens sometimes. We can't save everyone, but we try. And this was no exception."

Dowling made a calming gesture. "No need to get angry, Dr. Valentine. We're trying to get our facts straight. We don't need a formal statement from you now, but you may be called on to testify later."

Green grinned and added, "If you have any notion about not giving us a statement or testifying, we'll see that you're subpoenaed. So you'll do it. Whether you want to or not."

During the interview, Nick had been trying to figure out where he'd seen these men. Then it came to him. These detectives were the two men who'd brushed by him on their way out of Anna's house. And apparently they were still out to get her.

"Gentlemen, I hope you'll excuse me." Nick made a show of looking at his watch. "I'm due in surgery in a few minutes to assist with a frozen section. I trust you can find your way out."

He herded them toward the door. Nick figured they had no way to find out if he really was due in surgery. Besides, he needed a cup of coffee, and what they brewed in the surgeons' lounge was usually pretty good if you caught a fresh pot.

The detectives seemed content to go, but Green turned to Nick as they paused at the branch of the corridor where their paths separated. "Thank you for your time, Doctor. And I don't guess I have to remind you that what we've discussed was in confidence. It involves a case under investigation, so don't go talking to anyone about it, or you could find yourself in trouble."

Ross Donovan had told Anna to go home and try to relax, saying he'd call her tomorrow to set up a time for a strategy session. "And don't worry."

Don't worry. She'd just been accused of murder by two cops who seemed to think it was their mission in life to send her to prison, maybe even to death row. Don't worry, indeed.

What Anna wanted was a long soak in her tub, accompanied by a pint of Cherry Garcia ice cream and the latest issue of *Vanity Fair.* As soon as she got home, she bolted the door, took the phone off the hook, and set about preparing to make that dream a reality.

She'd been in the tub for about five minutes when she heard her cell phone ring. Drat, she'd forgotten to turn it off. Well, let it ring. She'd return the call later. But the phone continued ringing at five-minute intervals, and finally, like the constant dripping of the Chinese water torture, it wore her down. Swathed in a terry-cloth robe, Anna left a trail of water to the living room, where she snatched up the phone and flipped it open just as the call rolled into voicemail.

The display showed four missed calls, three messages, all from Nick Valentine. Well, she probably wasn't going to have any peace until she talked to him. Besides, she felt bad about the way she'd deflected Nick's attempts to build their relationship. He really did seem to care for her, and right now she could use all the support she could get. She dialed his number and he answered on the first ring.

"Nick, this is Anna. Sorry about missing your calls. I was in the tub."

Nick's tone was that of a mortician discussing final arrangements. "Anna, we need to talk."

"Sure." She looked around for a chair that would tolerate the water seeping through her robe. "Go ahead."

"No, not on the phone, especially not on a cell phone. Can I come over?"

"Nick, you're scaring me. And I've already had a bad day, so my coronaries don't need any more stress. What's this about?"

"Anna, I can be there in half an hour. It's important."

Anna dropped into an armchair, heedless of the upholstery by now. "If it's that important, sure. I'll see you then."

Forty minutes later, dressed in jeans and a tee shirt, sneakers on her bare feet, Anna looked through the security peephole of her front door and saw Nick on the porch holding a pizza box. As soon as she opened the door, he eased inside and slammed the door behind him.

"Nick, why all the cloak and dagger stuff?" Anna asked. "I told you, you're scaring me."

Nick dropped the pizza box on the coffee

table and turned to take Anna by the shoulders. He seemed to hesitate for a moment, then pulled her to him and hugged her. "Sorry. But maybe I'm sort of scared too. Sit down. I need to tell you some things, even though telling you could get me in trouble with the police."

Anna felt like she was free-falling from a great height. What more could go wrong? And how was Nick involved? She sagged onto the couch, patted the space beside her, and said, "Okay, let's hear it."

Instead of sitting, Nick began to pace. "I had a visit today from two detectives."

As Nick related his story, Anna tried to make sense of it all. Why did these men seem so determined to tie her to the illicit narcotics prescriptions when the DEA had already told her they were satisfied she wasn't involved? And now, the detectives were trying to hold her responsible for Eric Hatley's death, not as an act of malpractice, which was bad enough, but cold-blooded murder?

"And as they left, they told me this was an ongoing investigation, so I couldn't talk about it with anyone. I don't know what they can do to me for coming to you like this, but I don't care. It seems to me that you're in trouble, and I want to help." His forced grin held no humor. "After all, that's what friends do. And we are friends. Right?"

15

Nick used a paper napkin to wipe a spot of grease off the corner of his mouth. "So you already knew that Green and Dowling were trying to make a case against you?"

Anna nodded and pointed to her full mouth. She chewed the last bite of pizza and washed it down with a healthy swallow of Diet Coke. "Yes," she finally said. "Ross and I met with them at the police station earlier today. They must have gone right from our meeting to your office. What was it they said to you? 'Just getting their ducks in a row.' I'd better call Ross and let him know about this."

While Anna made her call, Nick fought to control his emotions. It seemed to Nick that, slowly but surely, her lawyer was monopolizing Anna's time and attention. His rational mind recognized the need for this, but the little green monster perched on his shoulder continued to whisper in his ear.

Anna closed her cell phone and dropped it into her pocket. "I had to leave a message. He'll call back."

"I know you need a lawyer in all this," Nick said, "but do you think Ross Donovan is up to defending you? Especially since this has turned into something really serious. I mean, you've told me he's an alcoholic. His drinking broke up his marriage and almost cost him his law license. Won't you let me ask around and find you somebody better?"

The look in Anna's eyes told Nick he'd gone too far. "The man is a *recovering* alcoholic," she said. "He's sober and highly motivated to remain that way. As for his competence, his ex-wife is the chief attorney for the medical center, and she's the one who recommended him. He's done a good job so far, and I don't intend to make a change now."

Nick threw up his hands in a gesture of surrender. "Okay, okay. I'm sorry." He pushed the empty pizza box aside and reached across the table. Anna hesitated, but finally put her hand out and Nick took it in both of his. "Anything else?"

Anna pulled her hand back and finished her soft drink. "We've got a couple of days, and I don't want to think about this anymore. I have to see Dr. Simpson in the morning, but I should be through by noon. Why don't we get together for lunch in the food court?"

Nick recognized the invitation as a peace offering, and he grabbed at it like a drowning man latching on to a piece of wood floating by. "Sounds great. I'll be in my office. Come by when you're finished."

They both stood. Nick reached for the pizza box and paper plates, but Anna said, "I'll take care of all this. You go ahead. I know you have things to do." She began gathering soiled paper napkins. "Thanks for coming by. Of course, I need to tell Ross about this, but I don't want you to get in trouble with the police over letting me know about their visit. I'll ask him to keep your name out of it."

"Don't worry," Nick said. "I'm not afraid of those guys."

"Well, you should be. They scare me to death."

At the door, Nick turned back toward Anna, but before he could say anything, her cell phone chimed the theme from *Law and Order.*

"I'm so sorry. That's Ross's ring. I have to take this." Anna pulled the phone from her pocket. "I'll see you tomorrow."

Nick closed the door a bit more firmly

than was necessary and trudged toward his car, wondering if Anna had assigned a special ring to his number as well. If Donovan was *Law and Order,* what had she given to him — maybe the theme from *Friends?*

Ross Donovan leaned back in his desk chair and cradled the phone between his neck and shoulder. He crumpled the Snickers wrapper and tossed it toward the wastebasket, missing by about a foot, before shifting the phone back to his hand. "You say that Green and Dowling are checking on Hatley's cause of death. How do you know this?"

Anna's voice seemed a mile away, as though by talking softly she could lessen the significance of what she was saying. "I can't tell you my source. I promised I'd keep his name out of this. They threatened him if he discussed a case that's under active investigation."

Ross snorted. "They were throwing their weight around. At this point, they don't even have a case. Besides, how hard would it be for me to find out who signed the death certificate? I'm your attorney. Don't start playing games with me."

"All right. They went to Nick Valentine. He's a pathologist at the medical center, and during this investigation we've become friends."

Ross wondered what Anna's definition of "friend" was, but he decided to let it slide for now. "So we know they weren't bluffing when they talked with us. Tell you what. There's a private detective I've used in the past — good man, knows how to find things out without making waves. He has some contacts in the local police department. I may ask him to make a few discreet inquiries."

Anna's voice got louder. "Is that necessary? I'm not sure I can afford any more fees."

"He owes me a few favors, so I can probably get him to do a little preliminary digging off the clock. If it begins to look like we're trying to keep you from being charged with murder . . . at that point I suspect we can work out handling his fees."

Ross waited for Anna to respond, but there was only silence on the other end of the line. Finally he said, "Anna, are you there?"

The little girl voice was back again, hushed and fearful. "Yes. I was thinking how simple my life was a couple of weeks ago. I can't help asking God, 'Why? Why me?' "

Ross shifted in his chair. "If it's any

comfort, I've had that same conversation with Him. I've asked the question when I couldn't stop drinking, when my wife divorced me, when I almost lost my license to practice law. Wish I had an answer for you."

"Oh, there's an answer," Anna said. "But only God has it. Then again —"

"What?"

"Maybe you're the answer."

After the conversation ended, Ross cradled the phone and stared at the ceiling. It was hard enough not to drink. It was hard enough to defend Anna against charges that seemed to worsen day by day. It was hard enough to remain professional in the face of the feelings he was developing for her. Now, out of the blue, she'd told him God might be using him. Ross began to chuckle. Maybe God really does have a sense of humor.

Mike Simpson opened the chart and fixed her with eyes the color of polished steel. "Anna, how do you feel?"

The response was automatic. "Fine."

Simpson shook his head. "No, don't just say 'fine.' You know what I mean. Any headaches?"

"Some, but Tylenol takes care of them."

"Vision?"

"That's all clear now. No fuzziness, no

double vision."

Simpson flipped a page, although Anna knew the checklist was in his head, not on the chart. "Weakness? Incoordination? Falling?"

"Nope."

Simpson eased onto the stool at the foot of the exam table on which Anna sat. "How's the thinking? Able to concentrate? I guess you know that's usually the last thing to clear after a severe concussion like you had."

Anna pursed her lips. If she told the truth — that she could think clearly now — that opened the door for Green and Dowling to put her on the hot seat and grill her some more. But to say otherwise would be a lie. Did God allow a little white lie if it kept her out of jail?

Simpson saved her. "I see you're having to think about that one, so maybe we'd better not rush it. Let's give it another week before you go back to work. I'll call Neil and let him know. I'm sure he'd want you to be one hundred percent before you get back in the OR."

Anna swallowed a couple of times, wishing she'd accepted the water the nurse had offered her. "Mike, I . . . I need to tell you something, but it's embarrassing."

Simpson's expression was neutral as granite. "I think I've heard just about everything at one time or another, Anna, so I doubt that you'll shock me. And it won't go outside this room."

"You may be getting a call from some detectives who'll want to know whether I've recovered from my concussion. They had me in for questioning, but my lawyer put a stop to it until I was in full possession of my faculties, as he put it."

"What's this about?"

"They're accusing me of deliberately giving a patient a drug he was allergic to, then easing up on treating the anaphylaxis so he'd die. They say they're going to charge me with murder."

Simpson closed the chart, marking his spot with a finger. "Well, I just thought I'd heard it all until now. Anna, that's the most far-fetched thing I've ever heard of. What does your lawyer say?"

"He tells me not to worry, but things seem to be coming at us faster and faster."

"Who do you have? I can recommend someone if you're not satisfied with this one."

Anna took a deep breath but still felt like she couldn't get enough air. "It's Ross Donovan."

Simpson frowned. "Name's familiar. Isn't that Laura Ernst's ex?"

Anna nodded.

"Didn't he . . . ? Wasn't there . . . ? I mean . . . He's practicing again?" Simpson rushed on, apparently trying to get past an awkward moment. "I recall Laura telling me once that her husband was a good lawyer. At least, he was then. But let me know if you need another name."

"Anna, sit down." Neil Fowler half-rose and motioned Anna to the visitor's chair across from his desk. "How are you doing?"

"Did Mike Simpson call you?" Anna asked.

"No, but I just got out of surgery." A faint line on Fowler's forehead from the elastic band of a surgical head cover and the wrinkles in his scrub suit confirmed this.

"Well, he just examined me. He thinks maybe I should be off another week, because of my concussion."

Fowler frowned. "I was counting on your coming back to work sooner than that." He pulled a pad toward him and scribbled a note. "I guess I can change around some of the staffing schedules. You take your time and get well."

He shoved the notepad aside and leaned

forward. "Anna, how are things in general? I mean, I got a call from the DEA and they've pretty much cleared you. Your new permit and number should be on your desk when you come back. But how about the other stuff? Your identity theft, for instance."

Anna ran her hand through her hair. "I haven't had time to deal with that. Now the Dallas Police are threatening to charge me with Eric Hatley's murder. They say I gave him a drug I knew he was allergic to, then held back treatment so he'd die of anaphylaxis."

"That's nonsense!"

"Not the way they put it together. They say I was supplying him with Vicodin 'scripts, and he'd threatened to go to the police and blow the whistle."

Fowler seemed calm, but she noticed that his knuckles were white on the arms of his chair. "That's absolutely ridiculous. I hope you have a good lawyer."

Here we go again. "Yes, Ross Donovan." Anna decided to meet the next comment head-on before Fowler could make it. "He's Laura Ernst's ex. He's had alcohol problems, but he's clean and sober now. I think he's doing a good job."

Lines creased Fowler's forehead. "Okay, but if you need a recommendation . . ."

"Thanks, but —"

"Dr. Fowler! Dr. McIntyre! You're needed in the ER." Fowler's administrative assistant stood in the doorway. "There's been an accident on Central Expressway. An eighteen-wheeler plowed into a loaded school bus, and that started a chain reaction pileup. Multiple casualties are on their way. They need all available surgeons in the ER stat."

Anna realized at once that she had two choices. She could beg off, citing residuals of her concussion, and buy herself another week before Green and Dowling could get to her. But an extra hand in the ER, maybe in the operating room, could mean life or death for someone. There was really only one choice, wasn't there?

"I'm on my way." Fowler was already shrugging into his white coat. "Anna, I don't guess you'll be coming, will you? I mean, if Mike told you to take another week off."

Anna's hesitation lasted only a second more. "No. Looks like you'll need all the help you can get. I'll come too."

In Anna's experience, the Emergency Room of Parkland Hospital was unlikely to be calm at the best of times. Even at three a.m., the waiting room was often crowded, the cubicles full. Today, the treatment rooms were occupied and the hallways filled with teenagers on gurneys. Will Fell and another junior surgery resident moved quickly from patient to patient, assessing injuries and performing triage.

Anna edged the door open and took in the scene in the waiting room. A harried security guard struggled to keep a tide of parents, all talking at once, from spilling into the treatment area. A senior nurse waved a stack of clipboards and pleaded, "Please let the doctors do their jobs. Take these forms and give us the medical history on your children. We may need to give them medications, and we need to know if they have any drug allergies." A chill ran up Anna's spine as she recognized that these words would always have added meaning for her.

She turned back to Neil Fowler, who stood at the junction of two hallways, direct-ing traffic and letting the confusion flow around him like rushing water around a boulder. "What do you want me to do?" she asked.

He nodded toward a dark-haired, teenage girl who lay moaning at the end of the hall. "Will thinks she has internal injuries, maybe a lacerated spleen. Check her out. If she needs surgery, OR 6 will be ready by the time you get her up there."

Apparently, the girl's parents had somehow managed to slip into the treatment area. They stood beside her stretcher, holding her hand and murmuring in Spanish. The mother fingered a rosary; the father wiped away a tear.

Anna grabbed a passing medical student, one she recognized from his recent rotation through her surgery service. "Matt, what are you doing right now?"

The young man seemed relieved to see a familiar face. "Dr. McIntyre. I'm here to help."

"Okay, then you're mine. Come on. Let's check out this girl. She has one IV running. Start a second one in the other arm, and while you're doing it, draw blood for H&H, 'lytes, cross-match for six units. Got it?"

"Yes, ma'am."

"Ma'am is your mother. I'm either Dr. McIntyre or Anna, depending on how well you do. Now move."

Matt whispered something to the girl's parents and they moved away, giving him room to work. Anna moved toward the head of the stretcher, looked down at the girl, and said, "I'm Dr. McIntyre. What's your name?" When the girl continued to moan,

Anna said, *"¿Qué es su nombre?"*

"Her name is Rosa Hernandez." The words were almost whispered, the voice a low baritone with the faintest trace of accent. "And she speaks English, as do we. She's just too frightened to talk."

Anna turned to face the parents, who now stood at the foot of the gurney. The father took a step toward her, his jaw clenched, tears coursing down his cheek. The woman continued to finger her rosary.

"Listen," Anna said, "we think Rosa has internal injuries. I may need to stick a needle into her abdomen and see if there's blood there. If there is, that would mean she's had a serious injury and would require emergency surgery. We might have to remove her spleen, sew up a laceration of her liver, even —"

"Whatever it takes, Doctor." The father's voice was low and intense. "Whatever we need to sign, we will do it." He began to roll up his sleeve. "If you need my blood for her, tell me where to go so they can take it. Just do it."

"Thank you." She looked at Matt, who was handing off the tubes of blood he'd drawn to a runner who'd take them to the lab. "Matt, get the Hernandez family to sign a permit for a four-quadrant abdominal tap, exploratory laparotomy, splenectomy, repair of internal injuries. You should know what to include. I'm going to find an empty cubicle and take Rosa in there."

"What about an MRI or a CAT scan?"

Anna was already pushing Rosa's gurney away. "Radiology's already overloaded and we can't wait. I'm going to do it the old-fashioned way. Four-quadrant belly tap. Find us when you've finished getting the paperwork done."

In the exam cubicle, Anna quickly gathered the supplies she'd need. After reassuring Rosa and injecting a local anesthetic, she inserted a long needle into the girl's abdomen in the right upper quadrant. The first tap yielded nothing. So far, so good. But on the second tap, when she drew back on the plunger the syringe filled with dark blood. Blood in the abdomen. Most likely a ruptured spleen. Maybe a lacerated liver. Perhaps even — please, God, no. Not a tear of the aorta. If that major vessel broke loose, Rosa could bleed to death in a matter of minutes. This was a surgical emergency.

Matt pulled aside the curtains. "Permit's signed. Hemoglobin's eight, 'crit twenty-five. The chems are cooking."

"What about — ?"

"They're cross-matching blood for her

now. I've asked for a unit of O negative stat, and I'll hang it as soon as it gets here."

"Okay, let's get her up to the operating room. We're going to OR Six. You'll be my assistant."

16

Anna broke all speed records for a quick change into scrub clothes. Soon she stepped away from the scrub sink, her dripping arms held before her, her mind focused on the operation she was about to perform. "Let's go, Matt. That'll have to do."

She bumped through the door into OR Six, and then it hit her. This was where it all started — with Eric Hatley's operation and the events that followed in rapid-fire succession, events that now threatened to end her career. Well, she'd go out fighting. The place didn't matter. What mattered was what she did here.

As she gowned and gloved, Anna studied her surgical team. Karen, the scrub nurse, chose instruments from a sterile pan and arranged them on the green-draped rolling tray that would be placed across the operating table for easy access. Anna nodded to herself. Karen was a battle-tested veteran of the surgical wars, someone who could be depended on not to crack under pressure. But when she saw the circulating nurse, Anna winced. Keisha was a new hire, fresh out of nursing school. Would she panic at a critical moment?

Matt stepped to his spot across the operating table from her. Below his surgical mask, his Adam's apple moved twice. His shoulders rose and fell, and Anna could hear the sigh. She knew what he was feeling. She'd been there herself once.

Anna breathed a silent prayer. Time to get moving. "Okay, prep and drape. Keisha, give her belly a couple of passes with Betadine. Matt, help Karen with the drape sheet. Anesthesia, are we ready?"

"Yes, ma'am."

Anna focused on the man sitting at the head of the operating table. Even with the surgical mask covering the bottom of his face, the voice and the eyes confirmed his identity: Jeff Murray, the junior resident who'd given Eric Hatley's anesthetic.

"Jeff," Anna said, "where's your staff man?"

"He . . . He's in the next room. We have every available OR going, so he has to staff two cases. But I'll be fine, Dr. McIntyre. Don't worry." The words expressed confidence that the eyes didn't back up.

No time to quibble. This was the team she had. "Okay, Jeff. Keep her as light as possible. Watch her blood pressure — I mean, watch it closely. Keep the fluids going, push the blood until we get the bleeding controlled."

"Right. She's got Ringer's running in one arm, a unit of unmatched O negative in the other, and the cross-matched blood is on its way up." He met her gaze. "I'm on top of this one. Really."

Anna turned back to the operative field. She picked up a gauze sponge with her left hand and held out her right. "Scalpel."

She felt the familiar pressure as Karen slapped the instrument into her palm. "Matt, get a clamp in one hand, a sponge in the other. Clamp the largest skin bleeders. We can deal with them later. As soon as we get the abdominal cavity open, be ready with the suction. There'll be a lot of blood, and you have to keep it cleared out so I can see."

Anna could see the drops of sweat already dotting Matt's forehead. He'd done well as a medical student on her service, but she was asking him to take a huge step up in responsibility. Well, he'd either sink or swim, and she couldn't waste time worrying about it.

Now she worked on automatic pilot. Skin incision, through the subcutaneous fat — thank goodness the girl was thin. Separate the muscles. "Self-retaining retractor." Matt was doing well, better than she'd hoped.

"How's her pressure holding up?" Anna asked.

Murray's voice was steady. "She was shocky when we brought her in, but with fluids she's holding at about a hundred over sixty. One unit unmatched O negative already in, first unit of cross-matched blood going in now."

"Keep me posted," she said. "Here we go. Opening the peritoneum. Matt, ready with the suction. Karen, we'll need a stack of lap pads —"

"Already up, Doctor."

"Thanks." Anna grabbed one of the large gauze laparotomy pads. "We'll need a bunch."

She incised the peritoneum, the tough but thin covering around the abdominal contents. Immediately, dark blood welled into the incision. "Left upper quadrant, Matt. Looks like a ruptured spleen."

In a moment, the bleeding area was packed off. Now Anna was able to identify the problem: a laceration running diagonally across the spleen. This was what she'd hoped for, one of the best possible scenarios. The spleen was important but people could live quite nicely without one, since other parts of the body would take over its function of making blood cells and antibodies. All Anna had to do was clamp off the blood vessels supplying the spleen and remove it. Problem solved.

Anna finally relaxed a bit. "Matt, you got a permit for splenectomy?"

"Splenectomy, partial resection of liver, bowel resection, whatever might be necessary."

"Good man. Okay, Karen. Let's get that spleen out of here. Bring up the vascular clamps." With the problem diagnosed and a solution in sight, Anna swung into teaching mode. "Matt, we're looking for the region where the blood vessels feed into the spleen. Tell me what it is and the procedure."

"The splenic artery and vein. After you ligate and divide those, you identify and clip the short gastric vessels."

As Matt described the anatomy involved, Anna's hands moved with efficiency and skill. This was what she knew, what she was good at, what she loved. It was good to be back.

She paused for a second as the thought crossed her mind. Soon, maybe as early as tomorrow, she'd be in an interview room with Dowling and Green. They'd already made it clear they were planning to charge her with the murder of Eric Hatley. It was very possible that she was performing her last operation. Well, if that was the case, she'd do a good job. And today she could add one more name to the list of patients who were alive because of her efforts.

"Rosa Hernandez. Fourteen years old. Exploratory lap, splenectomy. She's on her third unit of blood, just finishing her second bottle of Ringer's. Vitals are stable." As he gave his report to the nurse in the surgical Recovery Room, Dr. Murray's voice carried an authority Anna hadn't heard in it before. "Call me if you have any questions."

Anna wiped her palms on her scrub suit before offering her hand to Murray. "You did a nice job."

"Thanks, Dr. McIntyre." She noticed that his palms were still moist, but his handshake was firm. "I'm going to see if Dr. Jenkins needs my help in room four."

Anna watched him walk away. She knew that surviving the challenge of cases like this one supplied the building blocks of confidence that helped make a mature physician. She flashed on her own such experiences. She'd heard it said that to be a good trauma surgeon you had to be fearless. Her own opinion was that a little healthy fear never hurt. It was the doctors who were overconfident and thought they could do no wrong who always seemed to get into trouble.

"Dr. McIntyre?" Matt's voice at her elbow brought Anna out of her daydreaming.

"Yes, Matt?"

"I've handwritten an op note. I guess you'll dictate the formal one. Do you want to write the orders?"

Speaking of performing well under fire, Matt had done well also. She might as well let him spread his wings a bit more. "Why don't you write the orders, then show them to me? I'll sign off on them. While you do that, I'll talk with the family."

The Hernandez family was huddled together in a corner of the surgery waiting room. Anna tried to put a smile on her face as she approached them. She knew the anxiety, the empty feeling in the pit of the stomach that came when the doctor walked toward you with news that could wreck your life forever. She'd experienced it herself when her father was in Intensive Care after his stroke. No high-stakes poker player ever tried to read the face of his opponents with any more intensity than Anna did that day. But it was only when the doctor looked down at Anna and her mother and began, "I'm sorry" that the news became obvious. She'd vowed that, if she had good news to convey, it would be evident to the family as soon as she walked through the door.

"Is she all right?" Mrs. Hernandez looked up at Anna, her anguish and pain reflected in her eyes.

Mr. Hernandez sat grim-faced and stoic, obviously prepared to hear the worst and support his wife if the dread words were uttered.

"Rosa is fine." Anna had more to say, but the words were cut off when Rosa's parents jumped to their feet and embraced, first each other and then her.

"Thank you, Doctor." Mrs. Hernandez wrung Anna's hand. "Thank you for saving our daughter."

"Why don't you sit down and let me explain what we found?" Anna pulled up a chair so she'd be at eye level with Rosa's parents. "The force of the crash ruptured her spleen. We controlled the bleeding, then removed the spleen. It's a fairly common operation, sometimes done as an elective procedure for people with certain types of blood disorders. She'll function fine without it. We've replaced most of her blood loss, and she'll be able to build up the rest on her own."

They both began to speak at once. Anna held up a hand. "I'll answer all your questions, but first let me get back in and look at Rosa. She'll be in the Recovery Room until she's awake and stable. Either I or one of my staff will look in on her a couple of times a day, and the nurses will notify us immediately if there's any change in her condition. Why don't you wait here? The nurse will come and get you when it's okay for you to see her."

Back in the recovery room, she found Matt writing in Rosa's chart. "How're you doing?"

"I think I've got it covered," he said. "See what you think."

She took the chart and scanned what Matt had written. It all looked good.

"Do you agree with the morphine pump for pain?" Matt asked. "I can change it to IM Demerol if you want to." He lowered his voice. "Some of the older staff still like that, but I figure you —"

It felt so good to be back in action that Anna had almost forgotten her problems.

Now one of them came roaring back at her. Whether it was the look on her face or the way she shoved the chart back toward him, Matt's voice trailed off. "Dr. McIntyre?"

"Why don't you get Dr. Fowler to sign off on this?" Anna said.

"Did I do something wrong?"

"Matt, someone stole my DEA number and has been writing 'scripts for narcotics. I've had a hard time convincing the authorities to clear me, and even though they're supposed to have issued a new DEA number, I'm not sure the process is complete. Right now, I think it's best that someone else sign off on an order that involves narcotics."

Anna couldn't read Matt's expression. Did he believe she was unjustly accused? Was he sympathetic or suspicious? Was she justifying herself in his eyes or feeding the rumor mill she knew existed in the medical center?

"I'd heard a little about that," he said. "And I think you ought to know that none of us ever thought you did anything wrong."

As though embarrassed by his statement, Matt looked down at the chart. "I'll get Dr. Fowler to sign off on this."

"Thanks, Matt. I appreciate it."

"Thank you for letting me help. I'm applying for a surgery residency here at the medical center. Would you mind if I listed you as a reference?"

"I'd be honored," Anna said.

"Look, Glenn. You need to come clean on this one." Ross Donovan watched a drop of his sweat hit his desk blotter. He loosened his tie and moved the phone to his other hand. "I saw your name on the label. I know you're involved in this some way. I can make sure you go down for it, or I can try to keep you out of it. But I can't help you unless you tell me everything."

"Ross, you gotta believe me. I didn't think I was doing anything wrong. Honest." The last word came out like a strangled call for help.

The lawyer waited for more, but all he heard was heavy breathing. Okay, now it got tricky. How far could he push the man? "Tell you what. When's your next meeting?"

The answer came without hesitation. "Tonight at eight. The basement of St. Barnabas Church on McKinney."

"Okay, I know where that is. I'll be parked around the corner at seven-thirty. Find me and get in the car."

"You won't — ?"

"I won't tell your employer about this. At

300

least not yet. But I want the whole story. And you'd better level with me. If I find out you're lying, all bets are off."

After he hung up, Ross sat for a moment with his eyes closed. This was crunch time. If this meeting tonight worked out, he might be close to solving Anna's problems. Of course, if it didn't, he could be in big trouble, trouble that could have the police on him like fleas on a dog. It was times like this that had driven him to depend on courage in a bottle.

Ross pulled out the bottom drawer of his desk and probed without looking, ignoring everything else in the drawer, until his fingers found what he wanted. He pulled out a bottle and put it on the desktop. "Your Honor," he said, in his best courtroom voice, "I call to the stand Mr. James Beam. Mr. Beam is an old friend, one who has been with me through many difficult times."

Ross reached once more into the drawer and withdrew a glass. He held it up, and the rays of the noon sun passing through it cast a rainbow on the opposite wall. A bottle and a glass, companions he'd known for a long time. And oh, how he'd missed them.

One drink — one drink wouldn't hurt, would it? He knew what it would be like, could almost taste the smooth liquor rolling across his tongue, feel the burn as it hit his stomach, anticipate the feeling that followed. He uncapped the bottle and filled the glass almost to the brim.

Some ex-smokers carried a pack, testing their willpower and daring themselves to quit. Most didn't, though, because they knew that sometime, somewhere, they'd succumb to temptation. Stress, fatigue, even hunger were the enemies of the addict, whether their drug of choice was nicotine, alcohol, or narcotics.

Ross had decided to keep his stash intact, to test his willpower. His AA sponsor tried to talk him out of it. "Don't be around alcohol. Don't be around people who drink. Don't go into bars. Avoid cocktail parties. All you need is the opportunity, because believe me — the craving will always be there. Always."

If he ever needed some Dutch courage, though, now was the time. Ross was pleased to note that the surface of the amber liquid in the glass didn't move when he held it up. His hands hadn't always been this steady. He had things under control now. No problems.

He wasn't sure how long he sat there glass in hand, staring at the half-full bottle of bourbon. Then he walked to the window and raised the glass in a toast. To sobriety . . . or to oblivion?

Yesterday, he'd gone to an AA meeting and said, "I'm Ross. I'm an alcoholic, and I have ninety-nine days." If he went to a meeting tomorrow, would he be awarded a hundred-day chip? Or would he be saying, "I'm Ross. I'm an alcoholic. Yesterday I fell off the wagon."

He took a deep breath, then another. Finally, he turned away from the window. At the desk, he put the glass down next to the bottle and stared at them as though they were a magic crystal ball, holding all the answers to his questions. Would bourbon rule him for the rest of his life? In a single motion he swept both glass and bottle off the desk into the wastebasket. He heard the tinkle, smelled the fumes.

He shrugged. The cleaner would take care of the trash he'd created. Nothing could clean up the mess he had been about to make of his life.

Ross grabbed his coat and briefcase and left the office, not totally sure where he was going but knowing that wherever it was, he'd get there sober.

17

Nick took his frustration out on his cell phone when Anna failed to show. She had promised to come by his office and have lunch with him after her appointment with Mike Simpson. Nick had planned his day carefully so he'd be free for lunch, had even picked out a place off-campus where they'd have a little privacy. He'd gotten up enough courage to say some serious things to her, but now it was as though the earth had opened up and swallowed her.

When he hadn't seen or heard from her by one in the afternoon, Nick started calling. Her administrative assistant said Anna wasn't in and hadn't come into the office all day. Was there a message? Nick said he'd try elsewhere. No message.

Anna's machine at home picked up on the first ring, so he figured there were already messages waiting for her. Nick hung up without adding one of his own. When a call to her cell phone came up dry, he swallowed hard and decided to leave a message. He hated that. Voicemail messages were so sterile and impersonal.

He worked to keep his voice neutral — no urgency, no begging. "Anna, this is Nick. I thought we had planned on lunch. Give me a call when you get this. I —" He bit back the rest of his message and hung up.

Nick began to picture scenarios to explain why Anna was out of touch. Had Mike found a problem this morning? Maybe Anna had developed a late consequence of her head injury. What if she had a chronic subdural hematoma? At this moment, could she be suffering through the claustrophobic experience of an MRI? Was she once more lying in a hospital bed, or — oh, please, God, no — was she being prepped for surgery?

Nick's temples throbbed. He pulled a bottle of Advil out of his desk drawer and washed two tablets down with cold coffee. Of course, there was another possible scenario. He'd shoved this one into the back of his mind, but it kept creeping forward to stick its tentacles into his consciousness and stir his thoughts into unease. Had those two Dallas Police detectives, Green and Dowling, brought her in for more questioning?

He could picture her, sitting in an interview room being buffeted by questions and looking to her attorney for help. That last thought made him cringe. He knew Anna had confidence in Donovan, but Nick wasn't sure she should depend on an alcoholic, even if he was dry, or sober, or whatever AA called it.

"Dr. Valentine, call for you on line one." The voice on the intercom snapped Nick out of his thoughts before they could spiral downward any further.

He lifted the receiver. "Dr. Valentine."

"Doctor, this is Detective Green. You may remember —"

"I know who you are. What do you want?" Nick regretted snapping at the detective, but it was too late. Anyway, the man knew he wasn't a big fan, so how much more harm could Nick's tone have done?

Green went on, apparently unfazed. "We want you to come down here so we can get a formal statement from you."

"What about? That parking ticket I got last week? I'm going to pay it. Honest."

There was no humor in Green's voice. "You know what it's about, Doctor, so don't try to laugh it off. We need to get you on the record about Eric Hatley's death. Can you come down today?"

Nick held the phone near the surface of his desk and shuffled some papers. He knew what his schedule was, but Green didn't. How long could he stall? "Just checking my calendar. Can't do it today. And tomorrow's out too. How about next week?"

"How about we send a marshall down to your office with a subpoena? He can bring you back right now. Sound good to you?"

"No, not really." Nick decided to give it one more try. "Look, today and tomorrow really are bad days for me. Give me forty-eight hours to rearrange my schedule and get someone to cover for me. I'll come down Friday afternoon. Will that work?"

There was a murmur in the background, and Nick figured Green was conferring with Dowling. Good. Dowling had seemed like the more reasonable of the two. In a moment, Green said, "Friday at two p.m. Know where we are? On Harwood?"

"Yeah, I know. See you then."

Nick hung up, closed his eyes, and leaned back. The Advil hadn't touched his headache that bordered on a migraine. And now he had one more thing to add to his list of worries. "Lord, help me," he whispered.

Anna met Neil Fowler at the door to the surgeon's lounge. She gave him a brief rundown on the surgery she'd performed, careful to mention how Matt Ryan had functioned extremely well as her first assistant. "He's applying for a surgery residency here, and I hope you'll remember this when you review his application."

"Sure. Why don't you send me a memo — an e-mail will do — and mention this? I'll be sure that Peggy attaches it to his application when we get it." He moved toward the coffee urn. "I signed off on the narcotics order for your case, by the way. I'll be glad when the DEA gets that straightened out, and I know you will too."

He held up a cup and Anna nodded. When they were both seated with their coffee, Fowler told her about his own case, a bus driver whose face was so badly injured in the crash that it took more than two hours to repair the damage, realigning broken bones and meticulously sewing up lacerations. "Wouldn't you know it? Half our plastic surgeons have gone to a meeting in Chicago, so I got drafted. I haven't done a case like that in years."

"You know you enjoyed the challenge."

"Yeah, I guess you're right." Fowler tossed his empty cup into the wastebasket. "Do you feel okay? I know Mike told you to take another week off, but if you hadn't been here today, I'm afraid that little girl would have bled out. You saved her life."

"I'm fine," she said. "Just a little wrung out, I guess."

"Well, head home. I'll look in on your patient tonight. Call me tomorrow and let me know how you're feeling. I don't want to push you."

"Thanks. I'll stop by the waiting room and talk with Rosa's parents before I go."

At home, Anna dropped her backpack inside the front door and headed straight for the fridge. She pulled out a can of Diet Coke and trudged back to the living room, where she collapsed onto the couch and rubbed the cold container against her throbbing temples.

She closed her eyes but couldn't rest. Her mind kept going in circles that had no end. She remembered something she'd seen in geometry — or was it algebra? — called a Möbius strip. It was a paper strip twisted a half-turn and fastened together so it had no beginning and no end. Start to draw a line down the middle of it, and eventually you'd end up back where you started, with a line on both sides of the paper. Well, her problems were a Möbius strip, with no end in sight. The detectives who seemed determined to charge her with murder; the person or persons who were using her DEA number to write bogus narcotics prescriptions; the identity theft that threatened her credit, cost Eric Hatley his life, and almost convinced Nick she was HIV-positive.

That set her thoughts on another track — something she never thought would be a problem for her. Two weeks ago there were no men in her life. Now there were two. Each seemed fond of her and growing fonder, and that was nice. But they both had problems, and she wasn't sure she was strong enough to deal with her own difficulties, much less those of Nick and Ross.

"Lord, I need help." Anna wasn't sure whether she'd spoken the words aloud or just framed them in her mind, but they were certainly an outpouring of what she felt in her heart.

A loud banging at her door made her jump. What now? Her first thought sent a chill down her spine. Was it the police with a warrant for her arrest? They'd take her downtown and book her. Wasn't she supposed to get one phone call? What was Ross Donovan's number? She couldn't imagine they'd let her keep her cell phone in a jail cell. She scrambled through a pile of unopened correspondence on her desk until she found the slip with Ross's number on it. She started to stick it in her pocket, then changed her mind and wrote it on her palm with a Sharpie.

The banging continued. What else? Her mind raced. She'd never prepared to go to jail before.

"Anna, open up. I know you're home. I can see your car in the driveway."

At the sound of Nick's voice, Anna felt a mixture of relief and irritation wash over her. What was he doing here? She wasn't ready for company. She wanted to shower and fall into bed.

When she opened the door and saw the look on Nick's face, Anna's irritation melted.

"Anna," Nick said. "I've been trying to reach you all day. When I couldn't get you, I pictured all kinds of terrible things. At first, I thought maybe Mike Simpson found a problem from your head injury. I could picture you back in ICU, or on your way to surgery. Then I had visions of those detectives arresting you. I know it's silly, but I just had this bad feeling about you. I had to see you and know you're okay."

"Funny," she said. "I had that last vision myself when I heard you pounding on the door. So I guess we're both relieved."

"May I come in?"

"Of course. Would you like something to drink?"

In a moment, they were seated side-by-side on the sofa. "I'm sorry I wasn't around when you phoned," she said. "There was a huge pileup on the freeway, and I was scrubbed in on an emergency case. What was it you wanted?"

Nick decided this wasn't the time for the serious talk he had in mind. When he spoke with Anna about his relationship, he wanted her in a better mood than this. But there was still something Anna needed to know. He sipped his soft drink, but his throat remained dry. "I had another call from our detective friends."

"Which one? Green or Dowling?"

"Does it matter? Dowling seems to be a little easier to deal with than Green, but I get the impression they've played 'good cop-bad cop' for so long, they've kind of settled into those roles. I'm not fond of either one." Nick finished his soft drink in one long gulp. "Anyway, I got a call from Green. He wants me at police headquarters for a statement. Says he needs me on record about the cause of death in the Hatley case."

"But why? You've already told them it was nothing more than an adverse consequence of a medication we administered based on flawed information. They should worry less about going after me and more about catching the person responsible for that false information in Hatley's medical records."

Nick sighed and leaned toward Anna, as though he could add urgency to his message through his body language. "Anna, I went through all this when I shot that man years ago. I know how the authorities can twist your words and tie you in knots. Don't you think the police and the District Attorney can do that with my statement? I don't want to go on record. I don't want to give them even one word under oath because I'm afraid of how they might use it against you."

"Nick, I appreciate your concern. Don't think I'm not worried too. I'm supposed to talk with Ross Donovan tomorrow to plan our strategy. We're both afraid that Green and Dowling are about to arrest me."

Anna saw something flash in Nick's eyes when she mentioned Ross Donovan's name. Was it jealousy? Probably. Well, she didn't have the time or energy to deal with it.

"You've probably got a couple of days," Nick said. "I tried to put off Green until next week, but he finally pinned me down. I'll give them my statement on Friday afternoon. Be sure to tell Donovan when you talk to him."

Anna tried to ignore the way Nick said the name of her attorney. "Thanks for those two days," she said. "I probably had a week's grace, but I blew that this afternoon."

"What happened?"

After she gave Nick a brief recap of the day's events, he shook his head. "Anna McIntyre, you're something else. I'm not sure I could have done that."

"Of course you couldn't do that kind of surgery," Anna said. "You're a pathologist."

"That's not what I mean, and you know it. I mean the way you pitched in to help, even when you knew you might suffer for it in the end."

"Nick, that's sort of the heart of everything I believe. 'Do unto others as you would have them do to you.' I don't know if I have the words exactly right, but you get the meaning."

"You know, one of the things I admire about you is the way you've held on to your faith in the midst of all that's happened. I'm afraid mine's gone for good."

"That's not true," Anna said. "Your faith is right where you left it." She yawned. "I'm sorry. I can hardly keep my eyes open. I need to get some rest, but I appreciate your coming by. I'll call you tomorrow."

Nick opened his mouth, closed it, and then shook his head. "Sure. Give me a call."

Anna woke slowly, swimming toward the surface of consciousness. She remembered falling into her bed as soon as Nick left. She squinted one eye open and tried to read the red numbers of her bedside clock. Was it seven a.m. or seven p.m.? There was a little red dot illuminated beside the numbers. Good. She hadn't slept the clock 'round. Maybe she could do something productive for the rest of the evening.

Soon, fortified with a grilled cheese sandwich, she sat down at her desk to sort through the stack of mail she'd let pile up. Bill. Bill. Junk mail. Sale circular. Bill.

Anna discarded the junk and set the bills aside. She'd deal with them last. Her fear was that she'd open them and see more charges made by someone else. Ross had taken the material Anna had dropped off for him and assured her that her phone notifications and his filings would protect her from future unauthorized charges. But that was only part of the problem. She still had the feeling that her identity theft wasn't an isolated instance. And although she had nothing to substantiate it, she still wondered if it was connected to the unauthorized use of Eric Hatley's medical insurance that had indirectly caused his death.

She felt a figurative light bulb go on over her head. Before she could change her mind, she pulled out a phone book from the desk drawer and thumbed through it, searching her memory for the right first name. Please, don't let it be unlisted. No, there it was. She punched in the numbers and waited, the beat of butterfly wings roiling her stomach.

"Hello?"

"Mrs. Hatley, this is Dr. Anna McIntyre. Please don't hang up."

"What do you want? My lawyer told me not to talk with you."

Anna hurried on. "No, please. I just have one question, and it has nothing to do with your lawsuit. Do you recall your son telling you about problems with his credit card?"

There was a prolonged silence. "How did you know that?"

"So, in addition to his medical insurance information, he'd suffered other instances of identity theft."

"Just a few weeks before he . . ." There was a catch in the woman's voice, and Anna felt sorry for bringing back painful memories to her. "Not long before I lost him, he

316

called me and complained that someone had used his credit cards and run up a big bill. He started to contest the charges, but he never —"

"Mrs. Hatley, I'm sorry to bring this up. But if you have any of those receipts and bills, please, please don't destroy them. They could help the police find the person really at fault for your son's . . . for your loss."

"How do I know this isn't some lawyer's trick?" Now there was suspicion in the woman's words.

"Mrs. Hatley, you can talk with your own lawyer. Give the material to him to hold. Then it can only be released to the police if they have the proper papers. I won't be able to get hold of it. But believe me, it's imperative that information be preserved."

"I'll think about it." A loud click signaled the end of the conversation.

Anna cradled the phone and pulled a yellow legal pad toward her. She began to write, pausing for long periods between thoughts. She connected some of the words to others with lines that soon made the page look like the web of a drunken spider, searching for that loose end of the thread that would allow her to unravel the mystery.

■ ■ ■ ■

The ringing of her phone roused Anna from sleep. She raised her head from its resting place on her desk and squinted at her watch. Eleven o'clock. Who could be calling this late? Her father had told her once, "A phone call after ten p.m. is never good news." She had rarely experienced anything that proved that dictum wrong.

Anna picked up the phone, but had to clear her throat twice before she could answer. "Dr. McIntyre."

"I'm sorry to call this late, but what I have will probably let you sleep better." The urgency in Ross Donovan's voice was a marked contrast with Anna's fuzziness. "I just dug up some new information about that prescription bottle the police say links you to Eric Hatley."

The words acted like a jolt of caffeine. Anna sat up straight. "That's great. Can you tell me about it?"

"I don't want to seem paranoid, but I think we'd better talk in person about this, not on the phone. Can you come to my office at nine in the morning?"

Anna didn't want to wait ten minutes, much less ten hours. "Ross, you're awake and now I am too. Is there an all-night cof-fee shop where we could meet?"

"No, that's not a good idea. Getting this information tonight was risky business. If someone is following me and I meet with you now, that sends up a red flag and puts both you and me in danger. But if you come to my office tomorrow, it's just another lawyer-client conference."

"Can't you at least give me a hint what this is about?"

The hum of the open line went on so long Anna thought the connection had been broken. Finally, Ross said, "I've been won-dering all along if someone is trying to frame you for this."

"And?"

"Now I can prove it."

18

Ross closed his cell phone and stowed it in his pocket. He peered out of the shadows of the alley before stepping onto the deserted sidewalk. A faint light shone through the stained glass windows of St. Barnabas Church, but otherwise the street around him was dark. As he walked to his car, his head was on a swivel, searching for a presence he felt but could not see. He hunched his shoulders, clenched his fists, and lengthened his stride.

When he saw his car ahead, Ross breathed a little easier. Another hundred feet and he'd be safe inside. He wasted little time worrying that he might have put Glenn in jeopardy. Glenn had put his own neck in that noose. If anything, giving up the information tonight might help the man escape serious consequences. Right now, Ross's primary concern was for Anna. And with what he had, he should definitely be able to counter the police attempts to incriminate her.

As he neared his car, Ross heard a quick shuffle of footsteps behind him. He turned just enough to take the first blow on his shoulder, but his attacker adjusted quickly, and the second and third strikes were on target, right at the base of his skull. He dropped to his knees and put out his hands to brace himself for impact with the pavement. As everything faded from gray to black, he heard a voice, faint and far away. "Hey, what's going on?" Then there was nothing.

Anna was wide-awake now. That nap with her head on the desk might not have been the most comfortable one she'd ever had, but the rest, combined with the effect of Ross's phone call, had left her wide awake.

She wasn't going to sleep anytime soon, so she might as well get some more of this paperwork out of the way. Armed with a cup of tea, she shoved aside the legal pad where she'd been trying to connect the dots of her life and turned her attention to the stack of bills.

Anna took a sip from her cup and rolled her shoulders to relax them. She could recall when the only tension involved in opening her bills was wondering how she was going to pay them. Now she had to worry about whether the charges listed were her own or the work of someone else. Her latest MasterCard bill held no surprises. The identity thief, whoever it might be, apparently wasn't able to gain access to her new card number. Anna one, bad guy zero. The VISA bill was short — she generally used it only for backup — and like the MasterCard statement, it was free of unauthorized charges.

Her utility bills were routine. She expected no surprises, and there were none. As Anna wrote the checks, she watched her dwindling bank balance and wondered how she could afford the fee of the private detective Ross had mentioned.

Soon there was only one piece of mail left unopened: a large envelope marked "Personal." The return address was an unfamiliar one, a Dallas post office box. In Anna's experience, correspondence marked "Personal" was often part of a marketing scheme to entice the skeptical recipient to open the envelope. On the other hand, it might really be important, maybe medical information. She shivered as she thought of this last possibility. Was this yet another lab report, generated by a visit from someone using her insurance information? She still hadn't done anything to expunge that false report of a positive HIV test from the lab's records. She hated to have something like that floating around with her name and identifying data attached to it. That was one more thing for her "to do" list.

Anna slit the end of the envelope and pulled out a sheaf of papers with the heading "CSC Credit Services." Was this more bad news about her credit rating? As she read further, her eyes stopped at the line, "Your personal credit report." Then she remembered. When she'd first found out about the theft of her credit card information, she'd requested copies of her credit report from the three major companies that kept up with that stuff. The first two reports were in the packet she delivered to Ross. This one was just late.

Well, she might as well see if this one showed anything different. She spread the pages on the desk and picked up a red pen, ready to circle items that would require attention. When she reached the bottom of the last page, she frowned. There were two unfamiliar charge accounts listed. She was sure they hadn't been listed on the other credit reports. Sure enough, the dates showed they'd only been open for a week.

The name on the accounts was Anna Elizabeth McIntyre, but the address wasn't hers.

Ross had warned her that sometimes credit reports contained inaccuracies. He'd told her not to be surprised if she found some accounts, either old or active, that weren't hers. For instance, it could be a case of two people with the same name. Could there be two Anna Elizabeth McIntyres in Dallas? She pulled the phone directory to her and began to search. When she laid it aside, she was satisfied that, if she did share a name with someone else in the city, that person's phone number was unlisted.

So, what did this mean? Anna burrowed through the mound of papers she'd created and found her yellow legal pad. She entered the new information, but there was no instant flash of recognition, no sudden insight. Well, maybe it would look better in the morning. Anna yawned, stretched, and then padded off to the bedroom to snatch a few hours of sleep.

Anna poured a second cup of coffee and looked at her watch. She moved to her desk, where she picked up the phone and punched in a familiar number.

"Good morning, Dr. Fowler's office. This is Peggy."

"Peggy, this is Dr. McIntyre. Has Dr. Fowler come in yet?"

There was the expected exchange of good wishes, during which Anna felt alternate pleasure at being missed and shame that she wasn't at work right now. "He just walked in," Peggy finally said. "Let me tell him you're on the line."

In a moment, she heard Fowler's voice. "Anna, how are you today?"

"Doing pretty well. I was hoping to be back at work today, but some things have come up. Can you do without me for another day or two and let me try to tie up some loose ends?"

He paused long enough to make Anna wonder if he was about to deny her request. "Tell you what," he said. "This is Thursday. Why don't you plan on coming back on Monday. I'll schedule you to staff in the resident clinic that day, maybe a few cases in the OR on Tuesday, so you can ease back into things. Sound okay?"

Anna figured that would be fine, if she wasn't in jail by then. But there was no need to tell her chairman right now. "Yes, that'll be fine. And thanks for your patience."

Okay, she'd cleared the decks for the balance of the week. Nick's meeting with the detectives was on Friday afternoon. Green

325

and Dowling were obviously getting things lined up to ask a judge for an arrest warrant. Was Nick's statement the last piece of the puzzle for them? And, if so, could they get a warrant on the weekend? Did judges work on Saturday? Sunday?

What if Nick dropped by unannounced over the weekend just when the police came for her? That would be great, to have him show up at her door just as she was being led away in handcuffs. She silently asked God to show her a way out of the pit into which she seemed to be sinking day by day.

No need to sit here feeling sorry for herself. Time to get moving. By now, her coffee was cold. She shoved the cup aside and reached for the notes she'd made last evening. Maybe something would jump out at her this morning. Names, dates, addresses were scrawled across the page. Ideas came and went like shoppers at Christmas hurrying through the mall. Then it hit her.

The address for the new charge accounts, the ones she was sure weren't hers, was in her neighborhood. No wonder the address had tickled her memory last evening. She drove down that street every day on her way to work. Like most people, her routine was so set that she could navigate her way to the hospital on automatic pilot. But seen out of context, the address hadn't meant anything. Now it meant . . . what?

She let her finger roam over the page, looking for the other addresses she'd jotted down. Then she found it — another one in her neighborhood. She squinted to decipher the name scrawled above the address. Yes, that was it. Eric Hatley.

Anna looked at her watch and realized she was due in Ross Donovan's office in half an hour. Time to get moving. She could puzzle over her latest discovery as she drove. She'd almost forgotten Ross's phone call, telling her he had proof someone was trying to frame her. He'd sounded hopeful. Maybe deliverance was in sight after all.

"I tell you, I'm all right." Ross Donovan did his best to be emphatic and forceful, but it was hard when you were sitting on the edge of a gurney with your bare rear end hanging out of a hospital gown. "I don't see double. I don't hear bells ringing. I know what day it is and who's president. It was just a blow on the head. I've had worse than that playing football. Now let me have my pants. I have an appointment to keep."

The intern might have been young, but she knew she was in charge, and she refused to back down. "Mr. Donovan, the citizen who called the ambulance said a man was beating you with a club. That's assault, and it's a crime. I've notified the police, and they're sending someone to take your statement. You can't go until they're through with you."

This wasn't medicine, this was law, and now Ross was in his element. Talking to the police wouldn't help, and he knew his rights. "Doctor, I have no obligation, legal or otherwise, to talk with the police. This was a mugging, interrupted by a passerby. I have no idea who my attacker was, I'm not going to press charges, and it would take the police about five minutes to put any paperwork generated by my report into a drawer and forget it."

"But —"

Ross gathered his dignity, reaching behind him to hold his gown closed. "Do you have any medical reason to hold me? Are you going to force me to sign out AMA?" He figured that having a patient leave the hospital against medical advice would make the young doctor fill out a ream of paperwork, and he hoped this would be the leverage he needed.

She chewed on her lip for a moment before opening his chart and starting to write. "If you have a headache that Tylenol or Advil doesn't relieve, if you start seeing double, if you begin vomiting, if you find yourself stumbling or falling . . ."

Ross half-listened to the rest of the instructions. They had taken his watch along with his clothing and other valuables, but the clock on the exam room wall told him that if he hurried he would only be a few minutes late for his appointment with Anna. And after the events of last night, that seemed more important than ever.

Anna looked at her watch again. Nine-thirty. She tapped once more on the door of Ross's office, knowing there wouldn't be any response. The lights were off, and when she pressed her ear against the glass of the upper part of the door she heard only silence.

All sorts of scenarios ran through her head. Ross had hinted of danger last night. Had something happened to him? Was he lying behind the locked door, maybe in a pool of blood? She pulled out her cell phone and hit the "redial" button. She counted the rings as she heard them, slightly out of phase, first the buzz of her phone and then the electronic ring inside the office. She hung up when Ross's answering machine kicked in.

Try his cell phone again? There'd been no answer when she arrived here early for her appointment and anxious to hear Ross's news. She was punching in the numbers when she heard a "ding" from the elevator nearby. A few seconds later, Ross rounded the corner.

She almost didn't recognize her attorney. His clothes were rumpled and dirty, his hair mussed. He was unshaven. Her first thought was that he'd been drinking again, and her stomach clenched. What would this do to her case? She was already formulating alternate strategies when a sense of shame hit her. She'd completely ignored the possible consequences to Ross if he had slipped back into his old pattern of alcoholism. How could she be so self-centered? This was a man who had gone out on a limb for her, apparently put himself in danger last night. No, whatever he'd done, she'd help him through it. They'd deal with it together.

"Anna, I'm so sorry to be late. Let's go inside."

He pulled a small ring of keys from his pocket and opened the door. The smell of liquor made Anna's nostrils quiver. The office smelled like a distillery — or, at least, what she imagined a distillery would smell like. She'd been around lots of alcohol in her life, sometimes at parties, more often in the emergency room as she dealt with drunks and accident victims. There was no mistaking the aroma. She felt a tear form in her eye, but not just from the fumes. No question, Ross had been drinking.

The lawyer moved quickly to the window and fumbled for a minute. "Oh, man. I forgot. These windows don't open. Let me get rid of this." He picked up the waste-basket and carried it out the door. He was back in a few moments, drying his hands on a paper towel. "I'd like to leave the door into the hall open to let this place air out, but we need some privacy. Can we go to the coffee shop downstairs? I could use some coffee anyway."

"Yes, I bet you could," Anna said. "And maybe we can stop at the drugstore and get you some vitamins. I don't drink, but my colleagues who do tell me that large doses of B vitamins help them get over their hang-overs."

Anna could see Ross's expression change from confusion to understanding to indigna-tion. "Anna," he said, "I haven't been drink-ing. Actually, I was tempted to drink yester-day, but I dropped the liquor, glass and all, into the wastebasket. Apparently, the cleaning lady decided to skip this office last night."

"But what about your appearance? You have to admit, you look like somebody who's been on an all-night bender."

"Let's get that coffee," Ross said. "I have quite a story to tell you."

"Good morning. Coffee?"

"Yes, please." Ross turned over the empty cups on the table and inhaled the rich aroma of strong coffee as the waitress poured.

"Do you need a few minutes?" the waitress asked.

"Orange juice and an English muffin," Anna said without opening her menu.

"Two eggs over easy, wheat toast, crisp bacon." Ross drank deeply from his cup of coffee, then lifted it and held it out to be topped off. "And please keep the coffee coming."

After the squeak of the waitress's shoes faded, Ross leaned forward and fixed Anna with a steady gaze. "First, do you believe I haven't been drinking? I'd ask you to smell my breath, but since I haven't brushed my teeth since yesterday I think that might be unwise."

A hint of a smile flickered across Anna's

face. "Okay, the alcohol smell was in your office but not on you, so I guess you're clean. But look at you. Why were you late?" Her eyes traveled over him, and Ross became acutely aware of his wrinkled suit and a day's growth of beard.

He looked around, confirming there was no one within earshot. "Right after I talked with you last night, someone hit me over the head and knocked me out. I might have ended up in the morgue, but apparently a passerby saw the attack. His shouts scared off my assailant. I ended up in the emergency room at Parkland, where I practically had to fight the intern to retrieve my pants and leave."

"Who was the intern?" Anna shook her head. "No, never mind. Doesn't matter. Are you sure you're all right now? No double vision? No throwing up. No —"

Ross held up both hands, palms out. "I'm fine. I had a mild concussion, that's all. I've been given all the warnings. The important thing is what I found out before I was attacked with a club."

"And that would be . . . ?"

"When Green showed us that pill bottle with your name and Eric Hatley's on it, I noticed the pharmacy it came from. Yesterday, it dawned on me that I knew one of the pharmacists working there. I'd defended him on a DWI charge that almost cost him his license to practice. He still owes me big-time, so I called in the favor and got some information."

The waitress returned with their food. After she set down the plates and refilled their coffee cups, Ross continued. "The pharmacist — his name is Glenn — had an AA meeting last night, and I arranged to meet him in the neighborhood. If anyone saw us together, it would just be two alcoholics headed for a meeting. He sweated bullets the whole time we talked, and he couldn't get away fast enough after we were through, but I hit pay dirt with him."

Anna paused with her muffin halfway to her mouth. "What did you find out?"

"Glenn said a man approached him, one he'd seen a couple of times at AA. The man wanted a prescription inserted into the files at the pharmacy and a vial made up with matching data. No need to dispense the medication. When Glenn unfolded the prescription the man handed him, there were five one-hundred dollar bills inside."

"So he did it." Anna said.

"Actually, it took a little more than money to persuade him. The man said Glenn could cooperate and make a little money, provided he kept his mouth shut. If he didn't, Glenn's boss might find out about his alcohol problems. I really think that was the deciding factor."

Anna's face lit up. "So if those policemen come after me, we have a witness who can testify that I was set up." Her smile was quickly replaced by a frown. "And Glenn didn't give you the name of the person who approached him?"

Ross emptied his coffee cup and shoved it aside. "At AA meetings it's first names only, but Glenn didn't even recall that much about the man. So we know he exists, but we don't know who he is. He's probably only a go-between anyway, but if I could locate him I might be able to find out who he's working for."

Anna wiped a crumb from the corner of her mouth. "How can you do that?"

"I've already started. Last night, after I talked with Glenn, he went on to his AA meeting. I slipped in a bit later and sat in the back. He was supposed to give me a sign if the man was there. He wasn't."

"So we're at a dead end."

"Temporarily. But now we know that someone is trying to direct suspicion toward you, laying a false trail that diverts the police away from himself. And the attack on me tells me two things," Ross said. "One, our Mr. X is worried that we're getting close to him. And two, it's someone who knows I'm representing you."

"How — ?"

"Someone followed me last night. They didn't just happen to be there when I walked out of that AA meeting. They knew that you were trying to get at the truth, and they knew I'm your lawyer. Now, who could that be?"

Ross picked up the carafe the waitress had left behind and poured more coffee for both of them. He could see Anna concentrating, ticking off people on her fingers.

"Let me see," she said. "There's your ex-wife. She's the one who referred me to you."

"No motive there, although I'm sure there were times she would have liked to take a club to me, probably with good reason." Ross stifled a wry grin. "But let's put her aside."

"There's my chairman, Dr. Fowler." Anna ducked her head. "He knows about my problems, of course. And he has access to everything in the department, including my office and prescription pads." She looked up at Ross. "When I told him about you, he didn't seem too impressed that I'm being represented by an alcoholic. He offered to give me another name if I wanted one."

"We'll add him to the list."

Anna pursed her lips. "Then there's Nick."

"Who's Nick? Is that the doctor you told me about? The one who wants to help you?"

"Yes. He knows pretty much everything we've found out. But Nick's fond of me. Surely he wouldn't try to harm me. He . . ."

Ross waited, but Anna apparently decided to let that thought go unvoiced. Nevertheless, he certainly wouldn't give Nick a free pass just because there seemed to be some sparks between him and Anna. Time to move on. "You're forgetting some people."

"Who's that?"

"The police and the DEA. I've dealt with both agencies on your behalf. And my name is all over their records, so we have to consider them. And not just the people we know. There could be someone behind the scenes who has access to the information. Maybe more than one someone."

Anna looked up at Ross, an expression of utter hopelessness covering her face. "So I can't really trust anyone." She grimaced. "Except you, I guess."

Ross forced a smile. "Well, you know what they say. God works in mysterious ways."

19

Anna was in her car, halfway home from her meeting with Ross, when her cell phone chimed out the theme from *Law and Order*. She pulled it from her pocket and flipped it open, careful to keep her eyes on the road. "Ross, can you hold on? Let me pull over."

"Probably a good idea. You won't like what I'm going to tell you."

Anna inched her way to the right-hand lane and aimed toward the parking lot of a church, almost empty on a Thursday morning. As she brought the car to a stop, her mind ran through the possibilities for bad news. They seemed endless.

She picked the phone off the seat where she'd laid it. "Okay, I'm parked and I'm sitting down. Tell me your bad news."

"I keep a little portable TV in my office. I flipped it on to see if my attack made the news. It didn't, but something else did —

something that cuts our legs out from under us."

Anna felt her throat closing up. "What?"

"My witness, Glenn, works at a 24-hour pharmacy. He was due to come on duty at six this morning. When he didn't show up and didn't answer his phone, the pharmacist he was supposed to relieve got worried. He finally convinced the manager of the apartment where Glenn lived to use his passkey and check. He found Glenn lying on the living room floor, the back of his head caved in. The police are calling it robbery, but I don't think so. I think it was the work of the same person who tried to club me to death last night."

Suddenly, Anna couldn't catch her breath. She rolled down the windows but still felt oxygen-starved. "So we have nothing."

"No," Ross said. "We have something. We know what's happening. We just have to find out who's behind it."

"You mean you're still going to keep looking? Ross, you were attacked. The man you were with last night has been killed. You could be next. And if they come after you, they could come after me! We need to drop this. Now!"

"And give your friends Green and Dowling a free hand to railroad you right into

339

jail? Anna, the police apparently aren't going to let go of the idea that you're involved in something dirty."

"But they're wrong. And we know their evidence is either circumstantial or manufactured. So I'd never be convicted. Right?"

Ross's tone was that of a teacher explaining something to a particularly dense pupil. "Assuming you'd be found innocent — and the first thing they teach you in law school is not to assume that — do you want to be arrested, have to make bail, get dragged through the mud and tried in the newspapers before the case ever comes to court?"

Anna sighed. Ross was right, of course. "How long do we have? Nick meets with the detectives tomorrow afternoon. I don't think his statement will give them any new information, but you know how it's possible to pressure people into saying things that can be misinterpreted."

"I think getting that statement shows us they're about ready to move," Ross said. "They're dotting a few 'i's' and crossing one or two 't's' before they go before a judge to request a warrant for your arrest. I'd be surprised if they let it go until Monday. And it would be totally in character for them to make the arrest in time for the late news, leaking word to the local stations so there could be live coverage. I can see the video now. You in handcuffs, taking a 'perp walk,' flanked by Green and Dowling, who'll be smiling into the cameras."

It was more than she could stand. Anna's shoulders began shaking. Her eyes felt moist. She breathed faster and faster.

"Anna, are you there?" There was concern in Ross's voice.

She fought for control. "Yes, I'm here."

"Go home. Get some rest. I'll call my private detective friend and see if he can get any helpful information for us. I'll get back to you later today."

Anna made the drive home on automatic pilot as she struggled to find a way out of the net that appeared to be closing around her. The net. Made of threads. Tangled threads. She recalled the diagram she'd made the night before. Her address, Hatley's address, and the address for the bogus charge accounts in her name were all in the same neighborhood. Maybe this was the loose end she could pull to unravel the mystery. She'd go home, sit down with what she had, and pull on that string with a vengeance. It was important. Actually, it could turn out to be a matter of life or death — hers.

■ ■ ■ ■

Nick straightened his back, squinted, rubbed his eyes, and rolled his shoulders. He'd spent most of the afternoon glued to the microscope, and it was time for a break. The slides stacked before him represented previously living tissue, cut into ultra-thin sections, stained with special dyes, waiting for him to study them and render judgment. The chemistry lab down the hall might have reached a level of sophistication that allowed machines to carry out analysis and spit out the results in cold, impersonal numbers. That wasn't the case here. In this room, the fate of patient after patient depended on Nick's eyes and brain. Was the nucleus of that cell too dark? Were the natural borders of that tissue breached by invading cells? If this specimen represented a cancer, was it an aggressive type?

The ring of his cell phone startled Nick. Despite the jealousy he'd felt when he discovered she had assigned a special ring tone to her attorney, Nick had followed suit and given calls from Anna a unique ring. Right now he was listening to the faint tones of the old John Denver hit, "Annie's Song." He pulled the phone from the pocket of his lab coat and said, "Anna, what's up? Are you all right?"

"For now," she said. "Things are getting crazy, though."

"Like what?"

"Never mind. I just wanted to ask a favor."

"Sure. Anything."

"Just like that?" she said. "Aren't you going to ask me what I want?"

Nick leaned back in his swivel chair, pleased that Anna had called him rather than Ross Donovan. "Nope. If it's humanly possible, it's yours for the asking."

"I . . . may need to borrow your gun."

Nick leaned forward and his feet hit the floor with a slap of leather on vinyl. "No. Absolutely not." He took a deep breath. "I mean, why would you want — ? Anna, you don't know how to handle a pistol. You don't have a permit. What could you possibly need a gun for anyway?"

"I don't really know if I should tell you. If I get into trouble over this, I want you to have what the politicians call 'plausible deniability.' "

"Anna, I lost that when you asked to borrow the gun. If you're into something that serious, then the only way you're going to get my gun is with me on the other end of it. Now, will you tell me what's going on?"

In the silence that followed, Nick could picture Anna chewing on her lip and trying to decide what and how much to tell him. Finally, he heard her sigh. "Okay, I'll tell you this much. Last night I was going over my latest credit report and noticed there were a couple of accounts in my name with a different address."

"Do you think it might be someone with a similar name?"

"I think it's more than that," Anna said. "That address is in this neighborhood, about halfway between my house and Eric Hatley's. I'm not sure what's going on, but it seems to me that whoever stole my identity has some connection with this part of town. I intend to find them, and the place to start is the address on those new charge accounts."

"But —"

"No. No 'buts.' I don't have time to waste. Ross told me I may only have a couple of days before the police arrest me. The charges are ridiculous, and he thinks we can probably beat them, but there's no guarantee. Besides, I don't relish the idea of jail time while the legal battle plays out. So I've decided to take matters into my own hands."

"Look, I can't get away right now," Nick said. "I'll come by tonight. We can have dinner together and talk about this. Remember, I'm in this along with you. I have been ever since Hatley died."

It was as though Anna hadn't heard his last words. "Maybe you're right about the gun," she said. "I think I'll do a little surveillance first, and I shouldn't need a gun for that. Thanks."

"Anna —" Nick heard a click and found that he held a dead phone. He replaced it in the pocket of his coat and turned back to the stack of slides, already calculating how quickly he could go through them without sacrificing accuracy. He needed to get to Anna's before she did something foolish.

As she hung up the phone, Anna already regretted calling Nick. She wasn't sure why she thought she needed a gun. She certainly had no business with one. Anna had heard story after story in the doctors' lounge of homeowners who'd confronted a criminal, only to have their own guns turned on them. No, she was being foolish, letting her emotions overcome her common sense.

She wasn't a detective; she was a doctor. And even if she did manage to discover the person who had compromised her credit, stolen her DEA number, and indirectly caused Eric Hatley's death, what would she do with the knowledge? She couldn't very well call the police and say, "You need to come here right away. I think this person is a criminal."

The thing to do was call Ross Donovan, tell him about her theory, and see if his investigator could find out anything that would help her. In her heart, she knew that was the proper course of action. It kept running through her head, even as she dressed carefully in jeans, a dark sweatshirt, and scuffed sneakers. She kept repeating, "This is crazy," as she shoved her wallet in one side pocket, her keys in the other, and clipped her cell phone to the waistband of her jeans. Her mind told her, "You have no business doing this," as she climbed into her car and placed the scrap of paper with a scribbled address on the seat beside her. Finally, as she backed out into the street, she murmured, "God, I know this is crazy. But I have to do it. Please go with me. Protect me. Help me. Please."

She found the street and began cruising along it. This was a typical suburban neighborhood, populated with single-family homes set comfortably back from the street, front yards just large enough for a game of catch, backyards — most of them enclosed with chain-link fence — where dogs and children could romp. The house she wanted was in the middle of a short block, a one-story brick. The flowers and shrubs in the front bed were dead or dying, the grass was brown, and the "For Sale" sign in the yard told Anna why. She looked at the slip of paper once more. Yes, this was the place. But why would someone open a charge account and use the address of a vacant house?

She circled the block, went by again, did a U-turn and came back from the other direction. The blinds were drawn in the house. No car in the drive. No bikes or toys in the yard. No sign of life anywhere.

On this street, the driveways were in front of the houses, meaning the homes backed up to each other without an intervening alley. Unless someone crawled over the back fence, if Anna watched the front of the house she should be able to see anyone coming in and out.

Three houses down from the house in question, Anna tucked her car between two others and slouched down in her seat until she could barely see over the steering wheel. She wished she'd covered her hair with a dark baseball cap, but she was new at this spying thing. Maybe no one would notice her.

Anna started to turn on her car radio, but

thought better of it. Much as she'd like something to combat boredom, she didn't want any noise. She planned to listen, as well as watch. She fidgeted until she achieved the best compromise between comfort and hiding. Then she settled down to wait.

Almost an hour passed before Anna saw activity. She eased up a bit in the seat. A man in a gray-blue uniform walked toward her. As he came nearer, she could see a brown pouch hanging off his shoulder, resting against his hip. Just a mail carrier.

The mailman continued toward her, stopping at some houses, not at others. When he did stop, his body blocked Anna from seeing what he did. Then he turned in at the vacant house. Here she had a clear view of the man's actions. He opened the flap of the mailbox, reached in and pulled out a handful of envelopes. He thumbed through them, selected three to shove into his leather pouch, and replaced the rest. Then he closed the box and walked away, going back the way he came. She watched him until he got to the end of the block, where he climbed into a nondescript gray sedan and headed right toward her.

Anna ducked down until the mailman passed, then started her car, did a careful

K-turn, and dropped in behind him. Her education in tailing another car came from detective novels and TV programs. The only thing she recalled was that you should drop back and try to get other cars between yours and the subject vehicle. The problem was that this was a quiet suburban street, and there was no other traffic. Well, Anna knew the neighborhood. Maybe she could use that knowledge to her advantage.

At the first intersection, the driver of the gray sedan went through after barely tapping his brakes. Anna turned right, then immediately left at the next intersection. She sped up to reach the cross street first, where she looked to her left. The gray car went straight, so she did as well. Her quarry turned right at the next cross street. She pulled a map from the glove compartment and pretended to study it until he passed in front of her. Then she tossed the map on the seat and made a right turn, falling in a hundred yards behind him.

After two blocks, she watched the gray car turn into a strip mall. When she got there, the car was nowhere in sight. She aimed at a row of vacant parking places in front of an out-of-business cleaners, backing in so she had a view of most of the parking lot. She was scanning the cars, straining to see the gray sedan, when the passenger door of her car opened, and the man in the postal uniform climbed in.

He pulled a gun from his postal pouch and leveled it at her. "Keep your hands on the steering wheel. Don't make a move. Don't make a sound. Understand?"

Anna managed a weak nod and felt her stomach drop like an elevator in free fall. Why had she tried this? The man had spotted her easily. And she hadn't even had the presence of mind to lock her car doors. Why hadn't she left the investigation to the professionals?

"Okay, start the car. Both hands on the wheel, just like they taught you in driver's ed. We're going back to that house you were so interested in."

"Park here in the driveway." The mailman, as Anna had come to think of him, waved the gun for emphasis. "Folks will just think there's someone looking at the house. Fat chance! It's been vacant for six months, with no takers."

Anna put the car in park and turned off the ignition. She started to pocket the keys, but her captor said, "No. I'll take those. When we leave here, I'll be driving."

"I can drive you," Anna said.

When the man stopped laughing, he said, "You're not going to be in any shape to drive. I just hope the trunk of this car is big enough to hold you." He chuckled again. "Not that you're going to complain about being cramped."

He waved her out of the car. "I'm right behind you. I'll put the gun back in the pouch, but remember that I can pull it out and pull the trigger a lot faster than you can run."

"You don't want to do that," Anna said. "A shot would bring the neighbors running."

"Dream on. First of all, a shot from this pistol would sound about like someone bursting a balloon. And besides that, nobody is going to stick their nose outside if they think there's trouble. That's the American way. Don't get involved."

The mailman pulled a key from his pocket and unlocked the front door. He shoved Anna through and followed on her heels. "Sit over there," he said, waving toward a couch against the far wall. "The previous owners left us a little bit of furniture, so we have all the comforts of home."

Anna eased down onto the couch, edging to the left side to avoid a sharp spring coming through the cushion, while putting as much distance as possible between her captor and herself. "Can you tell me what's going on here? I was just waiting for a friend when you —"

"Shut up! I saw you following me. I'm not stupid." He held out his hand. "Gimme your wallet."

"Is that what this is? A robbery?" She dug her wallet out of her pocket and handed it over.

The man opened it to her driver's license and Anna could see recognition cross his face. "Dr. McIntyre. The name is familiar, and now I have a face to go with it. You're one of my best customers." He shoved the wallet into his pocket. "You won't need this anymore."

Anna's mind ran a mile a minute. Could she get the gun away from him? Not a chance. Maybe she could bolt and knock him down. And outrun a bullet? No, he'd been right about that. She had to let someone know she was here. But who? And how?

"Okay, I was following you," she said. "I wondered why you were picking up mail instead of leaving it." As she spoke, she shrugged her shoulders, moved around on the couch, grasping the sides of the cushion and adjusting it beneath her, making a show of trying to get comfortable. As she did so, her hand palmed her cell phone off its clip and dropped it between the cushions.

"You might as well know, since you're not going to be telling anyone about it. What you've stumbled on is a sweet little racket that provides my unemployment income."

Anna raised her eyebrows, inviting him to keep talking, while her finger searched for the right button on her phone. She knew she'd only have one chance. As soon as the mailman began speaking, she pressed the button . . . and prayed.

"Unemployment?"

"Yeah. I was a mailman. When too many government checks turned up missing, the Postal Inspectors started investigating. That's when I got fired. Actually, they didn't fire me — they didn't have enough evidence. They let me resign, which kept me out of federal prison. Unfortunately, it also kept me from drawing unemployment. So I figured, since I've still got the uniform, I'll set up my own unemployment fund."

Anna heard a few muffled noises from the sofa cushion. She tried to cover them with her next question. "So what are you doing? What does that have to do with this house on Shady Lane? And why are you holding me here?"

She made a move as though to stand,

causing her captor to say loudly, "Sit down. Remember, I've got a gun and I'm not afraid to use it."

"Take it easy. I'm not going anywhere. You're the one with the gun. How did you pull off stealing my identity?"

"Simple. I knew this route, so why not stay with it? I'd choose a different street every day, walking it after the regular mailman made his delivery. I knew the places where nobody was home during the day, and I'd check those boxes for things I could use: checks, credit card information, stuff like that. I hit the jackpot at your house. Not only did I get your credit card statements, I got the form for your narcotics license renewal. That's when I knew I'd moved into the big-time."

"I can see how you'd use the checks and the credit card information, but how did you figure out how to use my DEA number?"

"Oh, didn't I mention it?" the mailman said. "I took in a partner. Somebody who had an inside track on narcotics prescriptions and knew all about that stuff." He reached into his pocket and pulled out a cell phone. "Guess I'd better call him. I may need some help cleaning this up."

Anna could only hear one side of the

conversation, but it was enough to make her heart pound. "It's me. I'm at the house on Shady Lane with our lady doctor. I need help getting rid of her."

The man's expression hardened as he listened for a moment. "I don't care. Drop whatever you're doing. I need you here. Half an hour, no more. Remember, you're in this as deep as I am."

He shoved the phone in his pocket, seemed to consider something, and reached into his mail pouch.

Anna expected to see the barrel of his gun come out and spit its fatal missile at her. "Don't —"

The mailman's hand emerged holding a small roll of duct tape. "Shut up and stick your hands out. I don't want to have to watch you every minute."

With her wrists bound with silver tape that might as well have been handcuffs, Anna leaned back on the couch. She took a deep breath and opened her mouth, but her captor read the signs.

"Nobody's going to hear you scream. I told you, I know this neighborhood. The people on both sides of this house are at work right now. By the time they get home, I'll have shut you up permanently. Then I'll wait until dark, tidy up here, put your body in the trunk of your car and drive it some-place where it won't be found for a while. My partner will pick me up and that's the end of it."

The mailman started to drop the roll of duct tape back into his bag, then seemed to think better of it. "You know, I'm tired of hearing you ask questions." He ripped a strip of tape from the roll and slapped it across Anna's mouth, then grinned with satisfaction as he dropped the tape back into his bag.

Anna slumped into the cushion, totally defeated. Her hands were secured in front of her, palms together in an attitude of prayer. Prayer seemed to be all that was left for her right now. At least when the final moment came, she'd be talking with God.

Anna wasn't sure how long she sat with her eyes closed, sending up earnest peti-tions to heaven, before she heard footsteps on the porch followed by a firm rapping. She opened her eyes and looked up in time to see the mailman stride toward the door and open it.

At least she would finally see the person behind the scheme before she died. Anna fixed her gaze on the door, wondering who would come through.

She shuffled through the possibilities. Neil

Fowler? He certainly knew about narcotics prescriptions and had access to blank forms. But why would Fowler do such a thing? Was it a need for money, or had his position of chairman left him thinking that rules didn't apply to him?

Was it one of the DEA agents, Kramer or Hale? Or the detectives, Green or Dowling? Each of them would have the contacts, the specialized knowledge to make use of her DEA number. What better cover for criminal activity than carrying a badge?

Could it be her attorney? His story of a beating could have been faked to divert suspicion from him. And surely Ross would know the right people, either among the criminals he'd represented or those he'd encountered in his struggle to overcome addiction. Didn't Alcoholics Anonymous and Narcotics Anonymous sometimes meet together?

Was Nick involved? Ever since Hatley's death, he'd been after her to let him help. Was that so he could keep tabs on her activities? Had his apparent affection for her merely been an excuse to be around, to keep an eye on her? Had she been that badly fooled?

Or was it someone she hadn't considered? There were so many possibilities. And soon she'd have her answer. She'd know the identity of the person who'd betrayed her and ruined her personal and professional life. It was a pity she wouldn't be able to use the knowledge.

She pictured her last moments: a bullet in the head would bring total darkness and oblivion. Her lifeless body would be bundled in a blanket and dumped in the trunk of her car for its last ride.

Would her captor deliver the *coup de grace* himself or would he leave that to his partner, who was apparently the man in charge? She wondered who it would be and decided that it didn't make any difference. Dead is dead.

The mailman looked back at her. Apparently, assured that Anna posed no threat, he turned the knob and opened the door.

Anna craned her neck to see past her captor's form. The light was behind the man who stood in the door, silhouetting him and hiding his face. Then Nick Valentine stepped forward.

20

Ross Donovan sat at his desk, staring into space, replaying every word of his conversation with Glenn. Poor Glenn. What a terrible way to die. Ross shivered as he realized it very nearly was him lying on that stainless steel drawer in the morgue, his earthly remains identified by a tag on his toe. If he didn't stop, would that be his fate anyway? He knew he was playing a dangerous game, but there was no turning back now.

He arranged and rearranged the files and papers on his desk, shuffling them like a shell-game hustler on a New York corner. Maybe if he looked at things from a different perspective, considered the chronology, his next move would become clear. He started with the discovery that someone was using Anna's narcotics license to write bogus prescriptions. Ross opened the file labeled "DEA" and pulled out Anna's application for renewal of her license. He cleared a space on his desk and laid that form at the left end of it.

Then Anna had found her identity had been compromised and her credit cards used until they were maxed out. He shuffled through the stack to the pile labeled "Credit" and found Anna's latest credit report. That went next to the DEA application.

In the meantime, Eric Hatley showed up in the Emergency Room, the innocent — well, apparently innocent — random victim of a gang shooting. Because someone else had used Hatley's insurance information, he received an antibiotic that caused a fatal allergic reaction. From the folder marked "Hatley," Ross pulled the summary sheet from the man's pitifully thin hospital chart. He placed that next in line.

Then the police, in the persons of Detectives Green and Dowling, advanced the theory that Anna was guilty of murder, or at least manslaughter. Their key bit of evidence was the prescription bottle showing Anna had prescribed narcotics for Hatley. Ross now knew the label had been faked, but his witness was dead. Yesterday, Glenn had given Ross a blank prescription label from the pharmacy where he worked. Ross pulled that from the pocket of his coat and laid it alongside the other papers.

His eyes scanned the row, back and forth, left to right and back again. Nothing made any sense. There had to be a connection that tied all of this together, but so far the only connection was Anna. His legal training rebelled at the thought that kept running through the edge of his mind like something seen with peripheral vision. Could Anna be guilty of all this? Was Glenn's revelation a complex double fake to get Ross to believe she'd been set up? And then did some as-yet-unknown associate of Anna's assault Ross to make the story more believable? If that was so, then Glenn was beaten to death to keep him from recanting his carefully planted story.

No! That was too far-fetched. Anna was innocent. She had to be. He couldn't bring himself to think otherwise.

Suddenly, as though a filter had been moved aside, Ross saw it. There was the connection. He swiveled toward his computer and called up a program, entered information, scanned the results. Yes, that was it. But what should he do about it? He didn't hesitate. He had to go there, see for himself.

He pushed back his chair when his cell phone rang. "Ross Donovan."

The conversation that followed was short, but it galvanized Ross into action. He grabbed his coat, slammed his office door, and almost ran down the hallway toward the elevators.

When Nick Valentine heard his cell phone ring, his first reaction was a sigh. Would he ever be able to get through this stack of slides? He needed to finish the day's surgical dictation, and he'd never do it if he had to continually stop to answer calls. Then he realized that the tones he heard were a signal that Anna was calling again.

He plunged his hand into the pocket of his lab coat and fumbled to answer the phone before the call rolled over to voicemail. "Hello. Anna?"

But it wasn't Anna's voice that he heard. Instead, a male voice, faint and a bit muffled, was saying, "They let me resign, which kept me out of federal prison."

"Anna," Nick said. "What's going on?"

Then Anna's voice, faint like the other one but also strained.

"So what were you doing? And what does that have to do with this house on Shady Lane? And why are you holding me here?"

Shady Lane? That was just a couple of streets from where Anna lived. She'd talked about an address in her neighborhood that she thought might have something to do with the people behind her identity theft. Had she gone there? It appeared that she had — and she was in trouble.

The next words brought Nick out of his chair. "I've got a gun and I'm not afraid to use it." By the time the man finished speaking Nick was halfway out the door of his office. He took the cell phone away from his ear long enough to press the mute button.

His startled administrative assistant looked up as he rushed by.

"I have to leave. Life or death emergency. Call Dr. Rollins and ask him to finish the surgicals from today. I'll explain later." The last words trailed after Nick like the tail of a comet as he dashed down the hall toward the parking lot.

Anna couldn't believe it — didn't want to believe it. Was Nick at the heart of the scheme that had brought her here to the brink of her death? How could that be? Oh, Nick! She felt so foolish. She'd begun to care for the man. Care deeply, in fact.

Harsh words from the mailman interrupted Anna's pity party. "What do you want?"

"I'm looking for Anna McIntyre," Nick said.

Anna saw the mailman move forward to block the doorway and Nick's view of the room. Her captor's hand was already reaching into his mailbag. Anna tried to scream but the tape over her mouth did its job well. All she could produce was a weak, muffled sound that neither man seemed to notice. Well, if she couldn't warn Nick, she'd have to stop the mailman herself.

In a move she'd seen numerous times from the stands while in college but had never tried, she sprang from the sofa and launched herself at her captor in a flying body block. Although she'd never played football, she'd practiced medicine, and she knew where to aim. Her right shoulder took the mailman in the back where the bottom of his rib cage ended, right over the kidney.

By this time, the mailman's gun was clear of its leather hiding place and in his hand, but the unexpected blow sent it flying. Anna, her captor, and Nick all hit the floor. Anna looped her bound hands over the mailman's head from behind and began pulling backward with all the force she could muster. The man struggled and cursed, although the words came out in a strangled whisper. He clawed around for